LOVE ON ICE

ℬ

MARY RAY

Passion can melt frozen hearts

Author's Note

Although this is a novel—a fantasy to be enjoyed—I sincerely hope that readers will share the ideas of love, peace, social justice, and promote equal rights for all human beings...and bring them into their own lives, as well.

For the sake of world peace, I dedicate this book to those readers,

Mary Ray
Summer, 2015

Chapter 1 ❋ Anna

Anna was unhappy.

Her life had to change.

And soon.

But what did she *really* want to happen?

Her fingers were cold—nearly numb. She shivered. The cloud of breath that she saw when she exhaled was like watching life escape from her body.

She dug her gloves out of her pocket, and put them on. She could warm her hands, but nothing seemed to melt her freezing heart.

What caused restlessness to rumble inside her, like an approaching thunderstorm? She had a comfortable life—or so it seemed. Her husband was a good provider. He was a dentist. He was as reliable—in the financial sense—as the second hand on the hockey clock that hung on the wall above her. It annoyed her that it kept such perfect time. She watched its face, as it slowly ticked away the moments of her life.

In the most important way, though, she couldn't trust her husband. He was a cheater... and a liar.

There! She'd said the words—*almost* out loud.

But she didn't know what to do about his problem—her problem. How could she change him, and save their marriage?

She stood in her father's worn-down hockey skates, watching her twelve-year-old daughter, Emily in the center of the big rink, trying to copy the movements of her skating teacher. She had to keep it all together now—for Em's sake.

Anna shook her head, and wished she could be happy. Couldn't Bill just wake up one morning—like Ebenezer Scrooge—and be a changed man?

Ungrateful thoughts about her privileged life always triggered sickening waves of guilt.

Stop wanting things to be different, she felt like screaming, to anyone who would listen—or who might care.

She *should* be more grateful—and accept her lot in life. Shouldn't she?

What *was* her problem anyway?

Bill, her husband of thirteen years paid the bills, and she guessed, he probably loved their daughter—in a way that he could love anyone…

Her mouth tightened into a thin, angry line. What did Bill know about love—and, for that matter, what did *she* really know about it anymore?

And what about sex? Their marriage was sexless—for her. But maybe sex didn't have anything to do with love. Sure, Bill had flings with girls at the office, but hey, it *was* the 60's, and the sexual revolution was brewing. Lots of people cheated these days. In the movies, they called it getting rid of your "hang-ups"…So, was a little infidelity really something to end a marriage over?

And…it was her fault, anyway, she figured, because she hadn't wanted to be with Bill *that way*, for a couple of years now—ever since she'd discovered he'd been unfaithful the first time. Anna would never forget that raspy voice on the phone—she'd later learned it had been from Bill's just-fired, very hostile office manager, who'd said: "I'd want to know, if my husband was cheating on me—" And proceeded to give her details, dates, times, names...

But Anna had never said a word to Bill about that call—and maybe her marriage had really ended that day, two years ago.

She knew that if she told the *whole* truth—which she never had—there was a much bigger problem with her marriage: She couldn't be herself around Bill. He seemed to want her to be...*different*...than she was—ever since they'd gotten married—even long before all of his *flings* started happening.

What did Bill want? And why were they still married? She didn't know. But she certainly wasn't going to ask him. Not again. The last time she'd stood up for herself, it had ended in disaster.

It was last summer, and she and Bill were getting ready to meet his business partners for dinner. Anna had tried her best to look good for their big date. She'd trimmed and washed and set her hair—she didn't go to beauty parlors; there were pretty women in those places who *always* looked great—even when their hair was wet. Anna's hair was curly, and it tended to fly around her head like a giant ball of poodle fur—sort of like a wig. So, that night, she'd plastered it down with hairspray. She'd chosen a long black dress that she'd bought that morning. She'd even put on some lipstick.

Bill had come out of his bathroom, taken one look at her, and he'd cursed.

"Anna, you look like shit." His face was an angry red color. Nice language for a Baptist man, she'd thought—but she'd never dare say anything like that to him. He had a scary temper, when he got angry.

Now, she remembered how devastated she'd felt, and the pain and humiliation gripped her chest, as if the scene with Bill was still happening to her.

"What's wrong?" she'd asked him.

"We're going to the Country Club, for God's sake. Not some formal—funeral."

"Well, I'll not be changin' this dress. I like it. It makes me look thinner, and I think it would greatly impress Mr. and Mrs. Johnson."

His face couldn't have gotten redder, but it had; Bill had turned almost purple, and he'd said, "Must you talk—*that way*? Like some immigrant? It's embarrassing as hell."

Anna had been close to tears before he'd said that, but his last comment had pushed her over the edge, and she'd sobbed like a baby—and she couldn't stop. She'd thought about her family, and a powerful sense of loss came over her. Her father had been an Irish immigrant. Her mother had died in Belfast, when Anna was a toddler. Yes, her dad had been far from perfect, but he'd been the only family she'd had in this country—until he'd passed away, when Anna was in college. When Bill belittled the way she talked, Anna felt like he'd stabbed her very soul, and tried to kill whatever identity she had left.

She'd cried so hard that night that Bill had finally backed off, but he hadn't hugged her—or apologized. He'd merely said, "Look, Anna, you're a mess. I'll tell the Johnson's that you're not feeling well, okay?"

All she could do was nod, and he'd left in a huff, as if she'd ruined *his* evening.

Now, pushing off onto the ice, she tried to forget about Bill. She thought about her dad, like she often did when she skated. Her father had been her first—and only—skating teacher. Charlie O'Breen had been an aggressive hockey player who took no prisoners out on the ice. He'd taught Anna to skate—fast, and straight—from the time she could walk. She'd been the boy he'd never had—and wanted.

When Anna grew into a young woman—a woman without a mother to teach her how to be a lady—her dad rejected her interest in "girly" things…and her love for figure skating.

Her father loved "real man" country music, and he'd hated Anna's loved-themed "wimpy" songs—especially those sung by the Negro groups she enjoyed so much. She shook her head when she pictured her dad tough, and opinionated—and angry all the time. She remembered how his jokes grew even more hostile after a large cup of strong Irish whiskey—that awful smelling stuff he drank. Near the end of his short life, he'd sipped his deadly spirits, all day long, to ward off the shakes and seizures that finally killed him.

Anna sighed. She'd tried to help her dad, and to please him. And now, she wondered, if she trying to do the same for Bill. She couldn't please her dad, or make him happy, and she certainly couldn't please Bill…

What more could she do?

She didn't work at a *real* job—but she did work hard—keeping their home neat and clean. She scrubbed their huge house, from top to bottom. She cooked all their meals—even though Bill rarely ate at home anymore.

And, she *loved* being a parent to Emily.

Anna went to all Em's school activities, and she was on the parent committee. She drove Em to church youth groups on Sundays. Anna went to services sometimes, too, but she always went alone. Bill didn't go to church, but then, Anna knew that lots of husbands didn't—and Bill, with his very busy practice, was way too tired on Sundays to do anything but play golf, and take Em to his parents' even bigger house, for their weekly family brunches.

But...Anna did one thing for herself that did make her happy. During Em's ice skating lessons on Tuesday and Thursday afternoons, Anna designed and practiced her own ice dances to the songs that played in her head. She skated faster, now, hoping to escape thinking about her problems.

But, even here, in her favorite place, she felt sad. If her life was so full of luxuries, and parenting joys, then why was she feeling so terrible today?

Maybe it was because she was skating all alone in a dark corner of the arena. Maybe because Bill hated skating—and her music—and just about everything else she did. Maybe it was because her thirty-third birthday had come and gone last week, and Bill hadn't offered to celebrate it with her...And maybe there wasn't anything left to celebrate?

As she spun around, she put her hands on her hips, and pinched some puffs of fat around her waist—she guessed there was about an extra twenty pounds' worth there—but she was tall—so, she figured, she didn't look too big...but, so what? Who would notice anyway?

She shrugged, and hoped that all the bad feelings would go away, if she kept on skating and filling her mind with good music. So, she started to hum the melody from her favorite song by the Three Brothers. She'd listened to their songs so many times, that she knew them by heart.

She began to bend her knees to the rhythm. Snapping her fingers to the beat, she allowed her hips to swing from side to side.

Growing up in Atlanta, she's developed a passion for R&B music. Local DJs had filled her teenage radio airways with sensual—and sexually suggestive—love songs.

Although she was white—plain Irish, she called herself—the Motown Sound had always stirred her more deeply than any other kind of music. Promises of mind-blowing romance warmed her body. Some women read paperback novels for romance; Anna found it in the lyrics of her favorite soul songs.

At first, Anna hadn't noticed anyone watching her...As usual, the other mothers were sitting high up in the bleachers, on the far side of the massive indoor rink. They were so busy keeping track of their children's progress that she'd believed that she could do whatever she wanted in the little warm-up area behind the stands, and no one would really care...

So, she allowed herself skate with more feeling now. The lyrics in her mind seemed to magically transform themselves into her nerves, and the rhythm drove her muscles.

Turning to avoid slamming into the wooden half-wall, Anna glanced up into the bleachers, and saw a colored man looking at her. His black-rimmed glasses, his halo of dark hair, and his fuzzy beard stood out from the crowd of white women.

Was he was watching her?

Yes!

He was staring...

Her cheeks felt flushed, as if she'd been caught doing something wrong. Embarrassment burned her skin. She wanted to shrink down, and hide. Her fear of being judged for her weird dancing grabbed her by the throat. She knew the fear well. It had started years before, when her father and his buddies used to tease her about "sissy skating" to "jungle bunny music." Later, in her teenage years, her dad had condemned her suggestive dancing—that it was not right—not proper—for a good, Irish Catholic girl.

13

Catching her breath, she stood, and watched her daughter. Em's lessons lasted two full hours, and there was about an hour left. After a few minutes, which seemed like forever, Anna grew restless. She glanced up at the bleachers. The man with the black glasses was staring straight ahead.

Good! Leave me alone, and mind your own business!

She glared at him, feeling invaded—and very annoyed.

But now, since the coast was clear, she pushed off from the wall, planning to skate a couple of quick rounds, just to calm her nerves. Speed skating gave her a sense of freedom that was impossible to find anywhere else on the entire planet.

She skated faster and faster...trying to outrun the loneliness, and leave the sadness behind her, but those feelings seemed to follow her around the rink, like ghosts.

Was there no escaping her problems?

She knew she had to keep trying—for Em's sake. And it was here, dancing and flying around on the ice that she usually found some relief...

"Sorry Dad. I love you...but I *can't* end up like you! I will not! I won't leave my child all alone—and make her an orphan—like you've done to me." she whispered, like saying an angry prayer. But she knew anger was wrong—it killed her dad—and so she began to sing the kind of music that gave her life meaning, when nothing else seemed to make any sense.

She moved, skated and sang for love and happiness—like her songs promised.

But could love and happiness ever exist for her?

She closed her eyes, skating faster and wilder, almost out of control. She held her arms out, and raised them high in the air, reaching for something—or for someone—desire pouring from every fiber of her being. Craving, wishing, hoping her life to change…and, for a few precious seconds, she was totally transported—away from Bill, away from the sadness in her life…

And then she tripped. Her body slid across the ice, and her head slammed against the wooden wall—and her world went black.

Chapter 2 ❄ Abe

Abraham saw her crash into the wall. He felt as if he already knew her, and he'd reacted as if he'd seen his own child fall down.

He'd been secretly watching the strange, red-haired woman out of the corner of his dark-rimmed glasses, since he first seen her skating, alone, in the practice rink a couple of weeks ago. She was the only mother who skated, and she always skated alone. She'd race around, and sometimes she danced on the ice. It was pretty dark back there, but he could see her well enough.

She was kind of heavy—too chunky, for his taste, and with her wild hair sticking out, she wasn't anything like the hot chicks that he usually liked to watch. But he was curious about her. She was different than the other mothers—almost as different from them as he was, he joked to himself.

He assumed that their daughters were both in the same figure skating class. He'd never spoken to the woman—or to any of the other mothers, for that matter. While waiting for his daughter to finish her lessons, he'd sit by himself, far away from the clucking group of lily-white mother hens, with their bleached blond hair and their fancy jewelry hanging around their necks. From his vantage point, high up on the bleachers, he could hear them gossiping and complaining while they watched their kids with the teacher.

Sometimes he'd read or grade papers. But, sitting at the end of a row of empty seats and, behind a wide metal beam, he could—very slyly—peek around it, and check out the red-haired woman. She always wore a floppy hockey shirt, and black skates. *Men's skates?*

Sometimes he'd snicker when she tried to really dance on the ice—she had almost no control of herself at slow speeds—but when she skated fast, she was straight and strong, just like he'd skated, when he was a kid, on frozen lakes, up in Michigan.

Now, climbing fast down the bleachers, he jammed one of his basketball shoes against the edge of a seat, and he tripped—and nearly fell. He quickly caught himself using his super-fast reflexes. At least he still had those, he thought. The poultry didn't pay any attention to him, or to the noise that his body made, when his hand slammed hard against the wood—and no one seemed to notice the crumpled form of the woman lying still and lifeless, on the ice.

He was angry with himself for letting the woman catch him watching her. He was skilled at acting distant and aloof, and he'd made a big mistake—getting caught spying like that. A black man of his height and size had to be extra cautious about attracting attention—or appearing too interested in a white woman. He wore his full, thick beard and dark glasses like a mask, and—usually—his disguise, and his carefully practiced act, worked perfectly, when he was out in public—until today.

How could he have slipped up?

That was so stupid!

He'd learned to cope in the white world, for most of his adult life. But, now, his irritation with himself turned into fear about the woman, because her body—her sad-looking form—was still not moving.

His eyes never left her body, as he scrambled off the bleachers, and started jogging toward her. He was very agile for his height—over six feet. He'd been famous for jamming a lot of slick moves on the iced-over lakes around his grandma's house in Detroit. Growing up, his nickname in his neighborhood was "Ice Man" because he could skate like nobody else. No kid—or adult—could catch him, or even come close to topping the tricks he could do on skates. He was a natural.

When his grandma passed on, and he moved to Philly with his older half-brother, he'd switched to street skates. There, he became the fastest roller skater on the east side. But he'd kept the name, "Ice Man." It made him sound tough, and it had helped keep him safe from the gang members, who eventually had taken his brother's life.

Skidding to the wall of the small rink, he saw she was lying on her side, with both legs folded under her. The memory of a porcelain statue that his grandma had kept on her mantle popped into his head—a white woman in a robe, sleeping on a couch. He remembered asking his grandma why she kept a white person's doll, and she'd said, "Baby, they don't make colored lady statues like that…but if they ever do, I'd be pleased if you got me one."

And he'd tried to find her that statute—with a black woman on it—but he'd never found one—before she died—or since. Sometimes, when he went shopping with his daughter downtown, he'd still look around for that statue. He didn't know why. He thought about his Grams, now, and he missed her.

Suddenly, he saw that one of the woman's arms was moving. He jumped the gate. She was shaking her fluffy head around, and she started to push herself up off of the ice. His heart was racing, as he skidded to a sliding stop, and squatted down, next to her.

She was better looking, close up, he thought, and then he reminded himself that he was married, and he didn't play around anymore—not since he his daughter had gotten old enough to figure that kind of stuff out. But, he wasn't dead yet. He still did plenty of looking because his wife was…

"Ow!" the woman cried, interrupting his thoughts about his screwed-up marriage.

"Hey…hi…ah, are you okay?" he asked, gasping for air, realizing that he'd probably held his breath during his run from the bleachers.

Her eyelids were half-open now. Blinking, she stared up at him. A look of surprise flashed in her shiny green eyes, and she stopped trying to sit up. He'd never seen eyes quite like those before, and he found himself staring at her—something he knew he shouldn't do. But they were kind of spooky—like snake's eyes.

"Oh…um…who…?" She seemed confused.

She kept watching his face, and then she started to relax. She took a deep breath. Her mouth softened into a smile, and she seemed—maybe—happy to see him?

He didn't know what to say, or what to do. He looked around at the empty arena for help, and her eyes followed his.

"I fell, and hit my head, didn't I?"

He nodded, pushing his glasses up higher on his nose.

"How long was I out?"

He took in a breath, chewed on his lip, and hesitated. He didn't want to lie, but he didn't want to tell her the whole truth—that he had been watching her the whole time.

"Ah…I'm not *really* sure—I saw you…um, are you all right? Do you want me to call somebody?"

"Na…no, no. I'm fine. I can see okay, and my head—it doesn't really hurt—too much." She grinned, pushing herself up higher, into a semi-sitting position. "I'm tough…and, I've been told that I have a *really* hard head." She rubbed the back of her neck. "My head—and the ice—we go *way back*—I used to play hockey, with me dad."

She tried using her hands to support herself into a sitting position, but she slipped back down onto her thigh. "Oh…ouch! Well…I guess I'm still a *little* outta kilter…" She looked at him with a half-grin, but she seemed embarrassed. "I'm so sorry. Maybe you could let me borrow your arm—just for a second?"

He hesitated again. Touching white women was not something that he did. He'd never had one ask him to do something like this before. But when she reached out and grabbed his wrist, he reacted automatically, and he held her hand. He felt her strong grip as she grabbed his shoulders. His body tensed. He felt her breasts rub against his arm, and, when she stood up, her breath tickled his neck, quickly sending hot vibrations down into his chest.

He used his hands to support her shoulders, to keep her from slipping, but when he realized what he'd done—that he was practically hugging her, in plain view of the roosting hens from the skating club, he panicked. Stepping back, he almost let her go.

But he didn't let her go.

He felt strange—almost lightheaded. He could hear his heart beating in his own ears, and feel the blood rushing to his face, and he kept holding her…until she seemed strong enough to stand on her own.

What the hell was happening to him?

"Thanks…thank you, so much…" she said, as she wobbled onto her skates, and pushed herself away from him. But she was still unsteady, and when she leaned too far forward, he caught her with both his arms again, to save her from falling flat on her face. She was taller—and heavier—than he'd first guessed. The hockey jersey she wore covered most of her body, but she was curvy in all the right places...

"Oh! Wow," she breathed. "Maybe I *should* sit down for a couple of minutes."

"I think that's a *very* good idea," he agreed, and, holding her arms, he slowly led her toward the empty benches that coaches used for watching warm-ups and private lessons.

"Are you still dizzy?" he asked her, feeling some sincere concern.

"No. I'm fine...just a little shaky. Thank you, again, by the way. Asking for help isn't somethin' I'm good at." She gave him a weak smile.

He kept quiet, looking straight ahead, trying to stay aloof and detached, even though she was bumping up against his side and causing the vibrations to slide further down his body this time. He was starting to like the sensation of her body leaning on his. Touching her, and helping her, made him feel good. She was nice, and friendly—very different from what he'd expected. And there was something warm and kind in her voice, too. She had some kind of an accent...

But he couldn't let her know any of that, so he only nodded, scanning the bleachers, hoping nobody was watching them. He had a special *arrangement* with the Club. Because he was a college teacher, they'd considered his petition. He'd agreed to keep a low profile, and then, his daughter could take lessons with the white kids—on a trial basis. Of course, he wasn't an actual club member, but they'd given him permission to be here...as long as there were no...*problems.*

But none of the mothers were looking, and he was relieved—*and* he was glad that this woman seemed to want to keep talking to him. He was afraid to jeopardize his daughter's lessons, but a part of him felt exhilarated by the risky nature of what he was doing...

As they slowly made their way out of the rink, she continued to talk about herself. "You know, my father taught me to skate—but I think I already told you that. And my dad told me that I when I made a mistake, I'd fall...which, of course, shouldn't happen—"

"Falling...or making mistakes?" he interrupted.

"What?"

"What shouldn't happen—a fall, or a mistake?"

She stopped, and stared at him, and then she laughed. Her smile was quick and easy, and her whole face lit up with it.

"Well, I don't know! I guess, I never thought about it." She added after a pause, "I sure don't like making mistakes—and I've made a lot of those in my life, I have. You know, just today, I've been thinking a lot about them—about all my mistakes...and, then, today, I fell, too..." She looked down at the floor, watching her skates slide slowly along the ice, and then at his sneakers.

"Umm" he breathed, glancing at her face, and quickly turning away. He could remember faces without staring. It was one of his skills. He'd just seen her mouth for a couple of seconds, but he'd noticed that her teeth were almost straight, her lips were full, and crooked, and her freckled cheeks turned up higher on one side when she smiled. He liked that—the way she looked. Not perfect. But sweet...and, best of all, she seemed to like to talk to *him*.

"Me too," he said...and he instantly regretted the slip. *Don't reveal anything personal,* he reminded himself. That was one of his rules.

22

She giggled. "Yep! You know, you can't get this old, and not make some pretty big mistakes, right?"

He didn't know what he should say to that. He really wasn't thinking too clearly. She kept surprising him. She seemed so honest. It seemed like she trusted him—and she didn't even know him.

"I guess," he replied simply, trying to come up with some kind of safe strategy, and to regain control of himself. He wanted to get to know her, but he needed to stay hidden, and be cool.

As they walked together, he looked down at her worn out skates. They weren't lady skates. They were men's. And what was that accent? Irish maybe? He held her arm as lightly as he could, as he guided her gently to a front-row bench seat. He let her go, and she sat down heavily. He stood next to her, looking down at the skates, still wondering why she wasn't wearing lady's figure skates.

"Nice skates," he commented, and then felt stupid for his ridiculous comment.

But, instead of getting mad, and calling him a smart-ass, like his wife Georgie would have done, this woman just giggled...and not in a mean way. He quickly checked her face, and thought he saw a sad look there.

"They were my dad's. I lost him to the drinking," she said kindly. "I miss him, and wearing these helps me keep him close...if you know what I mean?"

He felt bad about what she told him about her father, but what should he say to her? He knew what it was like to lose family members...But he had no business staying here, and talking...

His thoughts raced.

He wished he could look into her eyes for as long as he wanted, and tell her all about his own family—his losses—his sadness—and his loneliness—but he didn't dare. He'd had nearly forty years of keeping quiet—hiding his emotions—especially from women—so he wouldn't frighten them—or maybe so he wouldn't feel his own pain…

But, now, he wondered if he had another problem. He'd avoided dealing with people—and his emotions—for so long—maybe too long. To avoid gangs, fights, and put-downs, he'd learned survival skills. In college, he'd kept his head down, his grades up, protected his GI scholarship, and avoided dudes who were looking for a fight. These days, on any city street in Georgia, he couldn't be too careful. Race riots were happening everywhere, since the murder of Doctor King.

His wife called him "Uncle Tom," and she was probably right. But what else could he do? He'd grown from being an over-sized boy to a hulk of a teenager, who looked old for his age…and then he'd become a very big man. People were afraid of him because he looked tough on the outside. No one except his wife and his daughter knew that he was as soft as a marshmallow, on the inside.

His students didn't really know him, either. He was a teacher at an all Negro technical college in downtown Atlanta. He'd been careful to conduct himself with great restraint there, too. He rarely revealed personal information about himself.

He'd never had a problem with the police. He'd seen family and friends die on the street, so he'd learned to play a role. He knew how to hide behind his mask—his beard, and his glasses, which were as big, and dark, and thick-rimmed as he could find. Lately, he'd been wondering, because of all the acting and pretending he'd done, if he'd lost his own identity. Sometimes, he wondered, if he knew who he really was at all anymore.

Now, he believed that he'd have to work extra hard at hiding himself, so this woman wouldn't be afraid of him. He wanted her to like him. He wanted her to talk with him—as a fellow parent, as her equal...

He longed to share the experiences and challenges of having a teenage daughter with someone who gave a shit about him. He needed to talk about the things that his own wife refused to discuss, because she was too damn busy, and she thought ice skating was just plain stupid.

He wanted help dealing with his only child, a headstrong girl, who was temperamental as hell...she was a tough little black girl who was trying to learn to figure skate from snooty, stuck-up white people.

But most of all he wanted to be *understood.* He realized that the red headed woman made him feel good because she was nice to him. She wasn't like the other mothers. This strange woman danced to her music as if it owned her, and she had the most *amazing* green eyes—eyes that seemed to like to look at him. He could tell that she didn't want him to leave...and, suddenly, he recognized it: she was lonely, too.

And so, he told himself, all he wanted was her friendship...and nothing more.

Chapter 3 ✳ Emily

Emily's eyes were glued to her instructor's skates. Carol, her teacher, was showing Emily how to shift her weight, and control the angle of their knees for the second time, because Emily didn't do it right the first time.

Emily watched Carol, and she wondered if she'd ever be able to skate like that. Even if she could skate half as good as her own mother did, Emily thought she would happy. She admired the way her mother practiced her ice dance routines in the warm-up area every week. Sometimes Emily wished that her mom would sit with the other mothers once in a while, though, and act more like them— like a normal mother.

But, Emily knew, her mom was different—she was *not* like the other mothers. She didn't do things the way that other people did. Her mom was kind of a rebel, her friend Steph said. And Steph was right. Emily never knew what her mom was going to do next, and sometimes that was fun—and sometimes it wasn't...

Now, Carol was asking the class to demonstrate moves for skating backwards. When Emily's turn came again, she strained with her best effort, pushing her knees in and out, stretching them almost to the breaking point. She started to slide backwards a little, but she felt scared, and stopped herself. She felt clumsy, and she nearly fell, tripping over her own skates.

She'd hoped her mom hadn't seen *that*, she thought with a sigh. Emily wanted so much to perform perfectly, but everything she did seemed to backfire. Carol said she was too tense, but Emily couldn't seem relax, way the other kids in the class did.

Emily didn't allow herself to fail—and she didn't like to give up. She always tried her best, like her parents had taught her to do. Her mother told her to always keep trying…and keep a smile on your face—no matter what. Her mom said she'd learned about that after her parents died. Emily's didn't remember her mom's parents. They'd died before she was born…but her mom always smiled, and she did her best, and her mother never cried, as far as Emily knew.

And Emily's father had taught her that failing was a very bad thing, and she would be punished by him, if she messed up. Emily knew he'd learned that from his father, who was a rich and very successful business man in town.

"Good try, Emily," said Carol. "Keep practicing. You've got the basic idea. Practice leaning your upper body into the turns a little more…and for heaven's sake, Emily, *just relax!*"

Emily nodded. Her stomach did a flip. Her eyes stung with tears, but she held them back.

Relax? How?

Her mother told her to sing in her head. Her Sunday school teacher told her to pray about it, and her father didn't have any advice, because he didn't even like skating. He just wanted her to quit.

Stuffing down bad feelings, and ignoring her upset stomach, she moved to the end of the line. She tried to focus on watching the next student. Jaheen—the only colored girl in the class—was out there now, perfectly performing each of the movements, flowing backwards—

and she was going fast, too. Emily shook her head. Why couldn't she be like *her*? Jaheen was so confident—and she did everything right.

Steph, her very best friend in the world, was standing next to Emily, and was shaking her head. "Crap! She makes the rest of us look *really bad*," Steph said loudly.

They watched Jaheen finish her turn in front of Carol that ended with a fancy spin.

Steph said, "What's with her, anyway? Did Carol say she could add a flip like that? What a show-off!" Emily cringed. Jaheen *was* really good, but she didn't want to rock the boat and disagree with Steph, so she kept her opinion to herself.

Jaheen glanced over her shoulder as she passed them, skating backwards. Emily was sure Jaheen had heard Steph, because she gave both of them a mean stare.

Emily didn't answer until Jaheen was far enough away, so that she wouldn't hear her. Emily tried to practice good manners. Steph, on the other hand, tended to push limits—and sometimes Steph could be downright rude. Steph liked to shock people, and her latest use of the word "crap" in almost every other sentence was a good example. But Emily really liked Steph, in spite of her crazy ways.

Emily knew her father didn't want her to spend time with Steph. He thought she was rude. But her mom was fine with their friendship. Emily knew her parents had argued about it—they disagreed about a lot of things. Just thinking about her parents fighting upset her, and she tried to put them out of her mind.

Emily looked at Jaheen, and, feeling jealous, she said to Steph, in a very low voice, "I don't know, Steph. I think she's really good...it's like she was *born* skating or something." She shook her head. "I mean, she only started with us in Beginner's a few weeks ago, and I don't think she takes private lessons—so why do you think she's—"

"Girls! Next! Stephanie? Your turn...let's see what you can do," called Carol, interrupting them, before Steph could answer. Carol was really nice, Emily thought. But she seemed to have eagle eyes and ears. She could zero in on a weak spot, or a problem in her students, within seconds.

Steph pushed off, and headed for the middle of the rink. While Emily waited for Steph, she looked over at the back rink, just to check on her mom, and something there caught her attention. Was that her mother, sitting with a *colored man* on the warm-up bleachers?

What were they doing? No! It couldn't be. Were they laughing and talking—like they were...*friends* or something?

Emily stared at her mother and the man, until Steph slid to a stop in front of her, blocking her view. Steph said excitedly, "Wow! Crap, Em! Did you see me? I did *great*...almost as good as little Miss Jaheen-the-Scream!"

Emily wasn't listening. "Oh...What? I...I'm sorry...I was..." Emily leaned around Steph, and pointed, "Steph, look over there, will you? I think that's my mom, sitting with—somebody—some guy." Emily pointed toward her mother. "Is that...is that maybe be Jaheen's dad? I mean, who else could it be? Nobody else here is...well, you know...colored—"

"Where?" Steph interrupted, squinting in the direction Emily was pointing. "Crap," she said. "How do you know that's Jaheen's...? Oh, yeah, crap, I think you're right! He's the only Neg...Wow..." Steph got quiet. For once, her friend seemed speechless.

Emily noticed that Steph's eyes were huge. As they stared at her mother, Emily felt her tummy ache coming back. When Carol called them back into the circle for repeat demonstrations, Emily couldn't seem to move. She felt frozen solid, watching her mother with…another man. And not just *any* man…

When Carol called them again, Steph grabbed Emily by the arm, and pulled her toward Carol and the other girls. Emily went along, but she was too distracted to really focus on the rest of the lesson. She kept looking over at the warm-up rink, and watching what her mother was doing, as often as she could.

Emily knew her parents weren't getting along at all. They argued behind closed doors, or downstairs, when they thought she was in her room studying, but she heard their angry voices and she knew they were fighting. She didn't dare ask them what was wrong. Her father said that children who questioned parents about "parent private time" were disrespectful, and they should be punished…and he *had* punished her, with some pretty bad spankings.

Emily was afraid of his temper. Steph said that her dad had problems in his brain.

Emily couldn't ask her mother about what was going on, either. It wouldn't do any good anyway. Her mother would just say "everything's fine, honey, don't worry," like she always did—and then she'd turn on her favorite radio station—the one with all the Negro singers. But, at least, her mother never had hit her. She would never do that— her mother said she hated violence. Her mom didn't know about the spankings because Emily had never told her about them. Her dad had only spanked her at his parents' house a few times. Her grandparents, the Smithson's, believed that God wanted parents to hit kids, so they would obey, and not commit sins.

She knew her mother loved her…and her father loved her, too—in his own way. But she wasn't at all sure that her parents loved each other.

30

Steph's parents went out on dates, without their kids. They went to the movies, they had dinner together at restaurants, and she'd even seen them kissing in the kitchen, when she'd been over at Steph's. It made her sad to think about her own parents, and how they never did anything as a couple—or even as a family, anymore.

Her father worked late—every night. Sometimes he was so late, Emily didn't see him at all before her eight o'clock bedtime. She'd be in her room, waiting for him to come home, knowing that her mom was wondering where he was. Her mother must worry about him a lot, because his office closed at six, and he never came home for dinner anymore.

Something was wrong, for sure, and she'd been hoping her parents problems would get better. She worried that, if things didn't change in her house—well, it made her stomach upset to think about what might happen. She was afraid to even tell Steph too much, because she was sure that talking about it would make it worse. Just last week, her Grandmother Smithson had warned her not to talk about family problems to *anyone*—because that could hurt people—and Emily didn't want to hurt anybody.

Now, Carol was calling Emily to take her last turn, but every time she tried to concentrate, Emily's worries about her family would jump into her head—and fly around in her body. Somehow, her fears went right to her legs, causing her to stumble. Usually, at the rink, she'd forget about her family's problems, but today, seeing her mother with another man—*a colored man*—watching her laughing with him, and touching him, made her feel too sick to skate.

Emily was relieved when Carol finally ended the class. Steph left, to run to the bathroom. Emily skated to a dark place under the bleachers, where she could hide, and still see her mother and the man who, she figured, was probably Jaheen's father.

Suddenly, she noticed that Jaheen was standing in the shadows, near the locker room door. Jaheen's hands were closed into tight fists, and she was staring at their parents, and she had an angry look on her dark, scrunched-up face.

Emily had a pretty good idea about what Jaheen was thinking.

Chapter 4 ✺ Anna

Anna's vision was clearing up, but the rest of her body was acting in very strange ways. She had a headache, and she expected that. But her heart was beating too hard. Her cheeks were flushed, and they were getting hotter whenever the tall black man looked at her *like that*—like he saw something in her face that interested him. She was alert enough now to figure out that he *was* the same guy who'd been watching her from the stands.

He seemed nice. He was sitting near her on the hard wooden bench, but he kept a polite distance. The seat was hard, and when he shifted his weight from one hip to the other, and she noticed that his pants were tight around his thighs. She could still feel his warm sweater where he'd touched her, and smell his musty after-shave.

"Well, thanks again, for…for helping me," she stuttered, squeezing her eyes closed and rubbing them.

"No problem," he said, standing up in front of her, holding onto the railing. She could feel him looking down at her. "You're sure you're all right?" he asked.

She reached for the railing and pulled herself up next to him. He started to lean over to help her, but then he backed away, as if he'd changed his mind about touching her again.

"Yeah…Wow…Where are my manners? Hi, I'm Anna—and that's my daughter, Emily, over there, skating in the class. She really likes working with Carol, and—

anyway, it's really nice to meet you…and thanks so much—again!" She knew she was talking too fast, so she stopped herself. She started to offer a handshake, but, seeing him turn away, she decided against it, and she laughed nervously.

"Nice to meet you, too, Anna," he said quietly, meeting her eyes for a quick second. Then he nodded toward the skating children. "I'm Abraham—and that's my daughter—Jaheen—she's in the same class as—" He seemed a little nervous, too.

"Emily," she finished for him. "Yep. Emily's twelve."

"*Emily*—and you're *Anna*," he repeated, with an apologetic half-smile. "Jaheen's fourteen, going on forty." His smile got bigger then, but it didn't last long. Anna watched him, as he looked at the class, and she tried to analyze his face—or what she could see of it. Most of his dark skin was hidden behind a monster-sized beard. His emotions seemed buried deep inside him, and there were few clues as to what he was really thinking about.

Any feelings that she *could* read in his face showed up in the tiny dark lines around his eyes—which were almost hidden by the big glasses. They crinkled up when he smiled. She guessed he was about her age—maybe a little older.

She decided that he was a very shy person, and he was kind of good looking. But she'd never really spent any length of time talking, face-to-face, at close range, with a black man, and when she realized that she was staring at him, she looked away. She felt her face grow warm again.

"Oh, right…Yep, they grow up too fast these days. They have to, because…well, you know, all of the violence, and—" She thought about the race problems that people were having in the south, and she wasn't sure it was the right thing to bring up to a black man, so, she changed the

34

subject. "*Abraham*. Nice name…Hey, I really appreciate you helping me out…and…it's good to meet you, too. I've seen you around—sitting up there, with the other parents. I usually just skate over here during the lessons…" she shrugged one shoulder, and feeling awkward, she added, "but I've seen your daughter skate. She's *very* good." She knew she was rambling again.

He nodded, shifting his weight from one hip to the other, looking everywhere but at her. "Thank you…I've always wanted her to learn how to skate, like I…"

Anna was even more curious now. She was curious—to a fault, Bill had told her that, whenever she asked a lot of questions. But now, she didn't care what Bill thought. She wanted to know more about *Abraham*.

"So, do you skate, too? I mean, did you, when you were a kid? Is that what you were going to say?"

He gave her a quick look of surprise, "How did you guess that I skate—that I skated—when I was a kid?"

She grinned at him. "Well, now, you kind of let that slip, but I can recognize a fellow skater. Look at the way you're standing…and moving your legs like that. It's hard to stand still in here, isn't it?"

She saw the lines around his eyes crinkle up again, as he continued to watch his daughter. He laughed and replied, "Okay, you got me…Yeah, I skated. It was a way to kind of, well, escape—from problems. Skating—roller, ice, street—it didn't matter…it was a great outlet for me." He paused to glance down at her, and a serious look crossed his face. "Skating changed my life, really…It might have even saved it…but…anyway…I'm glad you're okay now."

He touched her arm lightly, and turned, as if to walk away, but she could almost feel his reluctance to leave—and she knew she didn't want him to go, either.

There was something about him—he seemed a little bit sad—and maybe a little lonely—almost the same way she'd been feeling…

"I—I really think I know what you mean." The force of her words surprised her. She must have startled him too, because he stopped and turned to face her. His eyes were large, and glowing behind the thick glass lenses, like amber coals in a cozy fireplace. She felt a sudden need to tell him more about herself, and the words just tumbled out of her. "I loved to skate as a kid, because skating was the only thing that made me feel really free, you know, to be myself—and it still does." She added, feeling the heat in her face creep down her neck. "You'd think I'd have outgrown it by now."

He shook his head. "Na, you can't outgrow something like that." He said, moving his feet, looking down at his shoes. "Not if you really love it."

"I know," she said, looking down at his feet, too. "I just said that so I wouldn't sound so stupid. I don't think I'll ever outgrow skating." She saw him relax and lean forward on the wall, balancing his upper body on his elbows.

"It's not stupid—to love something that makes you feel…happy."

He was really kind and gentle, for such an intimidating-looking man, she thought. She realized that because he looked so scary, she would have never started talking to him, if she'd met him on the street. Now, she wanted to pour out her heart to him.

"That's what I think, too, but my husband—" Emotions about Bill began to bubble around inside of her. She was tempted to tell Abraham more about her life, but she stopped herself. *Who was this man?* Why did she feel like she could trust him with her secrets?

He looked over at her, and then he looked toward the arena. He waited, and when she didn't continue, he said, "The girls are learning to go backwards today...Who taught you to figure skate?"

"Nobody. I taught myself some moves. I'm actually learning from watching the class. My dad always wanted me to play hockey with him. He was tough on me, he was, bless his soul. I think he wanted a boy, but, ah, all he had was—was the likes of me—so...I guess I acted like one, to please him—I still act more like a boy than..." she giggled, nervously and shrugged. "My dad skated like a demon from hell, and he wanted me to skate the same way—to be like him, I think. But I always liked figure skating...and...sorry, I'm babbling...must be the whack on me head..."

He nodded, glancing, and grinning at her. "No problem. I've been told I'm a good listener...and not much of a talker."

Anna smiled and she felt a welcome sense of relief. She was really enjoying this—talking with this nice man, Abraham. She gripped the railing. The big and too - expensive diamond on her wedding ring pinched into her little finger, and it reminded her of Bill. She hadn't shared many memories or feelings about her father with Bill—the jerk. He never listened to her like this.

Abraham spoke softly, "So, tell me, do you skate now *because* of your father...or in spite of him? I'm guessing that's your father's hockey jersey..." She watched his eyes narrow, and then he looked away. "I'm sorry, I didn't mean to pry..."

His blunt comments shocked her. He was too close to the truth—and he was right. She leaned back, holding the railing in both hands for support, and she watched Em. Her eyes started to burn with tears.

He turned to leave, she reached out and touched his arm. "No...Wait. That's a fair question, it is...and...I'd like to tell you what I think—if you really want to hear it."

"Ah...yeah, well, that's okay. I'd better be going."

"No, please wait." She repeated.

He paced restlessly. She was afraid he might walk away, so she started to talk fast. "Yes! You're right...my father's life—and his death—is big part of me—of who I am. My mum died when I was a wee one. I'm an orphan now...and well, I actually love to skate for the way it makes me feel...and I want my daughter to learn to love it, too." She tried to catch her breath. "But I don't want her to learn the way my father taught me—all competitive and mean. So, maybe that's why I put Em in this class...so she'd have a good teacher—one who would, you know, respect her—and help her to express herself. You know, to show the world what's really in her heart."

She felt her cheeks glowing hot.

"Hmm." He shook his head, as if he didn't agree, and then he said slowly, "You could teach her. You respect her, I can tell. I don't think you're like your father at all...You seem very kind...and you have the skating ability..."

She saw him squeeze his eyes closed, as if he had a sudden pain in his head. She almost asked him why he knew she was a good skater, but then she realized he'd been watching her—probably more often than she'd ever noticed before.

So...she'd caught him! She could have confronted him, but she felt protective of him now. He was a good man—and he seemed to be able to read her like a book. Racial tensions were exploding everywhere, and she knew he was in an awkward, if not risky situation, just by talking with her, especially in this lily-white part of town, where he was almost a trespasser...

"Thank you, for the complement, Abraham," she said instead. As she smiled at him, she saw the lines around his eyes dance with some deep emotion—maybe it was gratitude?

"And when was the last time *you* skated?" she asked with a sly grin, watching the blades of her skates, as she slid them back and forth on the concrete. Her headache was gone now, and she was feeling energized, almost giddy.

He glanced at her, and he took a long time to answer her, if he was carefully choosing his words. "It's been awhile" he said flatly.

"Are you any good?"

He smiled again. "Maybe. I was…but, like I said, it's been awhile."

"I think they might have a pair of skates in your size over there."

Abraham followed her glance toward the rental counter, and sent her a look of alarm. "Now? I don't…I couldn't…"

She gave him a teasing look. "We still have an hour before the girls are out of class."

He laughed.

She nodded, and told herself that he was just another guy. Under all that colored skin, a man was still a man. She remembered the teasing from her father's friends, and she understood their need to compete. She'd learned, over years of playing rough hockey games with them, that no man who called himself a real skater ever backed down from a challenge on the ice.

Abraham looked at her now, searching her eyes as if he was trying to read her mind. "Well…okay…but I warn you, I am much more comfortable in a classroom, than on ice skates anymore…so, you promise not to laugh at me?"

"Hey, who am I to judge? I just woke up from a coma!" Anna giggled.

As he brushed passed her, the heat she felt between their bodies warmed her, and gave her a feeling of unreality. She felt like a teenager on her first date, not knowing what was happening, but at the same time, sensing that it could be dangerous.

"Hey, Abraham, what subject do you teach?" she asked to his back, as he walked away.

"History. Southside JC."

"Really? History? That was my major…"

He nodded with a sideways look back at her. She thought she saw another grin. Her eyes followed him closely, as he rented, tried on, and laced up a pair of the biggest skates she'd ever seen.

She fumbled around in her pocket for some lip gloss, and smoothed her unruly hair back behind her ears. She usually paid little attention to her appearance. She knew she was not a pretty woman. She had been called "good looking" when she set her naturally curly hair, and put some make-up on once in a while, but she'd never been told that she was beautiful. Men rarely gave her a second look.

Today, Abraham had looked at her a lot, and she was not used to having a man look at her, the way Abraham had…and Bill never did.

Bill. It had been almost an accident that they'd ever gotten together at all. Anna had gotten pregnant on the night they'd met. Bill had been drunk on too much beer. He'd given Anna something to drink too, and she never had remembered what really happened that night in his dorm room.

Bill was a *Christian,* and he had agreed—very reluctantly—to marry her. After Emily's birth, Anna dropped out of school, and worked to earn their living expenses. Because his parents were angry about their forced marriage—and, about the fact that they'd had sex— they'd only paid for Bill's tuition, even though they had tons of money.

After he'd graduated, Bill joined a dental practice in west Atlanta, and Anna stopped working to be a full-time mom. Anna tried substitute teaching. She'd shared her enthusiasm for history—and for social justice—with students. But when she'd explained that the causes of racial violence were shared by everyone in society, parents complained, and she'd stopped receiving teaching assignments.

Now, watching Abraham warm up on the ice, taking strong, straight strides with powerful strokes that nearly took her breath away. Her thoughts about her life with Bill were gone...And her feelings of loneliness had disappeared.

Chapter 5 ❋ Emily

Emily still couldn't believe what she was seeing. She stared in amazement at her mother, and the colored man—Jaheen's father. They were skating *together* laughing—almost dancing—all alone, in the back arena.

It was dark over there, but it was light enough for her to see what they were doing. The man was a much better skater than her mom. He kept her from falling a couple of times, but then he fell. Her mother pulled him up, and they'd held on to each other, giggling like kids. He'd let go of her mother, and she'd do some spins, but then he'd pull her back to him when she got too wobbly. Sometimes he held onto *both* of her arms, and they spun around and around, in circles together.

Someone touched Emily's shoulder and she jumped.

"Anything wrong, Em?" Carol asked.

Emily turned, and looked straight into her teacher's kind, old blue eyes.

"No."

Carol looked at her, like her mother sometimes did, when she didn't believe her.

"Something's bothering you. I can tell. You were very distracted in class today."

Emily shrugged.

"Um hum," Carol nodded slowly.

Emily didn't want to tell her teacher about her family's problems.

She glanced in the direction of her mother and the man. *Oh no!* She'd given it away! Carol had noticed, and was watching her mother and Jaheen's father, now, too! Ah, *crap*! There they were, in front of everybody—her mom and that Neg—skating together, dancing like they were on a date, or something.

"Is that your mom—skating with…is that Jaheen's *father?*"

Emily felt tears coming. She was so embarrassed. She didn't want Carol to see—anything! Her family problems should be *private*, like Grandmother Smithson had said. Or else, they could get worse…

"Oh my! They're ice dancing—well…I didn't know Jaheen's father could skate like that! Magnificent!"

Emily felt Carol looking at her again. Carol didn't seem too worried about a white lady skating in public with a black man, and that surprised her. Maybe she was just being polite…

Didn't Carol think that race was a big deal? Everybody did—except her mom. Her mom was different. Her mother was a *libraryal* or something like that. Her dad said her mother was wrong to be so open-minded. Her dad said it was a mistake to think that all races were the same. He said that God made people different colors for a reason. Her dad had never said what God's reason was, but she knew that she'd better not ask him stupid questions like that.

"Hmm. They have something really good going there…hmm. I'll have to tell…"

Oh no! Who was Carol going to tell? Her dad? That couldn't happen. Then her parents might get a divorce. And *that* would be terrible…

"Emily, lately, I've noticed that you've been worried—and upset—about something. But whatever is bothering you, I think it's been affecting your concentration in class." Her voice was so nice and soft, that Emily was having a hard time holding back the tears, and her eyes started to really hurt.

"Would it help to talk about it?" Carol asked.

Emily shook her head, no, but tears were dripping down her cheeks now. Her family was a mess. Her life was nothing like she wanted it to be. She wanted her parents to be happy, like the families she saw on TV—when her dad let her to watch TV—which was *almost never*. She just wanted a *normal* life.

And, now, today, her mother was making their family secret not a secret anymore—and that was so *wrong!* Carol could guess their family secret. And what would the other mothers think, too, when they saw what her mother was doing?

Why did she have to skate with a *colored man?* In front of *everybody?*

Carol reached out and gave her a quick hug, and turned Emily toward her. "Emily, you're a really good kid. You get out there, and you try hard, every week. I admire that in my students. So, if there's anything I can do to help, you, you'll tell me, right?"

Emily nodded.

"Are you sure you're going to be okay?"

Emily nodded again. No, she wasn't going to be okay.

"All right. I've got to start my next class. See you on Thursday?" Carol gave her a worried look as she turned away. Emily watched her skate over to the group of students who were waiting for her in the center of the rink.

As she wiped her eyes with her gloves, and skated toward the locker room, Emily wondered what she was going to say to her mother in the car. Maybe she'd try asking her mom to—to do what? She was just a kid. No one ever listened to her. All she could do was hope that her mother would just figure out how much she wanted a happy family.

Emily had been taught at church that God could work miracles. Her Sunday school teacher said that God's love could heal anything. Well, she thought, if God *really* loved her, and loved her family, too, then anything could happen.

So, as she sat down to take off her skates, she said a little prayer, and asked God for a big miracle.

Chapter 6 ❀ Jaheen

Jaheen could not believe what she was seeing. Her father was actually skating! He seemed to just fly around the corners, as if his blades weren't touching the ice at all. He raised his arms above his head, ending a round with a long, fast spin—and then he fell down.

Jaheen started skating toward the back rink, to go to him—to see if he was all right—and then she gasped, and braked hard. A red-haired lady skated up to him, and helped him to stand up! And they were—*laughing? Together?*

"Keep your hands off him, you bitch!" she whispered under her breath.

Her dad looked okay—more than okay—he was still laughing and touching the woman on her shoulder.

What the hell?

Jaheen looked up in the stands. The mothers from her own class were gone, but moms from the next class were climbing up to find seats.She started to worry about what these honkeys would think if they saw what he was doing over there: a black man skating—with one of *them*.

Wait a minute! He wasn't with just *any* woman, either. He was skating with that weird one who practiced, alone in the back rink, every week—Emily's mother. Emily, the little ratty girl in her class who couldn't skate worth a damn.

Jaheen's own mother had a bad temper, and the last thing Jaheen wanted was any more trouble at her house.

Her mother and her father were not a happy couple, and her mother yelled at him a lot—way too much. But her dad needed to stand up for himself more, too, she thought, shaking her head. So now, how could she stop that ugly white woman from causing even *more* problems?

In the past, she'd tried to help her parents get along with each other better, but nothing she did seemed to help them. In so many ways, Jaheen was used to feeling powerless to change her life, or her family's ways. She was a black girl with a mind of her own, and she had a plan. She figured that she had to learn to act white, if she was going to get what she wanted in life.

"You got to learn to get along in this world," her father always said.

But when her mother heard him say things like that—especially about getting along nice-like, with whites—her mom would go off in a rage. Jaheen had heard her mother say, many times, "Shee, Uncle Tom…when you kiss up on the outside, you die on the inside."

Jaheen noticed that Emily was standing in the corner, watching their parents skate together, too. Jaheen wondered what the kid was thinking about her own mother—flirting like that with a black man.

Then she saw Carol go over and talk to Emily. *Good!* Maybe Carol would straighten her out, and make the kid tell her mother to back off.

Why was Emily crying now?

What a baby, Jaheen thought.

Maybe Jaheen had almost felt like crying herself…But crying got you nowhere in this world, like her mother said. You had to be tough, especially when your skin was black.

Anyway, it was over now. Her dad was sitting on the bench, taking off his skates.

Better get going, she thought. He was always in a hurry to get her home for an early dinner—and wanted her to do her homework! *Yuk!* Her dad was always pushing too hard for her to go to college—just like he'd done. He was smart, and had won scholarships, but Jaheen knew she was only an average student, and even worse in math.

No, she had other plans. She was going to be a professional skater someday. On the way to the locker room, she did a couple of extra spins. For a few minutes, she was lost in a vision of herself in front of crowds, under spotlights, collecting medals. Skating always helped her to forget her family problems for a while. She'd have to talk with her dad on the way home in the car—talk some sense to him.

Inside the dressing room, a few girls were still there, taking off their skates, and putting on their street clothes and coats. She noticed Emily and Steph in the far corner. Jaheen hurried into a quiet corner far away from them, keeping her head down, not making eye contact with anyone, just like her dad told her to do.

She sat on an empty bench. While she unlaced her skates, she listened to the other girls' annoying giggling and their trashy gossip. She snickered to herself. *Losers*, she thought. She was glad that none of them ever talked to her. They were all stupid honkeys.

She was surprised when one of the girls—she thought her name was Wendy—called out her name, in a loud, screechy voice, from across the room. "Jaheen! Why was your dad hitting on Em's mom? Are they having a *love affair?*"

Jaheen, jumped to her feet. Without thinking—and forgetting her father's lectures about being polite—she snapped, and yelled, "What you sayin'? That bitch was goin' after *him!*"

Stephanie gasped from her corner. "You called Emily's mom a *bitch*?"

The girls in the room stared at one another. Jaheen felt her face and neck burn. She felt like she was going to explode. Jaheen looked at Emily, and their eyes locked. Then, she saw the tears falling all over Emily's face.

It wasn't just the crying that stopped Jaheen. It was that look of pain. It was the kind of pain that Jaheen had felt, when her own parents were acting stupid.

Was she feeling sorry for Emily? Maybe. But Emily's sad look had given Jaheen the few seconds that she needed to get back in control of herself. Jaheen knew she had to get along with these girls; it had been a condition for even being at the white-ass skate club. She'd been given special permission to take lessons from Carol because of her father. He had persuaded the club's board members that his only daughter had perfect manners. He'd given his, word as a college professor. He'd promised that she would obey *all* the rules—and those rules included no bad language—no fighting, and no disrespecting...*anybody*.

"I...I'm sorry. I didn't mean to call Emily's mother...*that*...I was just..." Jaheen stuttered, fighting her anger, struggling to stay calm, forcing herself back into the required role of acting nice, and being polite. After all, she was the intruder; she knew that she was not wanted there.

But, deep down, she was still boiling mad, because Emily's mother had made moves on her father. White on black. *"Use and abuse us"* as her mother said. But that wasn't Emily's fault. Emily couldn't control her parents any more that Jaheen herself could change her own.

And, it wasn't her dad's fault either. Her dad was so out of it when it came to women, Jaheen was sure that it *couldn't* have been his idea. He'd been tricked into doing something he hadn't wanted to do...but he had gotten out

49

there, and he'd skated for the first time in years, so that part was cool, she thought.

Now, Emily started to walk toward Jaheen. She wiped the tears from her face, and she turned to Wendy and the other girls. "Hey...Listen! There was...*nothing*—nothing wrong going on. Our parents were...they were just skating...like we all were out there." She hiccupped and sniffled. "They were just practicing a sport—our sport— just like playing basketball—or something." She glanced at Jaheen, and back to Stephanie. "Steph...Let it go. Okay?"

No one spoke.

Emily and Stephanie walked out together. Stephanie had her arm around Emily's shoulders.

Wendy and the other girls picked up their expensive-looking skate bags without saying a word. After they left, the room seemed to be filled with a silence that was so hot and heavy Jaheen thought she could almost smell smoke.

Chapter 7 ❀ Anna

Anna drove her pink Plymouth station wagon over the speed limit. The Brothers' new single filled the car with their special blend of soul and jazz. Anna was still feeling the warm flush of exhilaration from skating with Abraham. She glowed all over with some kind of new energy.

She tried to concentrate on her driving, but the images in her head were hard to ignore: Abraham's sly grins. The sound of his deep, kind voice. The way he joked and laughed about the mistakes he'd made in his life...

He'd made her feel good. He'd accepted her—just the way she was. He even seemed to like her. The more she thought about him, the more she noticed that she was having pleasant sexual feelings, too. Her breasts tingled, and the intense sensations, she had to admit, were something she was enjoying—but they were a little bit scary.

She noticed that Emily seemed more quiet than usual. Unable to keep the irritation out of her voice, Anna asked loudly, over the music, "Em, what's wrong?"

There was no response.

Emily's teenage moodiness had gotten a lot worse lately—she would turn thirteen soon—but right now, Anna was having problems dealing with her own emotions.

Anna sighed. "Emily, answer me...*please?*" she said impatiently.

Emily looked at her with narrowed eyes, and then she turned away. Talking to the windshield, she said, "How could you do it, Mom? In front of *everyone*..."

"How could I...? What are you talking about?"

"What do you *think?*" Emily snapped back at her.

Anna was surprised. It was not like Em to be rude. She seemed really upset.

Why would she be so...? Oh. Of course! Anna realized that Em must have seen her skating—with Abraham.

"Are you upset that I was skating...with *Jaheen's father?*"

"Slow down, Mom. You're driving too fast."

She was right, Anna thought, and she hit the brake. The car lurched, and then Anna reduced her speed. "Emily, honey, we were just practicing. Ab—*Jaheen's father* helped me to get up, after I slipped and fell. Did you know I knocked myself out on the ice today?"

There was no answer.

Anna wanted to change the direction of the conversation. "I still have a little headache. I don't know how long I was out..."

Emily didn't respond, and kept looking at the road ahead.

"He helped me up, and then we skated. He's very good. I learned a couple of new moves from him. He used to skate a lot, when he was growing up—in Philly and Detriot. I think that's why his dau..." She stopped herself. She realized that she was probably saying too much, and, as usual, she seemed to be making everything worse by over-explaining.

"Mom, you're *missing the point!* He's, you know..."

"What...? A man?" Anna was feeling defensive, and she was starting to feel angry at having to justify herself....and maybe she was feeling a little guilty, too.

"Well, yeah...*and*..."

"Oh...*and*...he's a *colored man*. Is that it, Em?" Heat rose fast into her face and neck. "You mean, his race makes him so different—that it's not okay for me to skate in the same rink with him?"

"Well, no...I mean, yes...Mom, you're *married*. Plus, Dad says..."

Here we go again, Anna thought. Bill's family legacy. His family's racism was being transferred to her daughter.

"I really don't care what your fath—," Anna said, and then she paused, trying to control herself. She understood that Em was upset about seeing her with another man—a black man at that, so Anna shifted into her best teacher-in-a-classroom voice. "Emily, I really don't *agree* with what your father says—and what his family believes. I think black people are equal to white people in every way." Anna sighed. "Your father and I—we *disagree* about that."

"Is that why you and daddy fight a lot?"

As if her face had just been slapped, Anna reacted to the question. She'd taken great care to keep her disagreements with Bill hidden—so Emily wouldn't know about their marital problems. Now, feeling guilty that she'd failed to protect Emily enough, she felt compelled to lie again—to cover up the lies she'd already told.

Barely breathing, Anna's mind was spinning. What should she say? Anna was tired and confused. Her head was hurting again. She was tired of the lying. It had felt so good to tell Abraham the truth about her life today...and he'd accepted her, mistakes and all...

Now, she didn't know what to do. She felt the need to protect her daughter, but she also needed to be honest, and she had no idea how to do either one of those things for Emily anymore.

Should she tell more lies? Or should she tell Em at least *some* of the truth?

Maybe it was her talk with Abraham. Maybe her head was still messed up from the fall. Maybe she was tired of pretending. Maybe it was her upbringing—her father never sugar-coated bad news—but the truth came flooding out of Anna's mouth like a water from a firehose: "Em...okay...yes. You know that your father and I disagree about race, and the reasons for race riots...And, yes indeed, he and I have had serious conflicts—about a lot of things—things that are very personal, between he and I—*and* the way he and his family are so strict with you—*and* the way they want you to think—and act—their hateful ideas." She took a breath. "I know I should have told you before, and I'm sorry...And I'm sorry that you've heard us arguing."

She took in another gulp of air, and she gave Emily a look that, Anna hoped, asked her daughter for understanding and forgiveness. Tears welled up in Anna's eyes, and she saw Em wiping her eyes with the back of her hand.

Anna chewed on her lip. She gripped the wheel with one hand, and she reached out for Emily's with the other. Squeezing her daughter's small fingers, she said, "But don't you worry, honey. Everything will be okay. Married people disagree all the time...and they can work things out."

Emily nodded, and said softly, "That's what God wants, doesn't he, mom? For families to stay together?"

Anna squeezed her eyes shut for a second, and took another deep breath. She thought about her father's beliefs, and how he'd taught her that it was wrong to act against God's will. But how could her father have been so sure about what God's will really was? And why was she so *unsure* about what she was supposed to do now?

Anna forced a highly practiced smile, but her jaw was tight. She nodded. "Like they teach you in church, honey...pray, and trust in God's will. And everything will be just fine...."

But Anna was lying again, and she knew it.

As she pulled into their circular driveway, she wished she didn't have to go inside their too-big of a house. She had a sudden impulse to keep on driving. She didn't want to talk to Bill tonight.

Something had shifted inside her at the rink today. Just for a little while, she'd seen herself, not as she pretended to be—the obedient wife who had no needs, no wants, and no opinions. She'd seen herself reflected in Abraham's kind and gentle eyes that was new and different. In his face, she'd seen a desirable, smart, attractive woman who had a talent. Not only did she have a talent for ice skating—something that Bill hated and denied—but she also had glimpsed a woman who had worth, and who deserved respect.

But her roots—her culture—and her father, had instilled in her a responsibility to God, family—and to a team. You didn't quit or disappoint God or anybody—not even if it cost you your own identity, and maybe even your deepest desires...

So, although she was tired of shaping herself into the mold of a marriage that didn't fit her anymore, she realized that Emily was becoming a casualty of her battles with Bill, and *that* had to change.

She loved her daughter, and her daughter's happiness came first. It was her job, as a good parent, to give Emily a family. She couldn't be selfish, like her father had been, drinking himself to death, leaving Anna all alone in the world. Being an orphan was terribly painful, even for adults, she thought sadly. Everybody needed their parents, even if those parents were far from perfect…

Through her shimmering tears, Anna said a silent prayer, vowing to try harder to fix her marriage, and save her family. *That* was her number one priority…and *that* was the right thing to do for her child…*wasn't it?*

Chapter 8 ❄ Abe

Abraham and Jaheen slipped quietly through the garage door into an empty kitchen. As usual, he noticed that the stove was stone cold, and the counters were bare. Their unwashed cereal bowls and spoons sat in the sink, where he and Jaheen had left them that morning.

He never knew what to expect, when he came home…but if he was totally honest with himself, he knew that everything *would* be the same. He'd given up hoping that his wife, Georgie, would change, and take back her kitchen—and rejoin their family. Dinners were almost always up to him to arrange. Usually it was carry-out—or leftovers from the previous day's carry-out.

Georgie, as usual, was busy—talking on the phone in her study, her voice echoing loudly around their large two story house. He could tell that she was on the line with one of her coworkers from the civil rights center. From the sound of the rising pitch of her voice, he knew for sure that she'd be awhile. He know her. She was just warming up for one of her rants.

He understood that Georgie was passionate about one thing: her involvement with the black community. She organized and led civil rights projects for Negro tenants in the inner city like a she was a frigging major general. Her second passion was for buying and selling real estate. She worked seven days a week, investing all of her energy into protecting her clients' interests, finding housing for the needy, and promoting racial equality—for "my people," she called them. They were worthy causes. Of course, he agreed it was important work, but it left her little or no time left for him—or for Jaheen.

And it was the way that she acted that got to him. She was so damn *bossy*.

She was planning to run for city commissioner, although, as a black woman, he believed that she had little chance of being elected. But he didn't dare tell her that. He didn't stick his neck out to offer his opinions anymore. She'd just wave his ideas aside—on good days—and, on really bad days, she belittled him about his peace-loving, "Uncle Tom" nature.

He tried to block out the sound of her voice, screeching with indignation, Georgie-style. He could hear her repeating to the unlucky caller all of the gory details of news he'd heard earlier on the radio—about another violent arrest at a sit-in on the steps of the courthouse.

"*Holy Jesus*...What? Yeah, well, honey, who do they think they are? Charlie...Yeah, I *know* Charlie's group wasn't planning anythin'...he was innocent...no, no, he was *not* trespassin'..." Georgie was nearly yelling now. He could imagine her face: rage dripping from her eyes, until her face twisted with it, and she looked like an old prune.

Abraham took Jaheen gently by the shoulders and said, "Baby," he sighed, looking toward Georgie's office. "Sounds like it's gonna be take-out again tonight, so run on upstairs now...and start your homework."

Jaheen returned his look with a frown.

"Dad?" she said, looking like she was about to ask him something complicated. She'd given him that look in the car, too, but he hadn't been in the mood to discuss anything serious with Jaheen—or with anyone, then...or now. For a change, he was glad that Georgie was busy. He wanted to be alone, and think over the day's events. He'd been trying to sort out what had really happened to him. He was thinking about it, all the way back home, in the car. He'd kept the radio turned up loud, so he didn't have to talk much; all he could think about was that woman…

"Honey, I know…Your mama's on another one of her important phone calls. But I'll be back with dinner in a few minutes," he said, as he grabbed two juice containers from the refrigerator. He slipped one into his jacket pocket, and tossed the other to Jaheen—who had lately started asking them to call her "J." She caught the juice, smiled at him, and she shrugged.

When she turned and headed wordlessly toward the stairs, and he was relieved to be alone.

He glanced at the closed door, behind which Georgie's tirade continued to ebb and flow—mostly flow, out of her mouth, he thought, like a tidal wave.

He guessed that today's racial incidents and arrests would result in more telephone calls to the community workers on her phone tree, so he scribbled her a message that he was going out to pick up barbeque at Sam's, and left it on the kitchen table.

He could have tacked the note to the refrigerator door, next to Jaheen's drawings, where they usually posted things, but he wanted to make a statement—he still couldn't help himself. It was just a small act, protesting the empty dinner table. He knew it would irritate Georgie when she saw it, but he didn't care. He wanted Georgie to cook for their family more—hell—*more?* She *never* cooked anymore—or even ate with him and J anymore. She spent all of her time on the phone, or out agitating, meeting, or marching, with her people. He and J were just slowing her down—getting in the way of her causes—taking too much time away from her real love, which, as he saw it, was to change the world.

Walking outside into the cool, gray fall dusk, he left his problems with Georgie behind, and he felt a smile slip onto his lips. Closing the car door, he started the engine of his rusty, wood-sided Ford wagon, he flipped the radio off. He wanted some quiet; he wanted to be alone with his thoughts.

As he drove, he allowed himself to absorb the full impact of what had happened to him. The excitement of meeting Anna, and the thrill of skating again. His head swam with images of the two of them, playing and laughing together…like children—like the fun he'd wished for, when he was a kid, but he'd never had.

Exhilaration surged from his chest and hit him in his empty stomach—where hunger was growing. Was he hungry for food? Or for…something else? He didn't know for sure, but it was like a gnawing…a craving.

He was looking forward to a spicy rib dinner, a really long shower, and settling down with new history book he was reading about the civil war. With any luck, Georgie would still be on the phone until late, so he could replay the events of the day, over and over again in his head.

For the first time in a very long time, he felt really, really jazzed. And there was heat in his body—and in his groin—a burning that he hadn't felt for many years. He drove slowly and carefully because he couldn't keep his mind off of the good feelings…

In the beginning, a long time ago, there had been feelings like that for Georgie. They had shared times of real passion during their first years together. Georgie had been aggressive in her lovemaking—and she was fit and sexy. But then J was born. She was a surprise baby. Georgie was restless, and had never wanted children. She was driven by a desire to right social wrongs. After she'd led her first protest march, it seemed to take possession of her.

They married for Jaheen, but he wanted a real marriage. He wanted to keep their passion alive. But between the demands of his teaching career *and* taking care of J—feeding her, driving her from school, doing housework...and he just got too tired to keep trying. He remembered the night of his thirtieth birthday. Georgie promised him a big celebration—a sex date. Jaheen was asleep, and they were getting it on. The telephone rang. She sat up in bed, and she switched on the light...She had reached out to answer the phone—right in the middle of sex!

"What the hell are you doin'?"

"It may be important, Abraham...I won't be too long."

"Georgie...I need to get up at six. I've got to get to sleep. I don't have much time..."

"You're just *selfish*. You know that? People are dying out there, and all you care about is your dick."

He remembered trying to hide his hurt and anger, but she'd seen right through him.

"Abraham, grow up! Don't you care about what I do?"

He hadn't known what to say, but his silence had given him away.

"I can see that you don't, you self-centered, white-lovin' bastard." He could still see the disgust in her face. "I'm gonna take this call in my study, so don't wait up."

Their sex life had dropped to mostly zero after that night. Since then, all of their arguments seemed to revolve around her radical political agenda. She always went overboard. She'd told him she was disappointed, when he wasn't as furious as she was about the way people of color were being treated; she accused him of not supporting her work for equal rights.

He told her that fighting wasn't the answer, and studying history had proven that to him. He just wanted to get along peacefully in the white world, like Doctor King, but she called him a "candy ass"…She said that he was weak, with no backbone, and he had no balls.

Her words had cut into him over the years, and now, her harshness, her appearance—she'd gained weight so she wouldn't "look like those skinny white bitches on TV," and her lack of respect for him had eroded his desire for her. She slept in her office. They didn't "date" anymore. She went everywhere with her pushy campaign flunky, Joe Johnson.

Abraham knew they were staying married because of Jaheen. Up until today, he'd thought he had learned to live with the loneliness and frustration. Sexually, he lived in a fantasy world, watching women from behind his mask. In real life, he buried himself in his work, teaching, writing courses, and, more recently, he had been outlining ideas for a new history textbook—and he still took care of Jaheen.

But today, something had changed. As he parked in front of Sam's Southern Heat Barbeque, he looked forward to two days from now, when he and Anna had agreed to meet in the back rink, during the girls' lesson, and skate together again.

Chapter 9 ❀ Anna

White foam and bright bubbles sparkled in the candlelight. Anna had sprinkled the water with her favorite rose-scented bath salts. She planned to forget her problems by soaking in the hottest water she could stand. Maybe the heat would dissolve the strange and powerful desires that were prowling around in her body, ever since she'd met Abraham…But they felt so good. Did she really want the feelings to go away?

Steam fogged the tall windows of her private bathroom. The last gasps of twilight peeked through the custom-made, stained glass windows that surrounded the antique claw foot tub on three sides. She'd lit candles in the wall sconces, and the light from the three separate flames bounced around the room, causing the high white tray ceiling to glow like moonlight.

She studied the room's rich woodwork, and the golden fixtures. She'd had nothing to do with designing the imposing, twelve-room, southern style mansion—except for this bathroom—her bathroom. Building the huge house had caused a big argument. Usually Anna gave into Bill's demands right away, but she'd resisted him about the size of the house; it was too big for three people, she'd insisted. So many poor Georgians were living on the street or in tenements…Anna had been so upset, that Bill had said he would increase the cash amount of his tithing to the church, where they were members…After that, he'd ended all further discussion.

So, Bill had gotten his way, as usual, and the house plans had been drawn and completed by Bill's father, William Smithson, Senior, who was one of Atlanta's more famous and successful builders.

Usually this room—and her tub—was her refuge. Locking herself in her bathroom allowed her a chance to be alone, and to relax. Bill couldn't interrupt her, or bully her with his stupid demands or complaints. But tonight, turmoil and confusion had followed her right into the bubbling tub.

Bill! Bill had his own massive shower, in his personal "man suite," as he called his bathroom-bedroom-office combination. He had a wet bar, and a redwood steam room that his father had imported from California. She'd bet he would like to show it off to one of his lady friends…

Bill's father. "That creep!" Just the thought of that man caused Anna to cringe out loud. She didn't like to admit it, because God didn't want people to judge, but she'd never liked Bill Senior—right from the first time she'd met him. On that day, Bill Senior had dramatically introduced her to his twisted views on social issues. She remembered their conversation like it was yesterday, and not thirteen years ago.

"Anna dear, there's been a great injustice done—and it needs to be corrected—"

"I agree, Mr. Smithson. All Americans should be allowed equal rights." Anna had interrupted. In her nervous attempt to be agreeable, she hadn't let him finish.

The handsome older man hadn't looked directly at her, but he'd continued on, with unbelievable composure. "Oh, my, my, no, child, that is *incorrect thinking*. Whites should rule the Negroes, like they had successfully done in the South, before the Civil War. Colored folks don't know what's best for them." He'd walked around the room, and spoke with authority, like a preacher. "Negros are like little black sheep…they have to be led, until the Lord Jesus returns to take the white folk home, to heaven."

At first she thought Bill Senior was joking. Then, realizing he wasn't, Anna had looked to Bill, hoping he would disagree with such nonsense. She'd stood there, speechless, waiting for Bill to say something *sane*, while she held onto her pregnant belly. She saw Bill drop his eyes to the floor, and then he changed the subject—and Bill started talking about his latest golf game!

Anna recalled another time when she'd lost her temper with both Bill and his father. Bill Senior had encouraged them to spank Emily—because she ate some candy. Emily was only ten years old then. Bill had agreed with his father, who was quoting something from the Bible about the value of beating children. Anna had exploded, taken Emily home, and Bill's father hadn't spoken to Anna since.

Bill's mother, Gwen, had never liked Anna, either. But Anna hadn't figured that out at first. Gwen had acted like a kind and friendly mother-in-law, and grandmother-to-be— in the beginning. When she'd first met the Smithsons, Anna's father had just died, and Anna had been sad—and ready to join the Smithson clan. She had no one, and she'd wanted—needed to become a part of their family. But Anna couldn't tolerate racism. Hate killed people. She'd seen what that had done to her father.

The last time Anna had seen Gwen, she and Emily had met her for a holiday lunch. During the meal, Emily had asked about Negro children who were being denied access to her church youth group.

"Baby girl," Gwen had said, glancing at Anna, in a slow, almost mocking drawl. "Some people are *born* superior to others. Negro souls have an animal nature, and God doesn't want the races mixin' together because it's not natural. Integration is not God's plan."

Anna had politely voiced her disagreement. "Gwen, that's not what I believe—and that's not what I want Emily to think. I want her to know that human beings were created equally—by God, and under our country's laws."

"Honey, your thinking was tainted by those silly Catholics—your father, and so many other ignorant immigrant foreigners—were sadly mistaken."

Anna would never forget Gwen's smiling face—lips that were smiling while they were speaking words of hate. That day, Anna realized that Gwen saw Anna, and people like her father, as horribly inferior—and she knew that she would never be a *real* Smithson—and after that, she didn't want to be a Smithson.

Anna sighed. Em…her little Em *was* a Smithson…a real one, by blood, and that would never change.

How could Anna save her daughter from becoming so hateful?

Anna watched the bubbles bursting in her tub. She thought about her hopes and dreams, of wanting a loving family, and how they were like the bubbles surrounding her body, popping and disappearing into nothingness.

Until today, Anna realized she'd been unable to move forward with her life because she'd wanted—she'd *needed*—to understand something that was impossible to know. She'd been trying to figure out what had gone so wrong in her marriage for so long, that she'd become obsessed with the question.

After asking the same question countless times, in countless ways, she still didn't have *the* answer, and she decided she would probably never know any answers that started with Bill's name.

Now, the real question came clear to her: What was she—Anna Margaret O'Breen Smithson—going to do?

She'd been stuck for too long. Her feelings had been frozen by fear….And, like today, she'd been asleep, knocked unconscious by guilt. But that was before…before she'd met…*him*.

Abraham Lincoln Brown. Why did someone name him *Abraham*? Was he Jewish? She didn't think so. She'd have to ask him…

But no, she couldn't ask him anything. If she was going to deal with her marriage, she'd better not see Mister Brown, or talk to him, ever again. He was too…sweet, too interesting…too…

Okay. Enough thinking—about Abraham. And about Bill.

She climbed out of the tub, and wrapped herself in a blanket-sized bath towel and flipped open the drain. She walked to the steamed–up mirror, wiped away a spot that was just big enough to see her eyes. They were so much like her father's eyes—plain Irish green.

"Help me!" She whispered, with all her heart.

And suddenly, she remembered a time when she'd broken a mirror by accident, and then she'd lied about it. She could hear her father's voice as the water gurgled from the tub. "Little girl, when ya lie, yer lyin' to yerself—and yer lying ta God."

Anna knew she needed to be honest. But who would be hurt, if she told everyone the whole truth?

But if lying was a sin then telling the truth, all the time, was the right thing to do.

Or was it?

Weren't there good lies, and bad ones? And big lies, and small ones?

She'd lied, to protect Emily.

She'd lied, to keep her family together.

She'd lied to herself, to keep from going crazy.

She gazed into the eyes of the confused woman in the mirror and asked herself: "What will it be, Plain Irish? The truth?...Or more lies?"

Chapter 10 ✳ Emily

Her mother was strangely quiet on the way to her Thursday lesson. Her mom had been acting funny ever since the talk they'd had about family problems. She guessed that her mother was upset about her Dad...but today, Emily wondered if her mom was thinking about skating with Jaheen's father again.

Were the two of them friends now? Could white people have colored friends? Emily didn't know anyone who had a colored friend.

The radio was tuned to her mother's favorite station, the one that played music for the Negroes, but it was on low, and usually her mom played it pretty loud. She thought about reasons why some white people liked colored people's music—and why her mom liked it so much.

"Why do you like that kind of music, mom?" she asked.

Her mother waited a while before she answered. "You know, Em, honey, I don't really know. Everyone...has—their *favorite* things in the world. You love country music—like my dad—your grandfather O'Breen—did. I don't like country at all. Everybody's different."

Emily nodded. That made sense.

"Em, why are you asking me about my music? You *know* that I've always listened to this station, ever since—"

"I know, I know. Since before you were my age," Emily finished for her. She'd heard her mom say that a thousand times.

Emily saw her mother smile, and Emily smiled, too.

Emily was feeling a little better about asking her mom questions since their talk about telling the truth, so Emily decided to try an honest question: "Mom, are you going to skate again today?" She watched her mother's face closely, looking for clues, ready to apologize, if her mom became upset.

She saw her mother's grip tighten on the shiny pink and silver steering wheel. Her big diamond ring flashed in the sunlight. Emily was glad to see that her mom was still wearing her ring; it meant that her parents were still married.

"Yes, I'm planning to, like always…but I know what you're going to ask me next."

Emily started to feel cold—kind of afraid—
and she wrapped her arms around herself.

"Go ahead. Ask me if I am going to skate with Jaheen's father again," her mother said with a sharp tone in her voice that Emily didn't like to hear. It didn't happen very often, but it meant that her mom was very unhappy about something.

Emily didn't answer. She stared straight ahead. Her stomach began to flutter—the way it had during Tuesday's lesson, when she'd watched her mother skating with….

Emily wanted her mother to skate—alone—by herself, just like she always did *before*…She wanted her mother to tell Jaheen's father that she was a married woman, and couldn't skate with him anymore because it was…because it was *wrong*. And, she wanted her mother to tell him that it wasn't right to skate with him because he was a colored man.

But she didn't know how to say any of that. And she didn't want to upset her mother, or be rude, so she said nothing at all.

She felt miserable.

"Have a good lesson, Sweetie," her mother said as she drove into the entrance to the ice arena. "I'm going to park the car, and I'll see you inside."

Emily grabbed her skate bag, and headed for the front door, running to catch up with Steph, who was waiting for her in the doorway of the lobby.

"Hey!" Steph called, with a happy grin.

Emily loved to be around Steph, and it was great to see her friend's smiling face today. They were a team—a perfect match. They knew each other's thoughts most of the time, and today was no different.

"Uh-oh…crap, Em, *what's wrong?*" Steph stopped and stared. "Don't tell me. It's your mom? She's going to skate…with *him* again?"

Emily nodded, afraid that tears might be coming. She was glad that Steph knew her so well, but she was worried…and embarrassed, for her mother, for herself— and for her family, too. Her emotions were so mixed up…

"I think she might. I don't know what's wrong with her. She's acting so crazy," she whispered to Steph.

"I know…Parents!…Crap. You know, they just get weird sometimes…"

"Yeah," Emily sighed. "I just don't know…I mean, I don't know what to do about it."

"Do about what?" Steph seemed confused, and Emily didn't blame her. She hadn't told her everything about her parents' arguments, or the way they were acting—being polite, never doing things together as a family. Emily hadn't had the nerve to actually say the word "divorce" out loud, to anyone—not even to Steph, her very best friend in the world.

Suddenly, Emily started to cry. She couldn't help it, and she started telling Steph everything, before she could stop herself. "Steph…my parents…they….they fight. They fight *a lot*. My dad never comes home—not until *really late* every night. I think maybe they're going to get a…a *divorce!*"

Steph pulled her over and sat her down onto the bench in the empty lobby. "Wow…Crap, Em! I didn't know…I mean I kinda knew *something* was wrong—I can sorta read your mind, ya know—but I didn't think things were *that* bad." Steph put her arm around Emily's shoulder. Her skate bag bumped up against Emily's arm, and it hurt a little, but Emily that pretended it didn't.

"Crap," her friend said again, still hugging her, and squeezing her against the bag, while Emily cried some more.

"Yeah…crap." Emily agreed, wiping her eyes with the back of her hand.

Steph pulled back and said, "It'll be okay, Em. I'll always be your friend, no matter what. We have each other. Things will work out—somehow…"

Emily started to get control of herself, and her tears were stopping.

"Ya know, our parents are just people. Yours are probably going through a *phase* or something—whatever that is. My parents said they did that—they had a phase, and then they got over it."

Emily nodded, swallowing. Steph's parents seemed happy. She took some deep breaths. "Okay, thanks," she managed to say. "Thanks, Steph, for being my friend."

Emily wondered how parents got over their phases, and if her parents ever would. It would be great if they did, she thought. Maybe there was still hope. Maybe they would solve their problems after all, and her life would be normal again.

"Hey...We are *best* friends!" Steph's voice was cheery.

Emily didn't know what she would do, if she didn't have Steph for a friend. She couldn't figure out how her life had gotten so complicated, but having a great friend sure made things better.

Steph looked at her with a serious frown. "You're worrying again. I can tell! Stop it! Come on, it'll be okay. Let's go in...if we're late, Carol will kill us."

Emily followed Steph toward the locker room. Emily was feeling a little better. But when she saw her mother and Jaheen's father, smiling and talking by the skate rental counter, her worries came flooding back, and her insides turned icy cold.

Chapter 11 ❋ Abe

Abraham's palms were wet. He was having trouble catching his breath. His heart was working too hard. But he could handle things. He'd just talk to her—maybe have some fun skating—and bug out...whenever he felt like it.

No risks. No problems.

More questions buzzed in his mind. Should he make an excuse, and just leave, right now? He could tell her he had a sore knee. He could go and wait for Jaheen at the mall now, and come back to pick her up...later...after Anna had gone home.

But his desire to be around that woman—and to skate with her—was strong. Wouldn't it be okay to skate with her, just for a little while? What would be so wrong with doing that?

Who would care?

But somebody might care, and he knew that he was taking a risk...

He closed his eyes. It was too late; there was no way that his legs would move his body out of the building—and away from a chance to be with her again.

When he saw her looking over at him, and she smiled; he felt his face light up like a flashlight. He couldn't stop his reaction.

She skated up to the wall near him, and she leaned on top of it. She seemed nervous, or excited. He couldn't tell which.

"Hi Abraham" she said, glancing up at him, grinning. "It's really windy out there today." She played with her hair. "How are ya?"

When she smiled, it seemed that time stopped—and so did his ability to make decent conversation. He was feeling the same weird something in his body that he'd felt when he met her the first time, just two days ago—half afraid, half excited...

He nodded. "I'm okay. How's your head?"

"Fine. Are you going to skate again today?" she asked bluntly.

He stepped back, surprised at her direct question, and he shrugged.

He needed more time to think. He needed to figure out what to say. He'd never intended to walk away, so why was he acting...so unfriendly, and so cold to her?

When he'd first noticed her today, she'd been sitting on a bench, bending over to lace her skates. The big, brown, bulky sweater she was wearing made her look like a small bear. But he didn't care too much about how she looked on the outside. There was something soft and warm that came from inside her that had gotten to him. In her green eyes, he'd seen something very seductive. It wasn't about sex; it was more about the way she'd accepted him—as a person.

So why couldn't he accept her kindness now? He felt like he already knew her. They had only met on Tuesday, but, since then, his life had been turned upside down.

In just forty-eight hours?

She was all he'd been thinking about. He'd replayed the memories of their first meeting over and over, in his mind: the way he'd felt when she'd leaned on him, and when they'd taken turns pulling each other up off the ice...and how she smelled. Sweet, like apples...

She was watching the kids in the main rink, sliding back and forth on her old black skates. He looked down at them, and she followed his glance.

"I know. I know...I'm a terrible burden of a skater. And...well, you know, now that I think about it, maybe my head isn't all that good yet. So it would be okay if we skipped it today..." she said in that cute Irish accent of hers.

She looked at him quickly, and then turned away.

He was more confused than ever now. Did she want him to skate with her again? Or didn't she?

Worried that she could read his mind, he mumbled, "No...yeah. Well, I'm...I'm...sorry you don't feel all right," and he looked toward the main arena.

Couldn't he put a sentence together anymore? He had his doubts.

The silence between them grew. It felt like forever, and it seemed like neither one of them knew what to do...He certainly didn't.

Maybe he *should* just go now...

She looked at his shoes, and she bit her lip. "Well, I'll be off now, and I'll leave you be...I just want thank you again, for helping me the other day—and for listening to my sad story. I know that I kind of scare people sometimes, because I say too much and..."

But she didn't move.

"No. It's not that..." He hesitated. Voices for fear and excitement were arguing so loudly inside his head that he was afraid she could hear them. He could still make an excuse; he still get out of this—this strange *thing* that was happening to him.

He looked over at her and he pushed his glasses up on his nose. His lips moved slightly, when told the voices in his mind to shut up, and go to hell.

"What?" she asked.

"No. Nothing," he said, in a tone that was too loud.

He saw her look of surprise, and, softening his voice, and using his best acting skills, he tried to apologize. "I'm sorry, Anna. I—"

"It's okay" she said, and looked away. "I know..."

He nodded his head toward the rental booth and he touched her arm. "Anna, I'm going over there, right now, and get my skates. And, if you want to...if you feel up to it—we can practice for a little while."

"Oh yeah! I mean...yes, that would be great. I'm fine. My head's good enough for a few rounds."

He happy that she seemed to be pleased about his decision to stay. "Nothing scares the Ice Man," he said with a slow grin at her as he began to walk away—some of his old confidence returning.

"The Ice Man? Ah, that would be you, now?" she called after him, laughing. He watched her eyes shine, like wet leaves in the rain. "Well, I'm...not scared of you, either...because...did ya know that I'm the Ice Woman?"

"Really?" He called back over his shoulder, waving his hand at her. Feeling silly with relief now—his ability to control himself was melting away. He tried to get it back, by standing tall, and taking some deep breaths. As he walked, he said to himself, "Yeah, that's right. The Ice Man knows the moves... and what he don't know, his Ice Woman does."

Feeling his face flushing, he hoped she hadn't heard that last part. He started jogging toward the skate rental booth, his heart racing again. He decided he should change his nickname to "Crazy Ice Man" because he was sure that he'd lost his mind.

* * *

Out on the ice, he thought about what he should do next. Last time, they'd sort of danced, but they'd only held hands and spun around—and they'd fallen a number of times. Now, he was doing straight laps to loosen up, and she was following behind, copying him—almost to prove that she could skate as fast as he did. His strides were aggressive, but she matched him, move for move. He had never seen a woman skate with that kind of power.

When they crowded together into a tight corner, going too fast, they tripped and fell over each other. They lay laughing, and out of breath, their backs lying flat on the cold ice. He felt the tension slipping from his body, and she seemed to be relaxing, too.

"Maybe we should slow down a little," he said.

She was nodding, still laughing. He looked at her, and felt warm all over.

When he could breathe easier, he sat up and extended both his hands to her. She took them into her own, and they struggled to stand up at the same time. He felt a jolt of electricity as she squeezed his hands. He met her eyes briefly. The intensity was too much for him, and he looked away, but didn't let go of her hands. Instead, he flipped into a backward skate, and he said, "Follow me."

She tried to synchronize her steps with his, but she was tripping over her own skates. But he kept an even pace, and after a couple of tries, she began to move with him. He pulled her closer in toward his body.

"That's it…good work, *Ice Lady*," he breathed down on her hair, avoiding her eyes.

Suddenly, she swung him around, switching herself into the backward position, and, leading him, she pulled him forward.

Grinning, she told him, "Two can play that game, *Mister Ice Man!*"

It took him a few seconds to recover from the surprise turn, and adjust to her lead. He started to laugh, and enjoy the sensation of letting go of control, as they eased into the slow beginnings of a dance rhythm. The feeling made him smile—but mostly because he was enjoying watching her happy expression. He didn't look away this time, and she was staring up at him, too.

"Dance with me, *you fool*," she laughed, but her teasing grin quickly turned to a look of surprise when he grabbed one of her arms with his left hand, and moved it to his shoulder, and then he lightly placed his right hand on her waist.

"Oh!" Her whisper was like a small gasp.

He felt himself melt into the formal dance position, and the thrill of their combined energy and closeness came over him like a hot cloud of steam. He felt that they were floating on air, and the blades of their skates were just barely skimming the ice.

On the third round together, their skates crossed and they fell down in a tangle of arms and legs. The feeling of soaring stayed with him as he lay on his back, laughing, gulping in gasps of air. He looked over at her, lying next to him, and watched her giggling like a school girl. He raised her hand high in the air, and bent it at the elbow, as if checking them both for broken arms.

"You okay?"

She nodded.

"Man, that was something!" he said, between gasps. He must have been holding his breath—almost the whole time, he thought. "Did you *feel* that?"

"Yah…Did that feel like we were flying—like birds— or what?"

"We just have to stay on our feet next time!" He laughed from his belly, in a way that he hadn't laughed in years. Lying still to catch his breath, staring up at the dim cage lights above them. He realized that he was still holding her hand, and she hadn't pulled it away.

She looked straight up, too. "You kept me going. If it weren't for you, I wouldn't have…"

"No!" He said, rolling toward her, coming up on one elbow. "*You* kept *me* going!"

"No, *you* kept *me* going. I couldn't have done *that* on my own…that ice dance thing—without you holding me—"

He shook his head. "Au contraire, Ice Woman. It was *you* who made that happen."

He continued to stare at her, both of them shaking their heads in mock disagreement, making silly laughing noises.

"Get real. It was neither one of you—it was, for the most part—an accident. You two are lucky that you both don't have broken legs," called a sharp voice from the wall below the bleachers.

Anna turned toward the voice and said with alarm, "What? Who's there?"

A compact woman with silver gray hair pulled neatly back into a bun stepped out on the ice. She was wearing boots and a long down coat. Abraham helped Anna stand, feeling like a kid in trouble at school.

"I said, what happened out there was pretty much an accident…a nice one, though. You two have ability—but no style, no coordination, you're both out of shape, and…honey, you need to get some real skates. Those are for playing hockey…"

Abraham glanced at Anna, and she rolled her eyes.

The woman in the coat continued to look at them as if they were a little bit insane, but in an interesting sort of way. "And…you'll have one hell of a racial problem, if you plan to compete as a pair," she added flatly.

"Who *are* you?" asked Abraham. He was on alert, feeling defensive. He instinctively moved protectively toward Anna.

She reached out her hand to him. "I'm Daisy French."

He looked at her blankly, and was about to ask something more, when Anna spoke up excitedly. "Oh my God! Daisy French! It is such a great pleasure to meet you!"

"I'm sorry, but I…" Abraham interrupted, shaking the woman's hand, using his most polite, barely-touch-a-white-woman handshake. Anna grabbed her hand, and shook the woman's whole arm. "Anna Smithson."

Anna turned to him. "She was—is—one of my heroes! Daisy French is one of the top skating coaches in the country…The Olympics…in—?"

"Nah, not one of the best—but I *was* pretty good back then, though. Thanks. I retired a few years back. But I like to keep my hand in. You know, a little judging, a little teaching…"

Abraham nodded, watching Anna's actions and reactions.

"You guys lookin' for a coach? I was serious when I said I see raw talent in you two—but I mean, it's *really* raw…a bit undercooked, if you know what I mean?" She grinned, and Abraham found himself liking her sense of humor.

He shook his head quickly, and noticed that Anna had done the same thing, too.

He said, "Oh no, no…but thank you. We're just—" He didn't know what they were, or how to explain their strange relationship.

Anna interrupted him, before he could finish. "Oh, no…That's right, no…we're not—" She hesitated, and then she added, "But thank you so much for the complement, though. Wow, it means a lot, coming from you!"

Daisy looked at them, up and down, with an intense interest. "Well…OK, but if you change your mind, here's my card. I could have you two ready for regional pairs in, hmmm, maybe, by spring."

As they both took the business cards that Daisy handed them. As she walked away, she turned, and repeated, with a sly smile, and with squinted eyes, "It would be interesting, working with the two of you…You have some good energy…there's some real sparks happening there…"

Anna smiled, and she said, "Aye. Yes, we are— we *are* a very unusual couple—of skaters," glancing over at him. He noticed her cheeks were starting to glow.

He smiled, too, and said, "It was very nice to meet you. And thank you again for the compliments."

He looked down at the business card, and turned it over a couple of times in his cold fingers.

Were his hands shaking, just a little?

Then, not believing that it was his own voice he was hearing, he said to Daisy, as she stepped around the gate, "We'll talk it over, and maybe we'll get back to you."

Chapter 12 ❀ Anna

"Abe, are you *crazy?*" Anna looked at him with her mouth open. He was watching Daisy walk away from them, and then he turned to face Anna.

"Sure…I'm a little crazy. But that's not the point….And, by the way, it's *Abraham.*"

"Okay—*Abraham*—tell me, what point am I missing?"

She immediately regretted her tone. Things were happening too fast. Her thoughts were mixed up with her emotions, and when she was upset or afraid like she was right now, she knew she could become a little offensive. She'd learned *that* life skill from her father, too.

"My *point* is, *Anna*, that maybe it couldn't hurt to get a little professional help?" he shrugged, but when he raised his eyebrows at her, she felt the seriousness in his suggestion.

"*Somebody* around here needs some professional help—and I think it's *you*, *Abraham*," Anna rolled her eyes at the ceiling, cracking a smile. There was no way she would perform in public; the idea scared her to death, but she didn't want him to know that.

He looked down at his feet, and she saw real hurt in his expression. She realized that she needed to stop jabbing him with jokes and sarcasm, and she said, "Abe—Abraham—look, I'm sorry. But you weren't really serious about training with Daisy, were you?"

She watched him adjust his glasses. His face was slightly damp with sweat, and his eyes behind the thick lenses took on a thoughtful expression. "Anna…" he began.

She liked the way he said her name. She decided she would call him whatever he wanted her to call him, so he'd feel good about her, too.

"…think about it. What we've got going here is—is pretty damn amazing—like Daisy said." He paused. "But, we don't really know what we're doing. Maybe just getting some coaching help from a pro—like our kids are doing—could be a good thing. It was just an idea…a crazy one, I know."

Anna felt her nerves come alive. The thought of performing—in front of anyone—especially Daisy French—made her feel sick.

She flashed back to her father, yelling at her after she'd missed a shot in a hockey game with his drinking pals, when she was only nine or ten. No, she couldn't be trusted. When the chips were down, she'd fold, and fail…She couldn't possibly perform in a team—especially a two-person team, with somebody good and kind, like Abe. She'd disappoint him, and that would be horrible…

But she didn't want Abe to see weakness in her. He'd run away if he knew how terribly afraid and inadequate she was.

"Yeah…well, aye, I agree with you. We were dancin' up a storm out there—for a couple of minutes. But…"

He looked so disappointed, that she wanted to make him feel better, so she added, in a soothing voice, "Well…I might be okay with getting some professional pointers—but public performances…ah, sorry, not my style, Abraham."

"Abe" he corrected her, his smile returning, big time.

"Okay, Abe," she squinted at him with a smirk.

"All right...and you can call me whatever you want," he said, with a chuckle, "but you know what I think?"

"What do you think?"

"I think that the reason you won't to skate in front of people because you're afraid you might make a mistake...and you don't like to make mistakes, do you?"

She felt suddenly exposed, and it hurt, like he'd punched her in the stomach. Her mind raced: He was right. She *was* afraid of making mistakes—and worse yet, she hated to fail. She was a terrible person and a terrible skating partner, and she knew it...and now he knew it, too.

Holding back tears took all the strength she had. Her breath came out like a sob. "You're right. If you and I were a team, I'd mess up, and I'd make you look bad," she whispered. She felt naked and defenseless, ready to rip off her skates, and get the hell out of there.

"Yep. So let's forget the whole thing," she choked. The tears were coming now, so she quickly turned away, but he was quicker, and, catching her arm firmly with his hand, he pulled her toward him.

"Anna, wait. Please." His eyes glowed like honey, and she felt a surge of strength flowing into her from his strong, cold hand. Through his thick glasses, which were starting to fog over, she could see his deep concern for her shining down on her face.

"*Please*, Anna. Just...just think about it. We could start with a lesson or two, and see where it goes from there. No commitments. No obligations..."

He released her arm, and, instantly, she missed the feel of his grip. She wondered if he was talking about more than just taking lessons together...and, she was ashamed to admit, the idea pleased her. She'd felt his power over her when he was holding her. She didn't want to look away from his eyes; it was almost like he was casting some sort of a spell over her...His kindness warmed her blood, and made her feel more like a woman than she'd had in a long time—if ever.

But doubts about her worth as a person—and as a woman—lurked in the back of her mind. Now that Abe knew she had problems, sooner or later, she was sure that he'd give up on her. Her act, her game of pretending, had lasted with Abe—how long—maybe two days? He'd already figured out that she was terrified of mistakes. And once Abe thought about it, and when he'd seen all of her flaws when they worked with Daisy, he was sure to reject her...criticize her, and find her an unworthy partner...just like Bill had.

Abe was silent. Was he thinking about how stupid she was? She sighed, watching her daughter skate with her class. She thought about what Em was going to say about her skating—in public view—with a black man that she hardly knew.

Anna finally said, "Give me some time, Abe. Let me think about it. You're right...I'm afraid. I'm afraid of performing in front of people. And you were right, I'm afraid of making mistakes, too. I'm really sorry—that I'm such a mess..."

There. She'd come clean with the truth, and she was ready and waiting for him to tell her that she was nuts, and he'd say goodbye to her forever. She waited for the bad news. She even half-expected Abe to get mad, and yell at her, like Bill did.

She let out a sigh, and waited, tensing and relaxing her shoulders, which were starting to ache. It seemed like an hour passed, but it was only seconds.

"Anna, I understand. I have my hang-ups, too...but I *do* know one thing for sure..." He stopped talking, and he shook his head. "I'm sorry. I shouldn't have pressed you about this."

She faced him. "No. What was it you were going to say? What do you know for sure?"

He turned to her, and he hesitated, and then he said, very slowly, "Well, what I know is that we all have to face fear in life, but we don't have to do it alone."

He paused, shifted his weight, and then he said softly, "My Grandma used to say that God sends us special people...people who help us through the bad times." He sighed. "I don't know that for sure. I'm not a religious man, but I do know that people make choices in this world...And, only you can decide if you want to face your fear, or not..."

She nodded. His soothing voice, the sweetness in his eyes, brought more tears. She smiled, and she said, "That's beautiful, Abe. I'd like to believe that. I hope it's true...Do you think that's the reason we met?"

He nodded. "You've really helped me, Anna. I owe you gratitude—not grief...so I don't want to force you into doing anything you're not ready to do."

"Thank you. But—but how in the hell did *I* help *you?*"

He looked embarrassed, and down at the floor, "I know I've only known you a short time, but...the way you treat me...you respect me—like an equal—like a human being." He added quietly, "Anna, meeting you has been really good for me."

She drew her lips together firmly, as she turned away. They both looked straight ahead, toward the main rink. Anna watched their daughters following the teacher, like baby ducks in a pond. Jaheen stood out as the only black child in the group, but she was, by far, the most skilled skater in the class.

"Your daughter is a very talented. I'm sure you're very proud to be her parent," she said, wondering about what sort of parent she'd be in her daughter's eyes, if she agreed to keep skating with Abe.

Choices. Abe had said she had choices to make. And he was so right. Should she face her fears, or run from them? He was offering his help...but Emily's needs were important, too. It would be so easy to stay stuck in misery...lying, and pretending, that her life was okay the way it was...and do nothing, risk nothing...

"I'll think about trying to deal with it—with my fears, but I can't make you any promises." She said. Then, she added, "And, just so you know, I think you've been really good for me, too. Honestly, you have."

A smile lit up his eyes. "Thanks, Anna. Well...okay. Whatever you decide—it'll be fine. I'll be here." He extended his hand to her. "Friends?"

"Yes. We're friends, Abe," Anna answered, grinning. And after they shook hands, Anna squeezed Abe's fingers, and he held hers for a longer time, too.

That was no ordinary handshake, she thought.

Chapter 13 ❀ Anna

Bill was late, as usual. Anna was nervous. Unable to sit still, she paced around the darkened living room. She weaved in and out of the antique chairs and the side tables with the fancy carved wooden legs that Bill's parents had chosen for the house. She swerved to avoid the wall with Bill's photographs of wild animals being hunted. She didn't like to look at those.

Violence of any kind made her feel sick. She'd turn down the volume when news about the race riots came on the radio or the television. She couldn't stand to watch—or even hear about—the arrests, the injuries, and all of the deaths. So many black Americans were suffering during protest marches that ended in violent clashes with the police...

How could some people be so hateful? Especially here, in the South, where Christian churches preached about peace and loving others. What was there to hate about black skin? People were people on the inside, weren't they?

Abe was sweet, polite, handsome, funny...But, no, she wasn't going to allow herself to think about Abe right now...

Bill. She had to focus on dealing with Bill. Abe had *nothing* to do with her problems with Bill, she told herself. She paced around the room, and passing the massive, cold, white marble fireplace. The gas logs looked almost real, even when the thing was turned off. More wasted expense for the sake of appearances, she thought. The gas logs had not been her choice. She liked *real* wood-burning fireplaces.

Scanning the gallery of photographs on the mantle, she felt her Irish ire building. Smiling for cameras, the faces she saw in the frames pretended that they belonged to happy people—but she knew none of them were happy in real life. They were actors. Acting as if they were happy—just posing...

Bill's parents. Did the belief that they were better than everybody else make them happy?

She and Bill: Unhappy with each other—living in different worlds, not even sleeping in the same bedroom.

When she looked at Emily's pictures, she began to cry. Such a sweet, vulnerable child!. Even though Em was a super-emotional pre-teen these days, Anna loved her with all her heart, and that would never change.

Anna wondered if she could fail to make her daughter happy tonight? Would she keep pretending to be happy, so that Emily could have her unhappy, "happy" family?

Anna was nearly consumed with nervous energy. She was determined not to fall asleep until Bill came home. She'd decided to have a talk with him—a calm, serious one—about their relationship. Like Abe had said today, you had to face your fears. She and Bill had postponed this conversation long enough, and she wanted to put an end, one way or another, to the strained silence between them.

She tossed herself onto the brown velvet fainting couch. It was the only piece of furniture she liked in this room because it was the most useful and comfortable, of all the useless antiques in the room. She'd been sleeping on it, every night, for the past few months. In the mornings, before Emily came downstairs for breakfast, Anna stuffed her pillow and blanket into the chest under the window seat, so Emily wouldn't know that her parents weren't sleeping in the same bedroom.

How had her life come to this?

Anna closed her eyes, and she immediately thought about Abe. She gave herself over to replaying his funny jokes, the way he teased her…and how he held her hand…and she found herself feeling sexually excited again.

No! Don't think about that, she told herself. Abe was just a friend. He seemed to understand her, like nobody she'd ever met before—man or woman.

Headlights flashed across the front windows, and she heard the garage door crank open. She sat up and smoothed her nightshirt, tucking her legs up under her, so Bill wouldn't see any part of her body. She had no desire for him to notice her in the sexual sense—and she hadn't for…? Wow, she thought. For *years!*

She heard him close the side door quietly, like a burglar in the night. When he walked out of the kitchen, she said, "Bill, I need to talk to you," she saw him jump, hitting his black brief case on his knee.

"Shit," he swore angrily. Bending over to rub his leg. "You scared the hell out of me, Anna," he said, as if it had been her fault that he'd hit his leg.

"Sorry," she said, feeling immediately defensive, as always. "I didn't mean to…"

"Why are you still up? It's late."

"I wanted to talk to you. You're never home for dinner anymore, so I thought I'd wait up. Do you want something to eat?"

He looked irritated. He raised himself up to his full height—much shorter than Abe, she noticed. He ran his hand through his thinning blond hair.

She watched him with a strange feeling of detachment. Even though he was good looking, she felt nothing in the way of attraction to him...nothing like she'd felt earlier today, when Abe...

"No, I had something on the way home—after my meeting—with the partners. We're planning to expand into the south side."

Anna nodded, feeling a twinge of resentment. She'd heard it all before. Bill and his fellow dentists were always building satellite offices, and recruiting more staff, or planning to expand. She couldn't understand why they weren't satisfied with the size of their practices. Their never-ending empire-building left them little private time for themselves and their families. Anna couldn't figure out why the other dentists' wives didn't complain like she had...But, once again, Anna thought, she didn't fit into Bill's life, or the way he planned to live it, in the future.

But, she didn't want to talk about his work. She wanted to focus on her immediate need, which was to try to start some kind of meaningful discussion with her husband.

"Hmm...Do you have some time to talk—about you and me?" she asked carefully. She was getting more nervous by the second.

"Now?" His gray eyes flashed an icy cold look at her. "You want to talk, *now*?" He looked at his watch. "Shit. It's late, Anna—"

"I know, but there's never any time anymore to..." she interrupted, trying to keep her determination strong.

He picked up his case, and started walking toward the stairs. "Maybe tomorrow..." He stopped, and glancing back at her, he added, "No, I forgot, I have a meeting with Fred after office hours....How about Saturday, at breakfast, before I go golfing with Dad?"

His question was not really an offer of a choice, Anna realized. His plans were always non-negotiable. Bill told her when he was available, and she was expected to accommodate his needs.

She watched him flip on the light on the landing, as he slowly climbed the stairs. He scraped the wall with his wedding ring, as if to show her how angry she'd made him. When he reached the top, the light went out.

She felt herself go limp, and, almost paralyzed with frustration, she seemed unable to move. Like floating down a strong river current, she was caught in Bill's wake, and she couldn't break free of his control over her.

She didn't have the energy to get up for her blanket and pillow. She knew she would be spending another night in the living room, alone. She had no desire to join Bill in their king-sized bed—and it was clear that he didn't want her there, either.

She snapped off the light on the table next to her, and stared up at the scrollwork that glowed in the moonlight on the high ceiling.

She wondered what her father would say about Bill, if he were alive. Was he watching the way his son-in-law was treating her? Had her father ever been that unkind to her mother?

She realized that she would never know those answers. Anna sighed, and rubbed her eyes.

"What should I do, Dad?" she said to the dark room.

In the silence, she pretended that she could hear her father's voice: "Lass, the truth hurts, but, little girl, lyin' to yerself, is like lying ta God."

Tough as he was, maybe her father had tried to tell her that she lived in a dream world. She'd thought that he was being mean to her, but now, she realized that, perhaps he had tried, out of love, to help her—in the best way that he could.

She was starting to believe that there were times in life when the truth was all you had. She dreaded talking with Bill on Saturday. There was really nothing left to say about their so-called marriage. It was over. It had been for a long time.

"I'm so sorry, Em!" she whispered into the dark. Hot tears were burning her eyes again.

Right then and there, she made her decision: She gave up on her marriage.

She thanked her father for loving her, and she asked him and God to forgive her for lying so much, for so long. She hoped her mother would understand, too. She imaged her mother was an angel, watching over her right now, because she felt so alone.

She wrapped her arms around herself for comfort, but the icy fingers of fear gripped her insides.

She got up, pulled her blanket from the window seat, and draped it over her shoulders like a robe.

"'Night, mommy, 'night, daddy. I love you." she whispered, in the voice of a child, to the ghosts of her parents.

Chapter 14 ✻ Abe

"Ow!" Anna cried, as she dove forward, head and hands first, skidding on the tile floor on her sore palms.

Daisy stood back, watching her, expressionless. "Try it again," she said flatly.

Anna scrambled up to a standing position, and began repeating the sequence of ballet positions that Daisy had shown her. Daisy was counting out loud for Anna's second try at completing a jump-turn that required landing a spin on one foot.

Abe suspected that Anna's feet and legs were as sore as his were. The intense hours of "dry land," practices that they had been enduring under Daisy's direction for the past week were wearing them down—physically and mentally.

Abe took sips from his coke, resting on the bench. He followed Anna's every move with his eyes. It was hard for him to stop trying to help her. But Daisy wouldn't allow it. He had orders to stay back, and let Anna master the new steps on her own.

"Daisy, it's just not the *same!* Sneakers don't slide into the turns, like skates do..." Anna said, in a voice as close to whining as he'd ever heard from her. She usually hung in there; she always worked hard, and she didn't hold back. But he could tell that she wasn't happy about learning all of this ballet stuff—and neither was he. He liked it a lot better when they were dancing on the ice, making up their own moves.

He felt protective of Anna, and ever since he'd met her, he realized that she'd found a place in his mind, and in his heart. He wanted to run to her now, and offer her comfort and encouragement, but there would be time for that…he hoped…and so, he'd wait until the time was right…

He was glad for his skills—his ability to act cool, and to restrain himself—until he felt safe enough to show his feelings. And he didn't want to upset Daisy, or change anything about the training sessions, no matter how tough or boring they were sometimes.

"Yes! See? You can do it, Anna…Now, just one more time!" Daisy called out across the hot and stuffy room. The space had mirrors on the walls, like a dance studio. It was great, he thought, because, no matter where he looked, he could watch Anna. She always wore a big shirt or a sweater, and loose jeans, so he wasn't sure what she really looked like under all those bulky clothes, but he liked to imagine it. Would she have big round curves, like Georgie, but kind of cream-colored? He'd never slept with a white woman before, but he'd seen lots of pictures—like in men's magazines.

Abe smiled at his memory of their first lesson with Daisy. He and Anna had been sitting together, against the wall, on this same narrow wooden bench. Like two school kids in gym class, Daisy had paced back in forth in front of them, barking instructions, laying down the rules…

Daisy had made it clear that she wouldn't hold anything back. She was, Daisy had told them, the most honest coach they would ever find. They were not to take any of her feedback personally—and then she'd gone ahead and made some very personal remarks that, in any other situation, would send somebody into a defensive rage: Anna was overweight and out of shape. She had to control her fuzzy curls, and pull her hair back into a tight bun, even for practice sessions. His beard was too bushy, his hair was too long, his glasses had to go—and he had to get contact lenses because they would offer him better vision—and a better overall look.

Anna understandably enough, had reacted defensively. Abe was used to hearing criticism—from his wife, and from people because of his color, and his racial features, so it had been easy for him to hide his feelings. But Anna was outspoken—and opinionated. She had been very opposed to changing anything. She'd called Daisy's suggestions "superficial."

And, Anna had clearly reminded him and Daisy that she had never planned to perform in public-*ever!*

But he'd started to trim back his beard and cut his hair—just a little—as a compromise. He made sure the changes weren't enough to upset Anna, and he hoped they would be enough to please Daisy. He'd also called his eye doctor—just to ask about the cost of contact lenses.

Deep down, though, the idea of *seriously* changing his looks bothered him, too. Completely removing his cover—the full beard, the glasses—the mask that had hidden his face over the years—made him nervous.

He thought about Anna's unwillingness to conform to the images of "normal" skaters, and he saw something in Anna that she didn't seem to understand about herself: she was a woman who could look beyond physical appearances. She had an outer blindness—and an inner vision—she had an ability to know people, deep down…She seemed to be color-blind. How else could she have found a friend in *him*? He was able to relax around her—more than he could with any other woman—or man. When he was with Anna, he felt safe and secure enough to open up, and to talk about…

"Okay, you two!" Daisy interrupted his thoughts, barking like one of the drill sergeants he'd had during his two years in the Army. "One last Samba sequence—together—and that'll be it, for today."

He tossed his coke bottle in the trash can, and joined Anna in the middle of the floor. His legs and his back were hurting, and he took his starting position stiffly. Was he getting old, or what? He offered his arms to Anna. Her hands were hot and sweaty.

He took a very deep breath, and he counted in a whisper, trying to synchronize his movements with the numbers that Daisy counted out loud for them. "Back, two, three, side, two three…turn, turn, turn, and lunge! And repeat…"

Whatever they did seemed to please Daisy enough to end the torture, but as usual, she was frugal with any praise; she dismissed them, saying, "That was a little better. Keep practicing. Your rhythm was a little off there at the end, Anna…but you did finish together. We'll try some music next time. Maybe that'll help. See you Tuesday?"

Abe nodded. He thanked Daisy, and looked at Anna with concern. He guessed that she was a little down, and maybe discouraged, but he was relieved when she said, "Yeah, okay, Daisy, thank you. See you then. 'Bye Abe. Have a nice weekend," and she disappeared into the ladies' locker room.

"How are ya holdin' up, Abe?" Daisy asked him.

"I'm good." He looked over at the door, which was closing behind Anna.

"You're worried about her, aren't you?"

"Umm. I guess."

"Can I give you some advice?" asked Daisy, looking up at him.

He smiled down at the little ball-of-fire of a lady. She never missed anything.

"Sure," he said.

"Anna's got growing pains, Abe. You know what I mean?"

"I think so."

"She's dealing with a lot of changes in her life. Her marriage. All the training. Maybe going public with your act…and you."

"Me?" Now Daisy had his full attention.

"Don't try to act dumb with me, Abraham Lincoln. You're too smart for that…Of course, *you*. The way you two look at each other—you should be on a honeymoon somewhere."

A high-pitched laugh—almost a giggle—escaped from him. "Daisy, I—"

But Daisy was shaking her head, cutting off his denial before he could say anything. She waved her hand at him. "It's none of my business, Abe….But I care about both of you. You two have talent, but what you really have is an amazing chemistry. When you're skating together, it shows."

He looked at her and nodded. It was true. She was right.

"I don't know where all this is going. But be careful, okay? I don't want to either one of you get hurt."

"I'd never hurt her, Daisy."

"I wasn't thinking about you hurting each other. The two of you wouldn't harm a fly. It would come from out there…" she pointed in the direction of the street. "There's so much hate in this country. If you do decide to perform in public, you'll be rocking a lot of quo off of the status that doesn't like black on white…"

"I know," he said, feeling the seriousness of her words. "I know…"

"Look, I won't quit you guys. I like working with you. But think it over. Talk it out with her. Make sure you both know what you're getting into. You have families to consider…"

"Daisy, can I ask you about—something—about that?"

"Maybe."

"Do you know what's going on with Anna's marriage?"

Daisy gave him a look that backed him off a little, but then, she nodded. "I can't tell you much. It's confidential. But I will say that there are problems—pretty big ones. Her daughter isn't doing well in her skating class because of…"

"Not because of me, right? Because I—"

Daisy cut him off. "If I thought that were the case, Abe, I'd be gone in a flash. It's not you—or her training. Like I said before, Anna's got to grow up. She has adult decisions to make. And those kinds of life choices are never easy…but she's the only one who can make them. Don't try to influence her. That would only backfire on you, and you might lose her forever."

Chapter 15 ❀ *Emily*

It was Saturday morning, and the phone rang. It caused Emily to jump. She'd been awake, lying in bed, thinking.

Who was calling so early?

She heard her father answer the call, and she was happy to hear his voice.

He was rarely home these days. Things weren't getting better between her parents. Emily felt like she was in the middle of a tug-of-war game that she didn't really want to play. Her mother was at one end of the rope, and her own desire to keep her family together, was on the opposing side. Back and forth, Emily's feelings pulled at her heart.

She felt upset about not having the parents she wanted—like the ones she saw on TV, and at other times, she felt sorry for her mother, who was alone all the time, because her father was never around.

After her mom had told her about some of the reasons for the fighting, Emily started to watch her parents, like a hawk. Her mom usually looked sad—unless she was skating. One night, she'd heard her dad say mean things to her mom. He was kind of polite, but not nice—if that made sense at all.

It felt good tell Steph about *some* of the things that were bothering her. Steph was cool, and Emily trusted her so much. During their talks, Steph had been helping Emily to figure out that her parents were human beings—like grown up kids—and they their problems—like everybody else in the world.

But Emily didn't dare talk to Steph when her dad was home, because if he heard her complaining, then he'd get mad…and she'd be in a ton of trouble.

Emily had called Steph last night. Her father had been out until after midnight. Steph had been really great, and she'd helped her to calm down. Emily had been so mad at her dad for not letting her go with the class on a field trip to the art museum. He'd said it was too dangerous to go downtown.

Steph had said, "Yeah, Em, like I told you, your dad is way too strict. My mom even says so. You can't do things other kids can—like eat sweets—or eat chips—or watch a lot of TV. Your dad doesn't even want you to ice skate."

"I know." Emily said.

"I feel real bad for ya, Em."

"But your parents got over their phase, right?"

"Yeah, they did, but I don't think your dad's in a phase. I think he's nuts."

Emily's stomach had felt sick when Steph had said that about her dad.

"Do you think your mom is going to, you know…div…I mean, leave him?"

"Maybe. I don't know." Emily had wanted to hang up, rather than answer her friend's question.

"My mom said that you and your mom can come over here. My dad's a lawyer, and he can help…"

Emily had felt too sick to keep on talking. She could only talk about her family problems for so long, and then she'd get really upset. But Steph had understood, and she'd told Emily to call her back anytime.

Emily hadn't been ready to share all of her feelings about Jaheen's father, with Steph. It worried her to see her mom skating with him—even though her had mother said that they were only training partners, they sure seemed to like each other a lot...

Now, Emily used her super-good hearing to listen at her bedroom door. She heard her father telling somebody on the phone that he'd be right there...and then, while he was going down the stairs, he told her mother he wouldn't have any time to spend with her, like he'd promised. He said he had a last-minute meeting, and then he had to go golfing with Grandfather Smithson's business partners. The last thing she heard was her father saying he was sorry to her mother, but it didn't sound like he really meant it.

Emily tiptoed back to bed, and tried to go back to sleep, but she couldn't. She wrapped herself in her pink Barbie doll quilt, and sat on the window seat in her dormer window. She looked past the dolls and toys that no longer interested her. Her old playthings weren't much fun anymore. If it weren't for her books, for skating, and for Steph, she didn't know what she would do.

She heard her father slam the front door. Since he'd come home so late last night, he hadn't used the garage—probably to keep from waking them up, she guessed. She watched him as he folded the top down on his car, and climbed into his little white convertible. She thought it was too cold for the top to be down. Before he drove away, he looked in the mirror and combed his hair.

Her mother came up the stairs, and Emily listened for her bathroom door to close. Her mother probably had waited up for dad, and slept on the couch again because he'd been so late...She picked up a Nancy Drew book, and started to read it, leaning back on the pink fluffy pillows in her window where she liked to sit and listen to the tweeting of the birds in the trees. The quiet house creaked, as the sun rose higher in the sky. Emily relaxed a little as she read, allowing the story to take her away from the reality of her family's problems.

Suddenly, she heard a soft, whimpering, like a kitten calling for its mother. As Emily got up and opened her bedroom door, she heard the crying sounds more clearly; they were coming from down the hall, from her mother's bathroom.

Emily listened, unable to move; she didn't know what to do. Her mother never cried. She thought about calling her father, but he was on his way to some important meeting. She could call Steph's, but it was too early...And she didn't know her grandparents' phone number.

She walked slowly down the hall toward the bathroom door. She could hear water running. She wondered if she should knock, or just go back to her room, and wait for her mother to come out.

Worries flashed through her mind. She thought about what Steph had said at school, a couple of days ago. They were having lunch together on the school lawn. The grass was dried brown, and the trees were shedding colored leaves, getting ready for winter. She and Steph both liked being outside in the fresh air, enjoying the sunshine; fall was their favorite time of year.

"Steph, what should I do—about my mom—and my dad?"

"I don't know, Em. Crap." Stephanie had said, crunching on her favorite corn chips. "Want some of these? They're great."

Emily had politely refused, sipping her orange juice, throwing the peanut butter sandwich her mother had made into a trash can. "I can't eat junk—I mean chips. My dad won't allow them in the house. They're bad for your teeth..."

"But your mom eats chips! I've seen her do it." Steph laughed.

"I think mom does things, just to make dad mad sometimes," Emily had said.

Steph had shrugged, "Maybe she does it to show him who's boss. Your dad is awfully bossy, ya know…"

"Well, Dad is…he *is* the man of the house, and my grandmother says that is the way it's supposed to be. Women are supposed to *obey* men. It's in the Bible."

"Really? It is? I dunno about the Bible rules, Em. My parents don't 'obey' each other. They work together, like a team—that's what they call it in our house—the 'home team.'"

"My parents don't act like that."

"Crap…" Steph had said, shaking her head. "Em, ya know, you're their kid…You *are* a part of your family *team*. Maybe if you'd talk to your mom—tell her what you think—about the way they're acting. She might listen to you—"

Now, Steph's advice ran through her head again. Maybe she *should* talk to her mom—and try to tell her how she was feeling. What did she have to lose? She was so worried about her family that she had trouble sleeping, and even eating right.

Something had to change, or she thought she was going to…

"Mom?" Emily knocked lightly on the door, hearing water running again. "Are you…okay?"

The water sounds stopped.

"What? Oh, yeah, honey…I'm fine…Just a minute. I'm just washing up…I'll be right out," her mother answered in a TV mom voice.

She heard a cabinet door close, the shuffling of clothes, and then the bathroom door opened slowly. Her mother's face was shiny and her nose was red. Her eyes were crinkled up and puffy, but she was smiling. Emily jumped forward to hug her mother with a quick, hard squeeze.

Her mother returned her hug, and held onto her for a long time. Her mother kissed her head. As she stepped away, she held Emily's hands. "I'm fine. Really. Thanks, honey…Are you okay?" her mother asked between deep breaths. Her voice was soft, the way Emily liked it.

"I'm, okay. Mom—are you…okay? You look…sad…" Emily asked tentatively.

"Aum…Oh…no, I'm happy to see your smilin' face this beautiful day. I'm fine, I really am." Emily noticed that her eyes were wet. Emily, started to feel like crying too. There was so much she wanted to say, but she couldn't find the right words. The hug had felt good; the two of them hadn't hugged much lately. Both of them wiped their own eyes with the backs of their hands, and they giggled together.

"Hey, come on, let's you and I go to The Pig for some strawberry pancakes…They're still your favorite treat…right?" her mother asked, with a little laugh.

Emily felt the tug of war starting up again. She didn't want to think about what her parents were doing wrong— or not doing right. Even though she desperately wanted her family to be normal—with a mother and a father—she wanted her mom to be happy like this, all the time.

She was tired of worrying about them. She decided not to her mother about anything serious. She was starting to think about pancakes.

"Sure, mom. Let's go," Emily said.

Chapter 16 ✱ Jaheen

Jaheen tried to concentrate on her homework, but it was impossible. Her mother's angry voice crawled up the staircase, and slithered under her bedroom door, like a snake.

Jaheen hated it when her mother yelled at her father. Their arguments always were the same, every time. Her dad would always be nice to her mom, at first. Then he would start defending himself—and try to talk her mother down. Then, when he got pushed too far, and he'd say some pretty awful things, and Jaheen didn't like that, either.

She tried to get in between the two of them before, and each time it had ended in disaster; she had lost her privileges for a week because she'd yelled "shut up"—and a few curse words at them—so since then, when they started the fighting, she'd put her radio on, turn it up, and pretend to ignore them.

"Just another Saturday night at the Brown's house," she told her sleeping cat through her clenched jaw, shaking her head. She finished copying another math problem into her notebook, and she then slammed the book closed; algebra could wait. She didn't see much use in learning to solve for "x" anyway. She had other plans for her future, and they didn't involve going to college.

Her brown cat's eyes were big and wide, and he was glaring at her. "Sorry, Cecil," she said to him, scratching behind his furry ears. "I'm going to be an Olympic skater. I won't need to know any dumb math."

She looked at her old canvas skating bag on the floor next to her bed for a long time, and then she reached for it, pulling it up, onto her lap. Rummaging through the end pocket, she found a scrap of paper with a phone number scribbled on it. She stared at it, trying to decide whether to dial it, or not. She'd never called a white girl before. She thought that it was stupid to worry about that, but she wondered what it would be like to talk with one on the phone. It was easy to chat with colored kids, but there was something different about this girl…and it wasn't just about her being white.

She picked up the receiver, and then put it back down again. She thought about Emily. She couldn't shake the memory of the girl's sad face when she'd secretly handed Jaheen her phone number at the rink last week.

Jaheen had been surprised by Emily's offer. It was the last thing she'd expected. She'd figured Emily wanted to talk about their parents…but she didn't know for sure if Emily wanted to actually do something about stopping them from following through with their crazy idea of skating as pair—or whether Emily was just mad, and wanted to fight about it.

From what Jaheen had seen at the rink, Emily seemed like an okay kid. She wasn't mouthy like her friend Stephanie. That smart-ass. And…Emily had looked pretty unhappy about their parents skating together, too.

But Jaheen had lost her temper, and gone off on Emily in the locker room, so she wasn't sure what to expect now. She had to be ready for anything. She could handle conflict, no matter how things went down. She'd learned *that* from her mother. She didn't plan to live her life cow-towing to people, like her father did.

The arguing continued downstairs...so, feeling determined and strong, she picked up the phone and dialed the number on the paper.

A woman answered in a friendly voice, "Hello...Smithson residence," she said.

Jaheen almost hung up. It was *her!* It was...*the woman!* She took a breath and tried to get ready to act nice and talk polite. It took all she had to stay on the line.

"Hi," she winced, and using her best white-person voice, she asked, "May I speak with Emily, please?"

"Um, sure...yes. I'll get her for you...just one minute, please. Can I ask who is calling?"

"Ah...just...one of her friends—from school—about homework." Jaheen lied.

Emily's mother hesitated, and then said, "All right. Hold on."

Jaheen breathed a sigh of relief while she waited, pacing around her room on the new pink shag carpet that her mother had bought her for her birthday. Then she heard someone pick up the extension.

"Hello?" said Emily.

"Hello...Emily?"

"Yes?"

"Hi, Emily. This is Jaheen—from the rink?" she paused. "You said that maybe I should call you. Can you talk?" She heard a click, and knew that Emily's mother had probably been listening the whole time. *Shit,* she thought. But she couldn't hang up now...Emily might think she was just messing with her.

"Ah, yes. Hello...Jaheen....Wait, just a minute," Emily said in a quiet voice, almost whispering. Jaheen could hear a door close. "I'm back. Hi," Emily continued. "Thanks for calling..." There was a long silence. Then

Emily said, "I'm, well, um…it's really weird, what's going on with our parents."

"Yeah, it's really, *really* weird," echoed Jaheen, feeling an unexpected connection to Emily.

"I don't know, really—I…" Emily didn't seem to know what to say.

"Yeah, I'm pretty upset, too. They need to stop those da—those stupid training lessons. Nothing personal, you know, to you, or your mom. It's just…really complicated."

"I know," Emily said, with sadness in her voice. "I don't know what to do."

"I've been thinkin' about it, and, I got an idea."

"Really? What's your idea?" Emily sounded suspicious.

"Well…We have to break them up. It's as simple as that. They shouldn't be doin' what they're doin'. If my mom finds out, all hell will break loose. It's bad enough in my house now—my dad has gotten some kinda *tude*—and it's getting worse since he started the training."

"Wait…what's a 'tude'?" Emily asked.

Jaheen snickered for a second, and then stopped herself. She took a deep breath, and figured she'd have to explain everything, like she was talking to a child—not somebody who was her own age. "Atti*tude*, girl. He's had a new kind of *attitude* that's getting' him in trouble with my ma. They're down there right now—fight…" She stopped herself again.

Emily was quiet.

Jaheen continued. "Never mind 'bout that…But what we have to do is to talk sense to 'em, before something bad happens. A Negro man has a lot more to lose than some whi—than your mom does."

"What do you mean?"

Jaheen shook her head. "Girl, don't you watch the *news*?"

"Well, sometimes…" Emily said, sounding embarrassed.

"Martin Luther King's dead! They killed him just because he wanted rights for our people. I don't want my dad shot because he's out there dancin' around in public with yo mama."

"Oh," said Emily. "*Oh….now*, I get what you mean." She sounded sincere, and she added in a louder voice, "So, what do you want *me* to do?"

"You could try talking to your mom. Tell her she's putting my dad in danger. I don't want my father shot…I love my dad…" Then she added, "And for God's sake, watch the news! Look at what's goin' on in White Town when black people just want to ride the *damn bus*—or eat lunch at a drug store…or…"

Emily was quiet for so long, that Jaheen was ready to jump into the phone—to grab her, and shake her. But she waited, remembering the skills her father had been trying to teach her about being kind and patient—until she seemed to run out of both of those things, and said, "*Emily*…are you still *there?*"

"Yeah, Jaheen. Yeah, I am. I'm thinking. I really don't know how to talk with my mom about this kind of stuff. I mean, my parents are kinda fighting, too…They tell me it's none of my business…to pray about it, and not worry about them."

Jaheen listened, biting her nails. That God talk. It never worked. Like her mom said, people had to take care of their own business in the world.

She was about to say so, when Emily said, "I love my parents. I don't want this to mess up my family either…and I don't want your dad to die…"

"Then you *have* to talk to your mom."

"I know."

"Will you do it? *Talk to her?*" Jaheen asked, firmly.

"I can try."

Jaheen was worried. Did this kid have what it took to talk about something serious with her *own mother?*

"Tryin' won't cut it, Emily. You've seen our parents together. They're getting big kicks out of those lessons—and from being together. If my mom ever saw that…" Jaheen had to stop herself from saying too much about her own mother's problems.

"I know," Emily replied. "I know this is important—to all of us—okay, Jaheen, I'll talk to her."

"When?" Jaheen's tone was demanding, and she knew it.

Emily was quiet again. Jaheen was starting to figure out that Emily was someone who didn't say things without thinking about them first. She'd have to go easy on her.

"I promise…to talk to her before our next lesson."

"Good!" said Jaheen. "Then, you'll tell me about what your mom says, when I see you, on Tuesday?"

"Yes, I will."

Jaheen hung up, thinking that if this didn't work, something more would have to be done to stop her father from making a total fool of himself—and maybe to save his life.

Chapter 17 ❀ Anna

Anna bit her lip. Questions flew around in her mind, like butterflies. They were hard to catch, and to hold onto long enough to try to figure out...and the answers seemed out of her reach all together.

Was that really Abe's daughter on the phone? Why the hell was she calling Emily? The two girls had never even spoken to one another—as far as she knew. Maybe they talked during the skating class, but did they have a telephone-level friendship? Since when? And why? They didn't even go to the same school.

Should she wait, and talk to Abe in person, on Tuesday? Or should she just go upstairs right now, wake up Emily, and find out what was really going on?

As usual, Bill was working late on another—probably bogus—meeting about the construction plan, and it was after ten o'clock...too late to talk with Emily tonight.

Maybe she should call Abe...

The phone rang.

"Hi," Abe said in a quiet voice. "Can you talk?"

"Abe? Hi! Yes...Bill's still at work," she whispered excitedly. "Wow. I was just thinking about calling you!"

"I think I know what about. Jaheen and I had a little chat tonight when I was tuckin' her in. Can you meet me someplace tomorrow? Maybe, ah, the college library downtown—in the afternoon? We should talk."

"Aye, yes, sure, I could meet you—tomorrow?" The butterflies flew from her head to her stomach. "Bill's taking Emily to his mother's for the day. How about around one?"

"One'd be great…I'll be in the reference section, on the second floor. There's a couple of private conference rooms back there."

Anna was already starting to feel excited about seeing him, face-to-face, in a not-so-public setting—alone—for the first time.

"All right," she said quietly. "I'll see you tomorrow."

Headlights flashed through the front windows as Bill's car pulled around the drive. She heard the garage door go up. Anna steadied herself, preparing for another unpleasant encounter. They'd barely been civil to one another since she'd stopped trying to make small talk, and started giving him a cold shoulder. Their conversations were thin and strained. She took a Daisy-style deep breath for composure and concentration, and picked up a magazine, ready to look interested in reading it.

The side door creaked, and she listened to him pace around in the kitchen. She heard the refrigerator slam shut, and the pop of a can opening.

"Oh. You're still up?" Bill said, barely glancing in her direction, as he walked through the living room, carrying an open beer. She took a peek at him. He looked tired. His tie was hanging loose around his neck, and his suit coat was hanging open.

"I was just about to go up and take a bath. How'd your meeting go?" She was pleased that she was able to stay so calm.

"It was fine," he said. As he walked toward the hall, he added, "Don't forget I'm taking Emily to my parents' tomorrow. I thought I would take her out to brunch at The Pig first—"

"Fine," she replied, cutting him off, relieved that he would be gone early. She'd have plenty of time to get ready for her trip downtown to meet Abe. "Em will love it—going out for breakfast twice in one weekend. I took her there today myself."

He stopped. She felt him staring at her, and she could sense his surprise. She flipped a page, and stared at it.

"Emily tells me that you're taking skating lessons now, too?"

"Aye. That I am." She knew he hated it when she "talked Irish," so she'd done it on purpose, just to irritate him. Ah...she sighed...old habits were hard to break. She decided that she should give up trying to teach Bill anything—and stop trying to change him.

"Hmm." He took a drink from the can. "What in the world do you hope to accomplish? Figure skating—at your age...and how much is *that* costing me?"

"I'm paying for it *myself*—from my father's trust fund."

He stared at her for what seemed to be a very long time before he started up the stairs. "Ridiculous waste of time and money..." she heard him mumble.

She wondered if Bill ever thought about the reasons why she'd become so distant from him—or why she'd stopped telling him about her activities...

But, then, did she really care what he thought about anymore?

* * *

It was a cloudy, windy day, and the threat of rain made the air feel heavy. Colorful fall leaves nearly covered the front lawn of the weathered, red brick college library.

Anna stepped carefully around fallen branches and swirling piles of leaves, as she climbed the cracked cement steps.

In spite of her resistance, Anna had begun to notice that Daisy's ballet lessons were helping to make her movements smoother, and more graceful—and her balance had improved. And, she'd noticed, when she'd dressed in a skirt and blouse this morning that she'd lost weight.

Inside the building, she was surprised to see leaves and crumpled paper littering the floor of the dimly lit lobby. She had an urge to grab a broom and clean the place up a little. Anna felt like a trespasser. She'd never been on this campus before—or even in this part of town.

She combed through her wind-blown hair with her fingers. She wished she could check herself out in a mirror, and brush her hair down, but it was almost one-thirty, so there was no time for that; she was already late.

She hurried past a sign that read: "Open: Sunday, 1 to 4, for students only." She wondered if she'd be asked to show an ID card. She tried to walk as quietly, but her loafers made loud clicking noises on the worn, gray linoleum floor.

There were a few young black students seated at some of the tables, and a few of them looked up, and stared at her. She wondered how many white people actually had set foot in here. The pretty young librarian at the front desk watched her intently, as she headed for the steps to the second floor. Anna forced a smile, and was glad when the woman said nothing.

Anna had been keyed up since Abe had called, and now she was getting more anxious by the second. Meeting him, alone, for the first time…feeling like she was an unwelcome intruder in this place—in his world—made her wonder about what it was that she was doing: could she and Abe ever really even be friends…outside of the rink?

But she kept on going. She wanted to be near him; she needed to talk to him.

At the top of the stairs, when she saw him, standing in the doorway of a tiny, glass-enclosed room, she felt a rush of good feelings.

At least she thought it was Abe. Something about him....looked different...

As she approached him, she realized his beard was missing. She felt her mouth drop open in surprise.

"Wow!" she took in a short, sharp breath.

She was stunned by the change in his appearance. Gone was the covering of dark curly hair that masked most of his face. He looked thinner, and his glasses seemed far too big for him now.

But the most startling thing about him was something she'd hadn't fully realized before: he was an extremely handsome man. His cheekbones were cleanly carved and shaped. His jaw was strong and square. The laugh lines around his mouth revealed much more about what he was thinking—or feeling. The overall picture was stunning.

"Hi," he greeted her, looking amused. "Glad you could make it."

"*My God*, Abe!" She whispered loudly, still staring. "Wow!"

His smile grew larger as he reached for her hand, and pulled her gently through the door. "Come on in...We can talk in here."

Once inside the small, brightly lit room, he closed the door behind them.

She turned to face him.

"*What's* going on here?" she asked, scanning his face. It was almost like meeting a stranger. She was so busy adjusting to his new look, that she had to stop herself from touching his cheek.

"No, it's what's *gone off of here!*" He laughed, touching his chin with his thumb. "Daisy said the beard had to go. So, last night, I...um," he shrugged, rubbing his cheeks with his palms, and avoiding her eyes. He seemed to be tense.

He pulled out one of the folding metal chairs from under the scarred wooden table.

"Please, sit down."

"I'm sorry, Abe...it's...it's just such a shock...to see you—without it..." Anna said, giggling, and sliding into the chair.

He pulled out the chair across from her and eased himself into it.

"I'm staring, I know, and I'm sorry, but you—" she said, biting her lip.

"So, do you think I look all right, without it?" he interrupted shyly, glancing at her.

Her heart went out to him. Seeing his insecurity made him seem so vulnerable—and suddenly, she saw the old Abe in his "new" face, and she smiled.

"Oh aye, yes, I do! I do! You look really fine! You're quite handsome...with or without all the fuzz, of course." Anna knew that when she slipped into her father's Irish, she was really anxious. But Abe didn't seem to mind—like Bill did.

He smiled. "Thank you."

She grinned back at him. She looked into his eyes, and he didn't look away. Anna felt warm all over—especially the now-familiar tingling in her seat, and she was lost in the enjoyment of the feeling.

He looked away, and stared down at his hands.

"Anna, we have a problem."

"Which one?" She laughed, nervously.

"Ah…right." He looked up at the ceiling. "Our daughters—Jaheen told me last night that she talked to Emily about—about us—about us skating together."

"I know."

"You do?" He looked at her with surprise.

"Aye. Yes, I listened in on some their conversation—the Lord forgive me—but I felt I had to…."

"Hmm." He nodded. "So you know that Jaheen's afraid that we are putting our marriages at risk—"

"I know, but that's silly, isn't it? We're just skating together…" She shrugged and looked at the blank chalkboard on the wall.

"Anna, there's more. How much did you hear?"

"Only a little girl talk at the beginning, and then I hung up. They sounded friendly enough—like they were gonna talk things over, ya know—between themselves." She looked at him, hoping he would understand her reasoning.

"Well…" He looked at the door, and back at her. "Jaheen also thinks that I'm in danger, because, we're an interracial couple—I mean skating pair. She asked Emily to try to convince you to stop skating with me, in public."

Anna's face flushed at the sound of the word "couple," and it took her a second to regain her focus.

"You mean your daughter thinks you're in danger—just because we skate together, at the *rink?*"

"Anna…Things like that—hate crimes—*are* happening everywhere—here, in our city—and all over the south. There's been violence against black men, for much less…"

"My God, I didn't think…Abe, I'm so sorry! I never meant to cause you or your family any harm." Anna bowed her head. "We can stop. It's not worth risking—"

"Hey, no!" He interrupted firmly.

Anna leaned far back in her chair.

He put his hand on her arm, and he shook his head. "I'm not going to let fear stop me. I told Jaheen, and I'm telling you...I'm not quitting our work together. It's too..." He rubbed his cheek again, and took a breath. "Anna, why do you think I shaved my face last night?" His voice had softened, but she felt the strength of his conviction.

She shook her head. "I don't know Abe...I—"

"I don't want fear and hate to run my life."

She considered his point. She was facing the same thing. Fear was running her life, and look what a disaster it had become...She scanned his face, and focused on his eyes.

"You want to skate—together...*with me*—that much?"

"Yes. Yes, I do" he said firmly, meeting her gaze. "I've considered the risks...There may be some, but I've decided that I want to keep training with you. I want see this through...wherever it leads."

She nodded, still worrying about him—and his family.

"But I want something from you, too."

"What's that?"

"I want you to make a commitment to compete with me, just once, in the spring."

Anna's body immediately reacted. She shook her head like someone had hit her. Like a wave of nausea, her stomach bubbled with fear.

"Abe! No, I—I can't...I..."

"You *can*, Anna! You *can* do it! I've seen you completely forget that people are watching you skate. When you lose yourself in the music, you're...it's as if you're singing with your whole body—the beat drives the way that you move your muscles, your arms, your legs..."

He took both of her hands in his, but she could hardly feel him. She was going numb. She couldn't look him in the eye. The idea of competing—of skating in front of crowds of people—the fear was almost unbearable. She shuffled her shoes on the floor, and stared down at the table, ask if she could watch her feet.

"Abe, I..." she slowly looked at him again Tears were starting to drop onto her cheeks. "I want to...with all my heart I really want to try, but...what if I can't go through with it? What if I mess up? I couldn't disappoint you..."

"You won't mess up. Trust me...Let me believe in you—until you can believe in yourself."

Anna was crying now, almost sobbing. She rummaged through her purse for a tissue. This conversation was not turning out the way she had expected, and now she was getting angry with herself for being so emotional...and so weak. Her father would have been disappointed in her. Maybe he was up there, this instant, telling her to buck up...and grow up. She looked at the ceiling, as if she could see him there.

"I don't know..."

She peeked at Abe through the veil of water that clouded her eyes. He looked miserable, and maybe even a little bit frustrated.

"I'm *so* sorry..." Anna sighed.

"Anna, stop apologizing for being who you are...and for feeling how you feel. It's *okay*...We'll work through this—together."

She didn't know how to respond. Such patience and kindness, coming from a man, felt strange—so unfamiliar. She didn't trust it, and she didn't trust herself.

"Thanks...thank you, Abe." She shook her head.

When she saw the deep care and concern in his eyes, she lost control completely. She stood up quickly, and accidentally knocked over the metal chair. The noise echoed around the tiny room.

She looked down at the chair, lying on its side on the floor, and she said, "Let me go…I need to go home now, Abe. I can only promise that I'll think about it. I've got to go…I'm really sorry…" And she left him sitting there, alone; his empty hands stretched out on the table.

Chapter 18 ❄ Abe

Abe waited outside the rink in his old leather jacket, dodging frozen rain drops, hoping to catch a glimpse of Anna's pink-finned station wagon. The roads were icy, and he worried about her, driving on the slippery highway. Truthfully, he wondered if she would even show up at all.

He hadn't heard from her since their talk at the library. He wanted to give her time to think. He shouldn't have pressured her. Like Daisy had warned him, Anna had some difficult decisions to make—and he understood how frightened she was about performing in public. He wasn't sure of all the reasons why she was so shy and afraid of competing...but, hell, here he was, a black man wanting to go public as an ice skater, and he wanted her to join him in that crazy idea—for what? A trophy? A few minutes of fame?

But he knew this was about more than just winning prizes, or getting recognition. It was about something much bigger. It was about expressing who they were—from deep down—from their souls.

Something really amazing had happened to them. He and Anna had met, and they'd discovered a common love for moving to music—the kind of music and lyrics that filled them with the rhythm of life itself...and, he believed, they could share their gift with the world.

It was their talent. It was what they did. It was who they were...

But when he thought about the all risks, he wasn't sure he had the right to ask her to continue on. She would have to agree—on her own, for her own reasons.

"There you are. Where's your partner in crime?" Daisy called to him though the half open door, shivering in spite of the full length coat that covered her tiny form down to her ankles. She was so short, it nearly covered all of her furry boots.

"Hi...I expect her any minute now," he replied casually, as if he didn't have a care in the world.

Ha, he thought. His acting skills were still working without his beard. He was freaking out inside, and Daisy couldn't even tell. "What's on the agenda for today?" He asked, walking to Daisy. He held the door for her, as they entered the deserted lobby.

Daisy had an access pass in her hand. She must have come in through the security door in the back, he thought. Daisy had called him at home, telling him that she had arranged for all three of them to meet at eight each morning, so they could start working with music in the main arena, before regular business hours.

"More torture," Daisy joked.

Abe had found a substitute teacher for his morning World History class, but he wouldn't have missed this, even if he'd had to cancel the class. His eyes wandered to the front windows, and then the lobby clock, feeling more anxious: eight-fifteen.

Where was she? She was never late...

"She'll be here. The weather's awful, and there's the commuter traffic..."

She looked at him curiously.

So she *had* noticed that he was worrying about Anna, he thought with a sideways look at her. Daisy was sharp. Too sharp sometimes.

"You know, I've worked with a lot of skaters over the years, and I've learned that skating is like any other sport." Daisy said. "Some athletes are motivated by a need to show off, some want to win awards, others want fame...and some compete just because—well, because they have to. Something inside them drives them to conquer their fears...achieve their personal best." She looked up at him. "I get the feeling that you and Anna have—that last kind of a need. Am I wrong?"

He sighed, and stared at her, giving her his full attention. "You are an amazing woman, Daisy French. How'd you get so wise?"

"Ha. You're a bit of a wise old owl yourself, Abraham...Hmm, but maybe it's just those glasses..."

He laughed. "I'm working on getting rid of these." He took them off and waved them at her. "Yeah. But, you know, you're right. What I'm doing—it has nothing to do with winning prizes. I can't stop now. Maybe it's—the challenge? I just hope Anna feels the same way..." He walked to the front window. "She might not go through with the competition part anyway." He shrugged, as if it didn't really matter to him—but it did.

"She's really afraid of performing, isn't she?" Daisy asked kindly.

He nodded.

"Well, we'll know soon...Fear is a powerful force. But I tend to think she'll go for it."

"Why do you think so?" He turned to Daisy. He felt hope growing in him.

"There's something that's stronger than fear, Abe. I saw it that first day, when I watched you skate together. Clearly, you love the sport...No question there. But there's an energy between you two—I haven't seen that kind of connection in my lifetime of coaching. It was like you could read each other's minds—"

"Thanks," he smiled, and hung his head, feeling like a little boy receiving a complement from his teacher.

"But, don't let that go to your head, Mr. Lincoln. Even though you're both strong and experienced skaters— and your technical is pretty solid now—your classical interp still needs a lot of work..." She shook her head.

"Yes, ma'am."

Her face grew thoughtful. "Something's not working with the choreography—and that surprises me—because when you're free dancing, you're really in sync..." She turned toward the arena. "Anyway, today, we'll try the ballet sequences, on the ice, with the Mozart. Hopefully, that will do the trick—"

"Hey guys!" Anna's voice cut her off. She was struggling to keep the front door open while carrying her skate bag, and a tray of steaming paper coffee cups. Abe rushed to help her. "I'm sorry I'm late. I stopped to pick up some breakfast treats for us...and the traffic was terrible."

She looked at Abe and she smiled at him. He was so glad to see her, he could hardly mask his big grin. He reached for the paper tray. He wanted to tell her how glad he was that she'd come, but Daisy interrupted.

"Anna, thank you," said Daisy, as she accepted the coffee and took a doughnut out of the sack. "We only have the rink until nine-thirty, so lace up, and I'll meet you inside. Hurry now!"

Daisy had been critical of Anna's weight, so Abe was glad Daisy hadn't commented on the sweets. He wanted today to be a good one, for all of them.

He took a bite of his doughnut, and a sip of coffee, even though he had eaten a giant bowl of cereal with

Jaheen at home, just about an hour ago. "Umm…delicious. Thank you!."

Anna sat on the lobby bench next to him, and he watched her devour her cruller out of the corner of his eye, as he drank some more coffee.

She licked her fingers, and he caught a glimpse of her tongue. He could feel heat from seeing it radiate down from his gut into his thighs.

"I was starved! The ice was bad out there—I guess I needed a little sugar."

Yeah, he thought. So did *he!*

He tried to control himself; he *had* to stop thinking about what it might be like to have sex with her.

"I'm glad you made it," he said, forcing his voice into an imitation of his favorite actor. "You're here…and I'm glad to see you, of course, but, does that mean you've made a decision?"

She looked at him over her coffee cup, and winced as she swallowed the hot liquid. She put it down. "Yep…I've made my decision."

"Well? Don't keep me in suspense…Ice Woman," his tone was joking, but everything inside him felt wound up tight, like a spring.

She raised her chin, "I've decided to…to do it. I'm gonna try my best…to not let ya down—"

After the second it took for him to register what she was saying, a big smile came over his face, and he couldn't stop it. He didn't want to. Before she'd even finished, he found himself reaching out to pinch her chin lightly between his thumb and first finger, like he did to Jaheen, when she'd made a good decision.

"Atta girl!" he said.

He watched her whole face light up, and sparkle into her bright green eyes. The range of feelings he was having—relief, excitement…and fear, was almost too intense, so he focused on finishing his coffee.

"Ah, excuse me…anyone out there wanting a skating lesson today?" Daisy's voice came over the loudspeaker.

Abe looked at Anna, and they laughed, as they jammed on their rental skates.

"We're gonna need to have Daze help us find some nice, new skates, don't ya think?" Anna asked him.

"Yep, I do. I don't think we'd have much of a chance of winning with these…"

She looked at him, and she crinkled up eyes. "I'm not thinking about the competition right now, Abe. I only promised that I'd try—and try to do my best, I will…"

"That's all I'm asking…and I promise that I'll be with you, every step of the way."

* * *

"No, no, *no*!" Daisy called from the center of the rink. "My God, do you people have *any* rhythm in your bodies *at all*? Geeze, Abe…at least you should…" Her frustrated voice crashed over the soft Mozart concerto that played from the overhead loudspeakers.

Abe pulled Anna to a stop and stared at Daisy. For the past hour they had been working to turn the "dry land" ballet steps that Daisy had drilled into them, into smooth dance movements that flowed with the classical music. Abe figured that they had the long runs down—and their spins were going pretty well, but, it was true, the shorter dance steps were absolute disasters. They'd both tripped and fell a couple of times, and everyone's nerves seemed to be on edge.

"I'm sorry, Daisy," Anna gasped, bending over to catch her breath. "I'm just not feelin' those ballet steps today…maybe it's the music…I don't know what's wrong."

Abe joined them. He hated the music, too, but he knew skating tradition—and competition requirements—demanded programs which were choreographed to traditional musical themes. He wouldn't rock the boat. He knew how to get along, and he was determined to comply, and to follow the rules.

But it was hard work.

"And, Abe, those damn glasses…You keep having to adjust them. It's distracting, and it interferes with your upper body follow-throughs. When are you going to get those contacts—and a better haircut?" demanded Daisy.

They were all silent for a moment. He felt like a child being scolded. Daisy's word sent him back to when his older half-brother had teased him, and hit him…and the feeling of shame crept up around his shoulders and neck. He bowed his head.

Anna looked at him. "Daisy, stop picking on him!" Anna blurted out, staring at Daisy now, with a look in her eyes that was—well, it was downright scary. He could see that she was mad, but, at the same time, he was touched that she was defending him.

"You're here to *help* us, not tear us down all the time…" Anna added, her hands resting on her hips

Daisy faced them with a calmness that Abe wished he could feel. With a quiet voice, Daisy said, "Believe it or not, I *am* trying to help you, Anna…and Abe, I am not being critical. I am giving you both *feedba*ck, which is necessary for your training…that is, if you still want me to continue to *try* to train you?"

Mozart, echoed from the rafters.

Abe nodded, "I do, Daisy," he said.

Anna glanced up at him. "Well, now, I do too—and I'm sorry, Daisy. I'm just tired. I want you to keep working with us, too."

Daisy looked at them with her most patient half-smile. She shook her head, as if she was dealing with two exasperating children, and said, "All right, then. Tomorrow morning, same time, same place—and Anna, no doughnuts, please."

Chapter 19 ❀ Emily

Emily knew she was performing better since her mother wasn't skating with Mr. Brown during her lessons anymore. Even Carol had said she had noticed a big improvement in her concentration.

She was standing next to Steph now, waiting for her turn to show Carol her backward figure eight. Emily felt relaxed, and ready.

Her mom was training in the mornings, and, that didn't worry her too much, because Daisy French was there watching them the whole time—and telling them what to do. Her mother complained about how strict Daisy was, and Emily was glad about that.

Emily tried not to worry about her promise to Jaheen. She was still planning to talk to her mother about quitting her training with Jaheen's father, like she'd said she would, but she kept putting it off. Every time she saw Jaheen, she thought about her promise. Jaheen always nodded and smiled at her...probably to remind her about their agreement.

Keeping promises was important to Emily. But she was learning that promises didn't always work out. Her mom and her dad had made wedding promises that they would stay together forever—before she was even born—and now look at them...

Did promises get old and just stop working—like an old radio?

Emily decided to ask her mom about promises later, on their way home, in the car. The subject of breaking promises would be a good way to start asking her mother about stopping her lessons. Her mom probably wouldn't listen to her, but she'd only promised Jaheen that she would *try* to talk her mom out of the training...

She thought that she'd better talk that out with Steph first. She pulled Steph aside during the break. They were sipping their juice and sharing a banana.

"Jaheen wants me to tell my mom to quit training with her dad. She thinks they could get hurt."

"Hurt by what?"

"Riots...or get divorces, or something..."

"Well, yeah, Em, That could happen. The riots are getting worse...Crap! I can't believe I'm thinking that Jaheen-the-Scream is right, but talking to your mom about—everything—that's what I would do..."

"Yeah. I know. I'm really worried about her, Steph— I've been watching the news—about the violence and riots and all—it's awful...and what if my dad finds out she's skating with a colored man?"

"Emily...you're up next!" called Carol, interrupting them.

"Go, Em! Show Ms. Jaheen what you can do!" whispered Steph.

Emily started her approach, her jaw set with determination. Her new-found confidence gave her some extra speed. She smiled and nodded at Jaheen as she whizzed past her, and the next thing she knew, a strange man in a white coat was shining a bright light into her eyes, and asking her if she knew what day it was...

* * *

"I've had enough of this *ridiculous* skating business." Emily could hear her father's loud talking. His voice

132

sounded funny, and far away, like an echo. It was coming from behind a tall white curtain. "*Look* what you have done to her! Filling her head with a sick need for a dangerous sport. And I want *you* to stop skating, too—you're just setting a bad example for *my* daughter!"

Where was she? Was she dead? Emily wondered, feeling very sleepy.

She could heard her mother crying, saying, "Bill, these things happen to children—to any child—anywhere...She could've—just as easy—fallen off her bike and hit her head, or..."

"*I don't care*," her father sounded really mad. "There will be no more skating for *my* daughter—or anyone else in this family. And that's the end of it. *End* of discussion!"

Then Emily realized that she wasn't dead after all. As her eyes slowly focused, she saw that she was lying in a white hospital room with big smiling elephants and jumping monkeys on the walls. Her head hurt, but she was very much alive—the sound of her parents' familiar argument had confirmed that.

They wouldn't be fighting if this were heaven, she thought.

She wiggled all of her fingers and toes, and they all moved okay. That was a good sign. Her left wrist had a thick white bandage around it, but if she bent it too far up or down, it hurt. Feeling too tired to try to move anything else, she looked around the room, with her eyes half open.

There was a bottle of something that looked like water hanging on a silver pole next to her bed. The water was dripping into a long clear tube that was attached to her right arm. She had never been in a hospital before. She had always been afraid of being in one, but she was feeling so relaxed and sleepy now, she thought that maybe hospitals weren't so bad, after all.

Her mother peeked around the curtain. "Hi, honey! You're awake!" she whispered with a big smile. Her eyes were red.

"Hi Mom," Emily said weakly, noticing that her mouth was dry. "Can I have some water, please?"

"Not quite yet, Sweetie." Her mom pointed to the bottle on the pole. "You're getting water from that bottle there, right into your veins, but I'll ask the nurse if you can have some ice." She stepped closer to the bed. "I am soo sorry you fell, honey. How do you feel?"

"My head hurts, and..." she raised her left hand just a little off its little resting pillow, "my hand does, too, if I move it too much."

Her mother kissed her cheek, smiling. "You are gonna be okay...Ya know, all the doctors say so." She had tears in her eyes. She reached for Emily's good hand, and squeezed it. "Oh, Em, I'm so glad you're going to be all right. I love you, honey."

"What happened to me, Mom?"

"You fell, and hit your head on the ice...Just like I did the other day." Her mother rolled her eyes, and bit into the side of her lip. "And you cut your wrist on your skate blade somehow, so there's a tiny crack in your wrist bone, but the doctor said you'll heal up real fast. You'll be as good as new, in no time at all..."

"Then why am I in the hospital?"

Her mother's green eyes were sad, but her smile was big, and her face was glowing white in the dark room. Emily was suddenly filled with love for her mother. She looked like an angel, and she was so happy that her mom was there.

"Oh...well, honey, you'll only be here for a day or two, just so the doctors and nurses can watch over you—

until your head heals a wee bit more…and your headache goes away."

"Will you stay here with me? I heard Daddy talking. Is he here too?"

"I'll stay with you as long as they'll let me…Your father—he had to go, but he'll be back tomorrow, to check on you."

Her mother quickly added, "But look! Your daddy brought you this nice big vase of yellow flowers, and a special get-well balloon!"

Emily tried to answer, but sleep was pulling her under. The last thing she heard before she drifted into a dreamy sleep was her mother showing her another gift—pink roses from her grandparents.

Chapter 20 ❋ Anna

Anna had begged the evening nurse to let her stay with Emily all night. The nurse was a kind Jamaican woman who had two young children of her own, so she'd agreed to bend the rules, and allow Anna to sleep in Emily's room.

Anna tried to get comfortable in the lounge chair next to Emily's bed, and, after wiggling around in all kinds of positions, she'd finally found one that worked well enough for her to drift off to sleep for a few hours.

Just before dawn, two young orderlies came in the room and woke them. The young men started to move Emily from her bed to a stretcher.

"Where are you taking her?" Anna asked with alarm. "Is anything wrong?"

"No, ma'am. We're just taking her down to radiology," one of the older boys in white answered.

"Mom? Will you go with me?" Emily asked.

"I'm sorry, she can't, honey. John and Jeff will take you down for an x-ray, but don't worry. It won't hurt," said a tall, black nurse, walking out from behind the curtain. "I'm Wanda, your daughter's day nurse," she added sharply.

Anna realized that there must have been a shift change, and her night nurse-ally had probably gone home. Judging from Wanda's cool manner, Anna figured it would be useless to argue, and so she meekly asked, "When will Emily be back?"

"It all depends, ma'am." Wanda sighed impatiently. "Emergencies are taken before routine x-rays, like Emily's. At least an hour, I suspect." Wanda looked at Emily, and smiled at her. "But we'll take good care of Emily now." She patted Emily's shoulder. "Mom, why don't you go on downstairs and get you some breakfast…and freshen up a little bit? And there's a real nice beauty parlor in the lobby. They do some good work down there…"

Anna cringed. She realized that she probably looked horrible to the nurse—her hair, her face—even her life— everything!

After the orderlies had left with Emily, Wanda stayed behind, and she said, "I heard that you'd slept here in your daughter's room last night."

"Um hum," Anna nodded, preparing to hear a lecture about breaking the rules.

"Good choice." She said. "I would've made the same one. Mothers gotta do what they gotta do—for their kids' sake. "

Anna was pleasantly surprised, and she gave Wanda a grateful smile.

Wanda turned to leave, saying, over her shoulder, "We moms got to make good choices—and take care of ourselves—so we can take care of our babies."

Anna watched her leave, and thought about what she'd said. Take care of herself first?

Hmm…How could she do that?

She looked in the mirror over the sink, and she had to admit that she *did* look pretty bad—and she hadn't been taking care of herself very well at all. Her hair were exploding in all directions, and her red curls were stuck together in bushy clumps. Her eyes were red from crying last night about: Bill!

Bill—that creep! Just thinking about him caused anger to flood her body, and she saw the hatred flash in the mirror. God, no! She didn't want to hate—anyone. Even Bill. Hatred was wrong. Hatred and bitterness had killed her father.

But she was *so* mad at Bill, there no getting around it. The terrible scene he'd made in the hospital hallway yesterday came rushing back: Bill and his parents had accused her of *causing* Emily's accident!

Gwen had said, that because Anna was obsessed with skating, she had caused Emily's interest in the sport— which, he said, was very dangerous—even life-threatening. After that, Bill Senior had chimed in, sneering, and saying that ice skating wasn't even a *real* sport...And after their tirade against her, Bill had forbidden Emily—*and Anna*—to skate, *ever again!*

Never in her life had she felt such rage toward anyone. They were so unfair, so irrational...She splashed cold water on her face, and ran a wet comb though her tangled hair.

Following Wanda's directions, she found her way to the hospital lobby.

What should she do now? She was tired. She was upset. It was hard to think straight...Where should she go?

Wanda's advice still echoed through the sleepy fog that clouded her head. She kept thinking about ways that she needed to take care of herself, to be strong, for Emily.

Eat something. Do something. Change something. But what?

She couldn't fight the Smithsons, or Bill, but at least she could make some good choices for herself—for Em.

Walking around the busy hospital entrance, she found the snack bar, and started to reach for a doughnut.

Not a good choice, she thought. Instead, she bought a banana and some orange juice.

While she ate, she strolled around a soothing water fountain, stretching out the stiffness from her night's sleep in the chair. She wandered past the gift shop, and the newsstand, watching people hurrying everywhere. Some were dressed in white—doctors, nurses, orderlies—and there were visitors carrying flowers, shopping bags, and gifts. She saw faces that were alive with purpose. People everywhere seemed to know where they were going—and the reasons why they were going there. She envied them…But at least, this morning, she'd already made one choice that was good for her—and for Em.

She felt lonely, and scared—like she was a child herself. She missed her father. She missed Abe. What advice would they have given her now?

Abe was probably tired of hearing her whining. He'd be nice, but…he was busy with his own family, and she needed to leave him alone.

And her father, bless his soul…he was probably pulling his hair out, watching her flop around, like a fish out of water, here in her messed up life on earth. Did people have hair in heaven? Boy, she must be really crazy to be thinking about something dumb like that, she thought.

She knew she wasn't really crazy, but she did have some serious problems to solve.

She decided to do something…

But what?

She hadn't done much to change her life. She was still living in misery with Bill. She hadn't really dealt with him;

she'd been avoiding him. She'd known her truth about her marriage for a while now, so why hadn't she acted on it?

"Please...help me to *live* my truth!" she said, almost prayerfully, out loud. Two nurses walked by and looked at her oddly. She ducked, and turned, and she almost ran the other way, her cheeks burning. She kept her head down, and, walking very fast, she nearly tripped over a sandwich board sign for the beauty shop.

She stopped and stared at it while she finished her juice.

She took a deep breath. It was time to make another choice. And she was ready for a change.

"Maybe I am crazy, but what do I have to lose?" she shrugged, and she went inside.

Chapter 21 ❀ *Abe*

Abe sat alone in his closet-sized office, leaning back in his antique wooden editor's chair. He rested his head against the closed door. It had taken him twelve long years to break in this chair just right. His feet were propped up on the worn mahogany desk; he'd cleared a spot for his long legs to fit in between the stacks of ungraded midterm essays.

His eyes scanned the piles of papers. He had to get to work on them, or his students wouldn't have them back by Thanksgiving—in time for studying for their final exams. But he couldn't seem to focus on work. It had been hard enough to show up for his classes lately. Somehow, his passion for teaching had taken a back seat to the demands of Daisy's increasingly complex training sessions.

And then there was Anna. She was never far from his thoughts. He was confused by the power of his feelings for her. She really wasn't his type. She was too tall, and, truth be told, he'd never found red-headed white women with freckles very attractive.

But she was a different kind of woman—like nobody he'd ever met. She got to him. She was funny, and she thought he was, too. She didn't seem to care about the color of his skin. She saw him as a *man*—and not a black man. When he was with her he felt like he was her equal—just another human being. And she accepted him as a friend—and she was his friend.

The light from his small desk lamp sent shadows onto shelves that were jammed with history books—most were from textbook salesmen who pitched their latest editions, giving him the teacher's copies to keep. In the past—until recently—his office and his books brought him comfort. He'd lived in a world of ideas, behind his mask...

He'd found tremendous satisfaction in teaching history to his students over the years. His Grandma had told him that he'd been named "Abraham," but not for the man in the Bible—he'd been named for the great president and liberator, Abraham Lincoln, and, she liked to say, one day, he too, would be a leader in the cause for human freedom.

He'd always thought teaching was his calling as a leader, but now he wasn't so sure...Hell, Georgie should have had his name, he thought. He just taught about history. Georgie was hell bent on making it.

He thought about his Grandma, and he wondered what she would think of him now, what she might say about what he was doing: Risking his family. Risking their safety. For—what? Sexual attraction? Ego? Pride?

He had these strange *feelings*—feelings for a married white woman, and he had been skating—dancing—with her, in public. Would Grams think he was being brave—being true to himself—or was he just being stupid?

His Grandma never approved of his skating. She'd worried that he'd get hurt, that it was too dangerous—and, honestly, he *had* skated recklessly, many times. He'd skated wild and fast to shake off the pain, and run from the rejection he'd felt, about not having a father—or a mother—a real family. He'd skated when kids put him down. He skated to prove he was tough. He skated instead of feeling...anything that hurt. When he'd fall, the physical pain was nothing compared to the emotional pain he carried around inside of him for as long as he could remember.

And now, he was married to a woman who rejected him, and who belittled him, too. He wondered that maybe he was like Abraham Lincoln, because he believed in keeping the peace, instead of waging war. He knew that fighting and violence would never bring peace. He learned that on the streets, and in the Army, and from the history books, but Georgie disagreed...

His Grams was gone now. She'd passed on years ago. While she was alive, he used to visit her in Detroit, and he'd taken Jaheen with him during summer breaks. Georgie never had—or made—the time to go with them. Georgie didn't have the time—for him, or for Jaheen now, either.

The telephone on his desk buzzed. It startled him. He was so lost in thought, that when he sat up, and his feet nocked some papers onto the floor. He grabbed the receiver. Bending down to retrieve the fallen essays under his desk, he answered with a low grunt: "Brown."

"Abe? It's me...Anna."

He reacted as if he'd gotten an electric shock, bumping the top of his head on the desk. "Ow! Shit" he cried out, rubbing the back of his neck.

"Oh, gee, Abe...I'm so sorry...I didn't mean to bother you at work..." Anna said.

"No...no. Anna, it's okay. I just hit my head. No problem. Hey, how's Emily doing?" He tried to sound calm, but he was excited by the sound of her voice.

"Not you, too? I don't want to hear about any more head injuries!" Anna said, trying to be cheerful, but he knew her well enough to hear the strain in her voice.

"Seriously. I'm fine. How *is* Emily doing?"

"She's much better, thanks. She gets to go home tomorrow. And the doctor says she can probably go back to school next week…" She paused. "You know, I had to cancel Thursday's practice…I've already called Daisy."

"Of course," he replied. He'd known it before, but he felt it now, on a very deep level, how much their skating together had come to mean to him. The week ahead suddenly loomed long, and empty, without the prospect of seeing her.

There was another long pause.

"Abe," Anna began tentatively. He didn't like the sound of her tone. There was something in it that made his stomach flip, like there was a fish swimming around inside of him.

"Yes," he breathed, squeezing his eyes tightly shut, rubbing the back of his neck.

"There's something more I need to tell you…"

"What is it, Anna? What's wrong?"

"It's Bill. He's…he's forbidden Emily to ever skate again. And he blamed me for the accident." Her voice was growing louder and higher as she talked. "He said, in front of his parents at the hospital—and even in front of the *doctor*—that I'm a terrible influence on her. He said that if I wasn't so crazy about skating…Well, that Emily could have died and the whole thing was my fault…" she broke off, her voice cracking into sobs.

"Anna, no." Abe said quietly, but anger was building in his chest. "Do *not* listen to that *bullshit*." He shook his head, and stood up, knocking more things off the desk with the phone cord. He paid no attention to papers and pencils as they fell onto the floor. "None of that is true, Anna! You've *got* to see that! He's just…just trying to control you—and Emily—with guilt, and…"

He tried to calm down; he didn't want to lecture her. He couldn't tell her what to do. Whatever she decided to do about Bill had to come from inside of her, and not from

144

him. He slapped his hand over his mouth to hold back giving her advice. Taking long, slow breaths, and he bit down on the base of his thumb.

"I know, Abe."

He listened to her whimper like a sad puppy. He wanted to reach into the phone, grab her, and hold her. He wanted to punch Bill in the face. He could do neither. Daisy was right. Anna had to deal with the changes in her life on her own, and all he could do was...what? Be her friend? That's *all* he could do. He was just her friend.

You are *so right*," she said, catching her breath, sniffling. "I've been thinking a lot about Bill—and how he treats me. It's all that I've been thinking about since he said those horrible things about me—in front of everybody. He *was* trying to make me feel bad—feel guilty...but...I didn't do anything wrong, did I Abe? I mean, I just wanted Emily to love something—the way I love it."

"You did nothing wrong, Anna. You're a good mother...Accidents happen—"

"Bill did something else too, Abe." She cut him off.

"What did that bast—what did he do, Anna? Tell me..."

She hesitated. "Bill has forbidden me to skate anymore. No more training, nothing...But you know what?"

"What?" he managed to ask, almost holding his breath while he waited.

"I told him he wasn't my *father*, he was just my *husband*," she said, with the same determination he'd observed in her when the going got rough on the ice...

"You know what else?" She didn't wait for him to respond. "He didn't know about you and me, about us skating together, until I told him. I thought that maybe he'd known all about our training sessions, because Emily tells him things…" Her words came faster and faster. "But he'd never bothered to ask me anything about what *I* was doing…He never seemed to care—until he saw that I was happy doing something on my own—something I might be good at. I think he just wants to control my life. And that's the real the reason he wants me to stop skating."

Abe felt his hands growing colder as he gripped the phone. "So you told him about us? About me?" he asked, worried about what might be coming next.

"Yep, I did. It all came out when he saw my haircut—after he told me I looked awful in short hair."

Abe sat down hard in his chair, in a full state of shock now, "You cut off your *hair?*"

"Aye…All off. Really short, Just like Daisy said I should," she said simply.

Abe's thoughts were racing. "So…wait. Let me get this straight: you're going to keep on—?"

She cut him off again, and an excited determination filled her voice. "Yes. I told Bill I wasn't going to *obey* his command—about skating. I told him I was going to keep training, with you and Daisy." Her voice changed, and she added tentatively, "I'm not sure how I'm going to pay her for now, until I can get some more money out of my dad's trust fund—Bill said he wouldn't pay for any skating bills anymore—"

Not being able to stop himself, he interrupted her. "Don't worry about the money. I'll handle the cost, for now. Does he know that—that I'm *black?*" His heart was beating fast.

"Ah, no. I didn't go into that. Why? Should I have told him that?"

Abe was struck again by the depth of her color-blindness.

But, just today, there had been another incident of a police beating. A black man had been hurt while being forced into the back of a squad car—after been arrested for using a white-only restroom.

Abe wondered why he hadn't talked with Anna more about the risks she was taking—being with him in public places, touching him, holding him during practices…How could he have gotten himself—and Anna—in such a dangerous situation?

"Can you get away sometime this weekend…and meet me again, at the library?" he asked, trying to keep his voice and his concerns under control.

"Maybe Sunday. It's Emily's day with her grandparents, if she feels up to it. What time? At one again?"

"Yes. Sunday at one would be fine."

"Abe?"

"Yes, Anna?"

"Did I make a mistake? Should I have told Bill *everything*? Was I wrong to stand up to him, and tell him off? I'm so mixed up…I feel really bad sometimes—about what we're doing—and then, you know, sometimes I feel really good about—"

"Anna, you didn't make any mistakes. But maybe I have. I think it's time that *everybody* knows *everything* about what we're doing—and what we plan to do.

"You do?"

"Yes. We are Atlanta's finest interracial skating team!" He took a deep breath, and laughed a little. "And, we are gonna make a little history, Ice Woman. Yes, we are gonna make ourselves some history…"

"Sounds like a plan, Ice Man."

He shook his head in disbelief. This woman had guts. But did he? He had a lot to think about, and there was something he had to do.

After he hung up, he felt relieved, but, his relief was mixed with dread. What was in store for them? Would they be accepted, or persecuted, for the color of their skin? Would people accept them as serious athletes?

Only time would tell.

Chapter 22 ❀ *Jaheen*

A cold north wind collided with Atlanta's warm November air. Tiny ice pellets sprayed sideways, against her bedroom window. Jaheen listened to the sounds of the storm as she struggled to figure out the right answers to the math problems she'd missed on her Algebra exam.

Her father had talked her into asking for extra help, and her teacher had allowed her to correct her test at home. Jaheen still believed that math was a huge waste of her time, but her father had explained, for the millionth time, that education was important—in case she ever wanted to follow in his footsteps, and go to college.

"Man, he's good at making me feel guilty," she muttered to herself.

She and her father had been out speed-walking together earlier that afternoon. She'd froze her face off the whole time, but she had wanted to show him how dedicated she was—getting fit for training—just like he was doing.

She'd reminded him about her goal—her dream of skating in the Olympics—and she didn't need to go to college. She was tough, and she was dedicated, she'd told him. She reminded him that she even had a boy's name—thanks to her mother, who wanted to name her something strong—and not give her some foo-foo white girl's name.

Jaheen was, her father had admitted, an excellent skater. Everybody said she had talent—

well *almost* everybody. Her mother didn't. Her mom wanted Jaheen to do something *important,* like volunteering at the civil rights office. Jaheen had to live in the real world. Her mother had lectured her about that, over and over...

But Jaheen knew that the world was real already. And when her father had warned her that white society didn't always recognize what a colored person could do—and, not like other sports—skating was definitely in the white world—she'd looked at him like he was nuts. What did he think *he* was doing? He was a *black man*, planning to compete on *white ice*, in *white public*, with a *white woman!*

Her dad was different lately—he had changed, she'd had to admit. He seemed more confident, and he was definitely more..."too big for his britches," like her mother said. So, Jaheen had decided to not ask him about skating with Emily's mother anymore. Adults—they acted crazy sometimes. Who could figure them out?

One thing Jaheen *did* know was that she didn't need math to win her gold medal. What she *did* need was more training. She wanted to work with Daisy French. When she'd asked him about it, her father said that she had to finish her classes with Carol first; then, he promised to discuss budgeting the extra money for more lessons.

Now, Jaheen was almost finished with her homework, when she heard her parents starting to raise their voices downstairs. As usual, the sound made her feel cold all over.

There they go again, she sighed, listening, and waiting for the argument to really get going. But this time, their voices got quieter, instead of getting louder—almost like they had sore throats. Were they really whispering?

What were they saying?

She had to find out.

She tiptoed out to the landing, and tucked herself behind the bannister in the stairwell, where they couldn't see her. She was thin and agile—she knew she had the perfect, world-class, skating figure. She didn't feel bad about eavesdropping; her future was at stake—her life plans depended on the decisions that her parents were making down there.

She strained to hear them, but she only understood bits and pieces of sentences. In low voice, her dad was telling her mom something about how he'd met Mrs. Smithson.

Then, she heard her mother's voice clearly. Her mother wasn't buying any of what her dad was trying to sell. Her mom was making rude remarks about the "wily ways of white women". Her dad told her to hush up. Her mother, of course, didn't listen, and she went on about Emily's mother, and how she was just using him, like all whites used blacks—like slaves.

For a long time after that, there was only silence. Jaheen waited, barely breathing. She was thinking. It surprised her, when she heard her mother call Emily's mother names, that she felt bad for Mrs. Smithson. Why did words like "bitch-whore" sound a lot worse, coming from her mother, than when she said them?

And it wasn't really true anyway. Emily's mother was a skater, and she seemed to really jive to it—Jaheen had seen it when Mrs. Smithson was out there on the ice, jamming with her dad.

Jaheen remembered the time that Carol had talked to her after that time in the locker room. Somebody must have told on her...and Jaheen knew that she could have lost her skating lessons that day, because of her temper.

"Jaheen, I know you are a serious skater. You're thinking about Olympic training, so I have something important to tell you." Carol had said, after pulling her away from the other girls.

Jaheen had looked down at the floor, but she had listened carefully to every word.

"Advanced skaters have to deal with tense and challenging situations out there, on the ice. In order to execute a flawless program—and to keep from getting hurt—they have to be calm and alert, at all times."

Jaheen had nodded.

"Do you know what I mean?"

Jaheen had nodded again, but this time, she'd looked at Carol.

"Good. I want you to practice staying calm—no matter what is going on around you. Can you do that?"

Jaheen had smiled, she'd felt so relieved. She'd been expecting a lecture. Instead, Carol had given her the best—and the most important—advice about training. Bad feelings affected her skating skills, and, if thinking mean thoughts hurt her performance, then she'd decided she would change her ways.

She thought about how her father was nice to everyone. He was even kind to white people. She knew her mother pushed him, to "tough him up for the real world," as she heard her ma say. But, Jaheen wondered, which one of them was right? Her dad seemed happier and much more calm, than her mom ever was...but...

Now, Jaheen's body tensed up, because she expected her mother to blow her top any second; feeling protective of her father, her stomach was churning so loud she was afraid they would hear it from downstairs.

How could she calm herself down when her parents started fighting like this?

But suddenly, when the two of them started to talk again—together—and have a normal conversation, she could hardly believe it. What was happening?

She shook her head in disbelief.

Parents.

She was getting a cramp in her leg from squeezing into her tiny listening corner, and her one foot was starting to feel numb, so she got up slowly to stretch.

"Jaheen, get back to your homework...and close your door—please!" Her father's voice made her jump and she bumped her head against the low ceiling.

"Okay," she answered, scurrying back to her room, rubbing the top of her head. Closing her bedroom door, she plopped down on her bed. She might as well finish her homework. She hoped that her wild and crazy parents would work things out...for her sake, and for all of them. After all, crazy or not, this *was* her only family.

Chapter 23 ❋ Anna

Anna propped her feet up on the couch. Listening absently to the wind rattle against the windows, she flipped through the pages of the book about ballet techniques that Daisy had given her to study.

She'd just finished with an hour of exercising in the cool, dimly lit living room, and she was satisfied that she'd done all of Daisy's homework. She'd practiced the stretches and the painful ballet positions—until her muscles were screaming for her to stop. Anna thought that Daze's workouts were unnatural, and they certainly weren't much fun, so she'd given herself a reward by free-dancing to her favorite soul music afterward.

Her legs felt like rubber. She sipped the warm herbal tea that Daisy had given her to try. It was supposed to calm her nerves. It seemed to be working; she was feeling very relaxed.

She was happy, too, knowing her daughter was upstairs, recovering without serious complications, from her fall. Anna looked up at the ceiling, feeling grateful that Em was back, doing her homework, in her own bed, in her own room. Faint music filtered downstairs from Em's radio. It was, Anna guessed, that latest group of boys from England—what were they called—the latest ones with the super-long hair? She couldn't remember. Em's interest in country music had certainly changed lately…

Anna smiled, and turned back to her book, trying to ignore nagging worries about Em's state of mind—and her own sanity. Could she take Emily away from the only home that she'd ever known? If she and Bill split up, then how would Emily cope with a family that was broken? Kids needed their parents. Her own parents had left her all alone in the world—and look what a mess she'd made of her life.

She was surprised to hear the key turn in the lock of the front door. It was only a little after six, on a Friday night. Could that be Bill coming home? *Already?*

Bill walked in, looking directly at her with an intensity she was not accustomed to seeing, and it set off warning bells in her head. He looked tense, and her body recoiled as if she was seeing a wild animal prowling into the room. Her heart started to beat faster.

"Hello," he said slowly. He seemed uncomfortable. That surprised her, too. He usually sort of swaggered around, as if he was in charge of the whole world—as if he knew more than anybody else—especially her.

"Hi" she answered, looking down at her book. The hurt from their argument in the hospital was still fresh in her mind. "You're home early," she managed to say.

Instead of going directly upstairs, as she expected him to do, he walked into the living room, and stood in front of the fireplace. He reached down to the controls, and he turned on the gas. She wanted to leave—get away from him—but she couldn't seem to move.

"It's really cold out there," he said, his back to her, as he warmed his hands over the struggling flames.

She didn't feel like making small talk. The sting of his accusations was still fresh. The picture of his face, twisted with outrage at the hospital, felt like it had been pressed so deeply into her brain that she'd never forget it.

All sports are risky; he can't blame me for Em's injuries, she repeated silently to herself.

She didn't want to start another argument, but the old one seemed to be starting by itself, in her head. She glanced at him through narrowed eyes and said nothing. Looking down at her book again, she hoped he would just go away.

"I've been thinking that maybe I owe you an apology," he said slowly.

Anna's body reacted as if she'd just been hit in the face. She couldn't believe what she'd just heard. He *never* apologized—at least, as far as she could remember. She was stunned, and unable to speak.

"I shouldn't have accused you of harming *our* daughter *on purpose*. I know you wouldn't do that."

She looked up at him.

Was he genuinely sorry? She couldn't tell. He was a good actor. He could lie, and he turn on a dime. She didn't trust him. She took in a long, deep breath and let it out.

"Thank you," she said coolly.

"That's *all* you can say?" His eyes were closing into slits now. His mouth became a sneer.

"What—what do you want me to say, Bill?" she snapped. The pain of the past—the days—the years— of abuse and betrayal seemed to pour from the very core of her body. She looked down at her hands, squeezing her book, as if she could hold herself back...

He moved slowly toward her, raising his voice, "You *could* say you're sorry, too—you know, for being rude to me, and my parents—for ignoring my *simple request* that you stop this...all this skating shit." She could see the rage in his eyes. "*Then*, just maybe, *then*, you could start *acting* like a *normal* mother should act."

Anna's feelings of being wronged by him erupted through her skin. Her own rage boiled in her blood, and her heart pumped it into her throat. She cried out, like one of the wounded animals in his hunting paintings. "*Normal?* You think, that telling me how to live my life, putting me down, criticizing me—the way I talk—my music—my skating—" she lowered her voice to a controlled whisper, "…and having *love affairs with other women…is normal?*"

He looked at her, and the color drained from his face. She was shocked by the power of the truth, and she could see the impact of her words on his body. His eyes closed, and, like unplugging a string of Christmas lights, they went dark.

Holy saints! Could speaking the truth really be that powerful? She was stunned.

As she watched him turn and leave through the front door and slam it, she felt her nerves humming. She'd never confronted him with the honest truth before; she'd never even spoken the words: "love affair" to him, and she had no idea where the strength had come from, to have done it now…but it felt good—and it felt right.

She thought about her father's message, that lying to yourself was the worst thing you could do, and she stared at the front door for a long time.

Finally, she flipped the light off. She'd decided to spend the night in her work-out clothes, but she was too drained to get up and change.

Lying the dark, she listened to her breathing as it slowed down. She felt strangely calm. She realized she had just faced something that she had been dreading for years, and she was still—breathing—she was still alive—and she was…okay. She was going to be okay…

She thanked her father, for loving her enough to teach her to speak the truth tonight. And then, she prayed to

God for help finding the courage to live it, every day, for the rest of her life.

Chapter 24 ❈ Abe

Abe waited in the library conference room for Anna, grading papers as fast as he could. Because he kept looking at the door so often, he had trouble keeping track of where he was on a page. He figured he could finish the entire class before she arrived, if he'd pay better attention to what he was doing.

But he was too excited to really concentrate. He had important news to share with Anna. His mind was jamming to fast. He was like Jaheen when she wanted something. He smiled to himself. She was so precious...and smart. He'd loved it when his daughter had asked him to help her learn to control her emotions—and stay calm. Ha! He laughed at the irony of that. Really? Abraham Lincoln Brown, trying to teach about self-control...right! He couldn't even think straight enough to do his own job. He laughed out loud at his own craziness.

His thoughts jumped to Georgie. What the hell was going on with *her*? He expected total knock-down, drag-out fight when he'd come clean about his plans for competing in public, with Anna, but Georgie was actually being half-way cooperative—almost nice—out of the blue. What was *that* about?

Was Georgie afraid that he was changing? He *was* changing—and fast.

Did she think he was going to quit her? Maybe he would. Maybe he should.

Maybe it had nothing to do with him. Georgie never missed a change to make in-your-face statements to white society...

Whatever Georgie's reasons were for not fighting him about his training plans, he wondered about her allowing him to spending money. After fussing and fuming because he'd not been totally honest with her about Daisy's charges—and he understood that part—Georgie had backed off, just like that! He snapped his fingers. She'd agreed to budget for Daisy's fees, and to pay for the cost of Jaheen's lessons, too...without a much of an argument. Why? He didn't know...but he didn't trust her motives either.

He'd been thinking about their money situation. They lived modestly. Bills got paid. He'd opened a college fund for Jaheen. But every time Georgie sold a house, she bought another rental in the inner city, so their money seemed to be tied up in investments. They'd blended their finances together, and Georgie had insisted on keeping the books, so he wasn't sure how much cash, or what kind of assets, they really had.

He took a big drink of his soda. He had to let all of that go, and focus on his work.

Grading papers as fast as he could, he finished the final stack. He usually felt good when all his work was done, but not today. He was on edge; too much was happening...

The door sprung open, and Anna almost flew in the room. She did a little dance that looked like an Irish jig, and she smiled down at him. He looked at her, and all he could do was stare with his mouth open.

"Well, now, what do you think? Like the new me?" She laughed, turning around and fluffing out what was left of her hair. "Shocking, isn't it?" She ran her fingers through top of her short curls—her *very* short curls. Her eyes were shining and they looked bigger than ever. She looked like a model out of a fashion magazine.

"My God," he finally said. "I can't believe how...how *great* you look!"

"So...you *do* like it?" She said, her eyes were teasing him, half-flirting with him, and it was working.

He fought for composure; this was one more surprise to add to the list of all the changes. "Oh, yeah. I *really, really* do," he stammered.

"Good!" She laughed. She bounced down into one of the chairs, looking at the piles of essays. "Wow, that's a good lot of papers you have there."

"Um...Yep, I just finished grading my mid-terms." He was finding it hard to collect his thoughts. "Hey...Um. Wow, you know, I have to just look at you for a minute."

And he did. He stared at her, taking in her new look. He was getting erect. He crossed his legs, coughed, and he said, "Daisy will be thrilled."

She looked down at the table, and waved her arms at him. "Enough looking now..."

He shouldn't have been staring so long, he realized. "Sorry. I..." He paused and looked away, feeling awkward. "Ah...never mind. Anyway, now, I have a couple of surprises for you, too."

"Okay, but I have something to tell you too—but you go first," she said, pulling her chair in closer to the table next to him, and she touched his arm. He could feel the resolve that he'd had to stay cool melt away at her touch—and then he felt a twinge of guilt, thinking of Georgie, and what he *hadn't* told her about his sexual attraction to this woman.

He coughed again. "Anna, you'll never believe this—I'm still in shock myself. Georgie knows about our plan—I

161

told her—*everything*—and she agreed to support me—my training—our training." He was perspiring now, and he reached for his handkerchief to wipe his upper lip and forehead.

"You're kidding?"

"No! Last night we talked—and she actually listened to me. And…well, it was a little rough at first, telling her, but she calmed down, and she's okay, with what we planning to do—to train for the competition."

"Really?" Anna half-smiled, but leaned back, away from him. "That's…that's good news, Abe. I-I'm happy for you—and Georgie."

He sensed she wasn't telling the truth. What was she really thinking? He wished he knew what she was really feeling. He wanted to ask her, but, instead, he said, "Yeah… well, I'm happy for *us*. For our *team*, Ice Lady. Me and you. We're gonna go to the top—together."

She smiled and nodded, but she was growing more subdued.

"Are you—all right?" he asked tentatively.

"Oh, yeah. No, I'm fine. I'm just, you know, thinking about the competition thing again."

He nodded. Was she telling him the truth? He couldn't tell…and even if she was hoping that things were bad between Georgie and him, she wouldn't say it. She was too sweet…too polite…and too married.

"So tell me. What's your news?" he asked, his good mood was not so good now.

"I had a talk with Bill last night."

"How did *that* go?" He was at full attention now, staring at her.

"It didn't…We had a major fight," her eyes clouded over with sadness. "I lost it." She looked down at the table,

162

pushed some papers away to make room for her arms, and she leaned forward onto them, hiding her face.

"Tell me about what happened, Anna," he said quietly. He lightly touched the back of her neck. His fingers began to move in circles, on their own, as if he had no control of them. He started to massage her shoulders, and he reached a short way under her sweater as far as he dared. He couldn't stop himself. He smelled the flower scent of her shampoo, and he played with the bottom of her curls, just to find out if they were soft as they looked.

She didn't seem to notice—or to mind. He didn't know which.

"It was *awful*. Bill came in, after my workout...He was home really early—I don't know why. That *never* happens, you know?" She lifted her head, and looked at him, as if she wanted him to agree with her, so he nodded, and he pulled his hand away. "He was nice at first. He apologized for being a jerk...and then, I don't know, Abe. I just lost it..." She started to sniffle.

He didn't know what to do next. Hold her hand? Offer to hug her? He really wanted to wrap her in his arms, but his old survival skills kicked in, and he decided against doing anything at all.

"What did you tell him?" he asked, offering her his handkerchief.

She took it from him, looked directly into his eyes, and said, "I told him he should apologize for trying to control me, for putting me down all the time—*and for cheating on me!*"

Once again he found himself totally unprepared for this new information.

"He's been cheating on you—with other women?"

She nodded, and looked away. "Yes." She looked back at him. "I have proof, and if I believed all of the rumors, he's done it a lot. Abe, I feel *so stupid*—"

"Anna! Don't say that about yourself. You are *not* stupid! Geez…You are…an intelligent, smart—and wonderful—woman." He stopped himself, knowing he probably had gone too far, but he didn't care. He was angry—for her—and for her daughter. All of a sudden, the truth dawned on him. He recognized it because it was his truth, too. He said, "You've been trying to keep your marriage together—for your daughter's sake, haven't you?"

She nodded, tears falling onto her lips. "Aye…Abe, I've been lying to myself for a long time. I thought if I just—I don't know—kept trying…hoping—praying—that things would change…then, Em could have the family she wanted…like the one I never had…"

He took his handkerchief out of her hand, and lightly wiped the tears from her face with it. God, when her eyes were wet, they sparkled like emeralds, he thought. He found himself becoming sexually aroused again. He was irritated by that. This was not the time…nor the place.

"My dad told me that the worst thing you can do is to lie to yourself," she said, anger showing in her eyes. "And he was right…I have been lying, Abe. I've been a *liar*—I have been lying to myself—to everyone—about my life, for a long time…"

"To protect your daughter," he finished for her, and she nodded.

He leaned away, back into his chair. He was breathing hard. He crossed his legs, hoping she wouldn't notice how excited he was. He was insane, he thought. She needed him to comfort her, and here he was, acting like—like some kind of horny monster.

He didn't know how to help her. He was glad that she was telling him about her pain, but his mind was racing too fast. She was saying "...and from now on, no matter what, I have to be honest—with myself, with Bill—with Emily—with you—with everybody."

She looked at him, waiting for his response, but all he could do was try to absorb what she'd just told him: Her marriage was on the rocks. Her husband was cheating on her.

So many questions flooded his mind at once. Was she was on the verge of leaving him? What would Bill do to her if she did? And what would he—Abraham Lincoln Brown—do about his own marital situation, if suddenly his Ice Woman was divorced, and available...?

She calmed down, and she stopped crying. She looked at him. He tried to guess what she was feeling...and he tried to guess what he was feeling, too.

He only knew one thing for sure: he no longer felt sexually excited now.

* * *

Anna felt good about finally telling Abe the truth about Bill. When she'd been so emotional at the library, Abe had been so understanding. She knew that she'd started to rely on Abe. He had become her friend. She cared for him so much—*too much*—and that wasn't right. She was determined to stay in control of herself, and her feelings for Abe—and hide her attraction to him. Abe and Georgie were getting along better, he'd said, and that was a good thing—for him, and for Jaheen.

But when she thought about sharing Abe with another woman—even if the woman was his own wife—she felt jealous. Georgie was lucky to have a husband as wonderful as Abe...

And Anna didn't want to be like Bill, either. She would never cheat with a married person—and never lie—well, *almost* never lie. Anna hoped God would forgive her for all of the lying she'd done in the past...but she'd have to lie just a *little more*, so no one would know that she had feelings for a married man. Surely, God would understand the difference between *good* lies and *bad* lies.

Now, she followed Abe's car as closely as she could. It was almost dark, driving through the middle of downtown Atlanta, in the shadows of the tall buildings—and the cold that rain misted on her windshield.

She didn't know where Abe was taking her. It would be a *big surprise*, he'd said, and she'd trusted him completely.

Why did she trust him so much?

Something just felt so good whenever she was with him. From the first time they'd skated together, and he'd danced with her on the ice—before Daisy had showed up, hammering them with her endless exercises, diets, ballet steps, and classical music—there was a bond between her and Abe, and Anna wanted to hold on to that special connection.

Anna's favorite radio station was on, playing a new R&B hit single that she loved. The beat was strong, and the lyrics were rough, but the message of the song was about loving, not hating, people of different races and beliefs. It lifted her mood even more.

She stopped at a red light, and she smiled at herself in the rear-view mirror. She played with her hair. Thank you, Daisy! This haircut was a great idea, she thought. Abe seemed to really like it, too. She pictured his smile of approval when he'd checked out her new look. He was so cute when he smiled, she thought. He was amazingly handsome, without that beard...more thanks to Daze!

Abe made a quick turn off of the highway, and she swerved to keep up with him. She wondered where in the world he was taking her. They drove through an older, run-down neighborhood that she'd never seen before. Kids were in the street—lots of colored children. Riding bikes, playing with basketballs—out in the freezing rain? She could see some of the kids staring at her. She wanted to duck her head below the dash at each of the stop signs. She wanted them to know she liked them—loved them all—and they had nothing to fear from her. In spite of her desire for good will, she realized that she felt afraid. She was far away from the safety of her quiet neighborhood.

She was relieved when Abe finally stopped and parked his car in front a warehouse. But when she saw the condition of the building, her uneasiness returned.

"What the hell?" she whispered to herself. "Where *are* we?"

He motioned for her to park next to him on the cracked asphalt. She pulled over, and he walked over to her car.

"Get out, Anna, and lock your car," he said, very seriously.

She looked at him, her mind full of questions but, trusting him, she did what he asked. He walked to the back of his car, and he opened the trunk. She followed him, and looked inside—and couldn't believe what she saw.

Chapter 25 ❋ Abe

Abe looked at the surprise in her face, and he couldn't stop himself from laughing. Her mouth was open and when she bit her lip, with that chipped tooth of hers, she reminded him of one of the chipmunks that lived in his backyard.

She looked up at him with raised eyebrows.

"I'm sorry," he said, unable to contain his laughter. He was feeling more than a little giddy. They were about to try out an amazing idea that had come to him just yesterday.

On the way over he'd been thinking about the possibilities...if she divorced Bill...

Life was good; thank you, Jesus!

"Abe...are those *roller skates?*" she asked, watching him take the women's pair out of his trunk.

He handed them to her. She took them from him reluctantly, looking them over as if they were alien creatures from outer space.

"Yep, they sure are," he breathed in, knowing he was grinning like a cartoon cat. "Sorry, Anna...I didn't mean to laugh. It's just that you were so...cute...that look on your face. You didn't expect *this*, did you?"

He reached past her for the men's pair of roller skates, and his arm passed lightly across the front of her sweater. A shiver shot through his body. He lifted a small portable record player from the back of the trunk, tucked the men's pair of skates under his arm, and slammed down the trunk with one foot. They had to hurry. This was not the best part of town.

"Well, now, no, I had no idea..." she trailed off as he turned away from her, motioning with his head for her to follow him.

Wordlessly, he led her toward the old warehouse building. He looked around, scanning for any problems. He felt good about her willingness to follow him. She seemed to trust him—at least enough to not to shoot him down with a million questions, like Georgie would have done. He knew that this part of town was completely foreign to someone like Anna, yet she was brave, and open to trying whatever it was that he'd had in mind.

They stepped through the garage doors, which were wide open, swinging back and forth, with each gust of wind. The locks were rusted and long broken—or maybe stolen. The place had been vandalized lots of times, he assumed, given the amount of wood pieces and metal pipes that were scattered around on the floor. They stood together, looking around the empty space. It had no usable contents. A set of broken windows lay on the ground. Electrical wires hung from cement beams high above them. The walls were sprayed with gang markers, and an old basketball hoop was attached to one wall, drooping down into a far corner. The tall side windows had been blown out or smashed, allowing plenty of light, and a cool breeze, to flow over the expansive concrete floor.

"Wow," said Anna. "What a wild place! Who owns this?"

"One of my students told me about it. He said some rich developer—some sleezy slumlord—owns it..." he answered, setting down the record player on the floor next to his skates. "The electric's still on, though, if you can believe it." He was focused on connecting the cords as quickly as possible, his hands shaking with nerves.

She looked around the massive space, and then back at Abe.

"I am assuming you want me to put these on?" she said, still looking doubtful, holding out the scuffed-up white skates, spinning one of the wheels with her thumb. "You know, I've never tried roller skating before..."

"Trust me. It's not that different. You'll see. Just try it," he urged with a quick pleading look. He put on the record album, dropped the needle, and the sultry, rough sounds of a new popular soul song began to play.

She smiled at him with her lips tightly pressed together, and bobbed her head to the beat. He recognized that look: the sexy one she always gave him, whenever she was feeling the music, and getting ready to move with it. He knew she loved this song, and he'd made a special trip to the record store to buy it. He really liked the tune, too, and he'd hoped the music would inspire them—a lot more than Mozart ever did.

They laced up their skates to the music. It was blasting loud, and talking wasn't possible.

Abe stood up on his skates, and restarted the song. He offered his hands to her. She wobbled to a standing position with his help, and she gave him her sad look of helplessness. As usual, when she look like she needed something, he had a powerful desire to help her. They held each other's hands, as they shuffled their skates around, to get their bearings.

Rolling on wheels was far less smooth than gliding on ice, and turning was a good deal more difficult, too, especially on the uneven surface, but his old moves were coming back to him.

"Use the rubber things on the front, if you want to slow down or stop," he yelled in her ear, and she nodded.

He pulled her out onto the middle of the concrete floor, skating backward, still holding both of her hands. She watched her feet like a beginner, keeping her knees stiffly locked.

"Bend your knees!" he told her. She did, and he could feel her began to flow along with him more easily.

The song finished, and the next cut started. It had a long instrumental intro, in a slow, smoldering, Cajun rhythm that seemed to envelop them. He began to pull her from side to side, swaying his hips, shifting his weight. He moved his arms in a dance position. He felt her start to relax. She seemed to get the rhythm, too, and she responded by leaning into his waist and against his hips. He let his body take over, and he stopped thinking about what to do next...and her moves began to copy his.

Then something unexpected started happening. She had pulled him in close to her. Maybe he'd done it first—he couldn't tell who started it, but they were pressing against each other, and his body was feeling shots of heat everywhere they touched.

He realized that they were now slow dancing as if they were joined together, and it was effortless. There were no contrived ballet moves to try and remember. They weren't following any kind of a plan for each step. He felt loose and relaxed—and hot and tense—all at the same time. He stole a quick look at her face, and saw her smiling up at him.

The song ended, and she tripped trying to stop, falling into his chest. She looked up at him with her big, shiny eyes that took his breath away.

"Wow, that was *something!*" she laughed, out of breath.

He was breathing hard, too, but not just because moving the roller skates had taken that much physical effort. He couldn't stop looking at her creamy skin, her pink mouth, her parted lips, the way her white teeth flashed...

The next song came on—her favorite—and she pushed herself back, away from him, trying a spin on her own, holding onto the fingers of his hands for support, swinging her hips to the beat. The words to this song were erotic, repetitious, and demanding: love, love...you got it, I want it, share it! And, instantly, as if inspired by the words, he slid in toward her, moving into her body, almost aggressively. He turned her around, into a spiral, grabbing her lower body, then sliding his arms along her sides, ending by holding her arms high in the air, "I want it...give it to me" he mouthed the words of the song, as if he was coming onto her for real, never taking his eyes off of hers.

She began to mirror his actions, surprising him with her own aggressive moves, pursuing him whenever he backed off, lip-singing back to him: "give it to me...share the love". They played with one another's faces, and arms, acting out the words, sometimes pantomiming, sometimes just locking gazes, coming within an inch of kissing, and stopping. Their acting out with the lyrics intensified, until Abe thought he was going to explode. When the song ended, and they were locked in an embrace that, he figured, would make anyone watching blush, and want to give them their privacy.

The record ended, and the room was quiet. All he could hear was their deep breathing. They separated, and he had to bend forward and work hard to catch his breath. He looked up and saw her grinning at him. The next song came on, but Abe didn't move. He was blown away by what had happened, and he stood in front of her, shaking his head. He'd suspected that the problems they were having with Daisy's program designs had been about the music, but he hadn't expected this...

She was laughing and rolling backwards, away from him, "Wow, Abe, that was *amazing!*" she said. He was breathing heavily, too.

Suddenly the music stopped. Sounds of slow clapping echoed through the silence.

"That was quite the performance," said a deep voice in a slow southern drawl.

Abe and Anna turned toward the two white, uniformed police officers who were approaching them. One was tall, and the other was very short and fat.

"You two are trespassing on private property," the short one said, his voice flat, and almost mean.

The tall one shined a bright flashlight onto Abe's skates, scanning his torso, stopped at his crotch, and then passing the light up into his face, blinding him. Abe raised his hand to cover his eyes, his heart racing.

"Put your hands down, *boy*, and hold your arms out, away from your body," said the short cop, loudly.

"Sorry, officer, I was just..."

"Shut up, Roller Derby!"

The second cop, the tall one, clicked on his flashlight, and scanned Anna as well. His eyes lit up, and his face softened. The two cops exchanged glances. Abe recognized the look: an interracial couple.

"Has this man been bothering you, ma'am?"

"No...not at all, we were...just practicing," Anna said confidently. "We didn't mean to harm anything...We're so sorry—really. We shouldn't have trespassed...We'll just get our things, and be on our way..."

"Not so fast, Miss..." said the short one. He looked at their hands, slowly and dramatically, he added, "Ah.

What's this? Your both *married*...to each other, I assume?"
He sneered at his question, as if he already knew the
answer, staring at Abe with obvious contempt. "Let's just
take it on over to the station, and see if this here owner's
gonna need to press some charges..."

Abe kept is eyes focused on the floor. The tall one
reached for Anna's arm, while the short one put handcuffs
on him roughly, "Don't you worry. We'll call yer
husband—and yer wife, too" he said in Abe's ear with a
snarl, "Let 'em know—that you're both *okay*...both here
together and all. They must be *really* worried about ya'll...
and what you been doin'," pushing Abe from behind.
Skates still on, Abe tripped, and fell forward onto the
concrete. Unable to stop himself he felt a searing pain as
his face hit the floor.

"Abe!" Anna screamed.

Abe felt his body go limp, and he saw a flash of
light—and then blackness.

Chapter 26 ❀ Emily

Emily had always wanted to explore the *monster house*—Steph had named it that. Emily's grandparents' home *was* a monster-sized mansion. Emily never been alone in their house before, and she felt excited about being to be left here, all by herself—until Tilly, her grandmother's maid, came to stay with her.

It was Sunday afternoon, and Tilly's day off, but, because her father and her grandparents were freaking out about something—Emily had no idea what had upset them so much, but it must have been really bad—and they had left together, in a big hurry. Grandmother Smithson had called Tilly, who had promised to be over, in about an hour, after she did something for her church.

Emily wondered what was *really* going on. Her father and her grandparents said they were going downtown. Somebody called on the phone, and they were all whispering, and talking in the study for a long time, with the door closed. When they'd come out, they had on their Sunday smiles, which Emily knew were phony. Her father told her there was a business emergency, and they would all be gone for a couple of hours. But Emily knew her father was lying. He—and Grandfather Smithson—never did business on Sundays—the Lord's Day. So, Emily wondered what they were doing. It had to be really important. They never left her alone in the house. She wished she could have called her mom, and gone home, but Grandmother Smithson said her mother wasn't at home.

Emily hadn't dared ask them any more questions. Her father reminded her she was not to question adults—about anything.

So she'd decided to call Steph, who—no surprise—picked up on the first ring. She and Steph could read each other's minds.

"Hey, guess what?" Emily asked her friend.

"What?"

"I'm all by myself—in the *monster house!*"

"No way!"

"I am. I told my dad I was okay here alone, but this place is creepy. Like a museum. What should I do?"

"Well, did they lock the door? There was another race thing today downtown."

"Let me check." Emily hurried to the door, and tried the doorknob. It was locked. "Yep. It's locked. I'm waiting for Tilly, their maid, to come over and stay with me."

"She's a Negro, right?"

"Yeah. I wonder why Tilly works for my grandparents. They don't like colored people."

"I dunno. Maybe she just needed the job." Steph answered. "Hey, why don't you take a look around? You know, do some snooping? You said you've never been upstairs. Now's your chance!"

Emily thought about Steph's idea. She'd get into a lot of trouble if she got caught. But, maybe she could go upstairs—just to find out more about her grandparents. She really didn't understand them. They never talked much about themselves. All she knew was she was named after her great-grandmother Smithson, who was a plantation owner's wife—and they had slaves who picked their acres of cotton.

"I don't know if I should—"

Steph cut her off. "Why shouldn't you? They're your *grandparents,* for crap's sake. I can go anywhere I want in my grandparents' houses." Steph was getting more into the idea now, Emily could tell. And when Steph had an idea…watch out! "They're your family, Em. They're house is practically *your* house."

"It doesn't feel like it's my house. I don't really know a lot about them. They never tell me anything." She sighed. "Maybe I *should* go upstairs. Just for a minute…and look around." She looked at the front door. "I'd better hurry up though. Tilly might get here early."

"Okay…Tell me what you find up there. Be brave, Em! Do it! And call me back!"

Emily hung up, and she hesitated, looking up at the curved wooden stairs to the second story. This was her family's house, she reminded herself. And Steph said it would be okay. Her mother didn't have a family…and Emily wanted a *whole* family—one that had grandparents. She wanted to feel close to this family, and she didn't know how to do that. Maybe if she saw where her grandparents slept, they would seem more—more *real?*

Excited, she ran up the stairs as fast as she could. The upper hallway was wide, and long, and it had a lot of closed doors. It looked like a hotel. She started to feel nervous, wondering if she should just go back downstairs and forget the whole thing. But her curiosity, and her strong desire to feel like she was a part of this family, pushed her to keep on exploring.

Steph had said, that if you really wanted to find out about a person, look in their bathroom cabinets, and so she decided to look there first. She went into the only open door—which looked like a guest bathroom. Everything was neat and tidy. Fluffy white guest towels with a big "S" were draped over each of the racks, and the medicine chest had a new toothbrush in a package in it. Nothing interesting there.

She wandered into the next room—a bedroom, but it was mostly empty. The bed was made, and there was nothing in the closets.

The next door led to a giant bedroom. She peeked inside. A blouse belonging to her grandmother was lying on the bed. She tiptoed inside, and noticed there were two more doors—one opened to a bathroom, and the other led to—was that another bedroom? Walking faster, she saw that the other bedroom had her grandfather's clothes in it. She sort of knew what that meant: her grandparents were living in separate bedrooms—just like her own parents did.

Steph had told her that, when parents had their own bedrooms, it was a sign of a divorce, and the idea made her feel cold all over. Suddenly, Emily felt terrible. This was not what she'd wanted to find, and she felt awful for snooping. She hurried toward the stairs, just as she heard the front door opening.

She saw Tilly come in the front door, and lock it behind her. Emily stood, frozen, on the stairs. Tilly noticed her right away and was looking up at her!

Emily's heart was racing. She tried to not look guilty. There was no reason for her to have been upstairs, and Tilly probably knew that, too. Oh, man, her father would kill her, if he found out she'd been up there snooping around.

"Hey, honey child, how are you doin'?" Tilly smiled, looking up her with what Emily. "My, my, you've grown up since the last time I saw your little self."

Emily caught her breath, and held her up her left wrist that was still in wrapped in plaster and tape as she slowly walked down the stairs. "Hi, Tilly…I was just checking—

on my cast," Emily said, lamely, feeling dumb for not being able to come up with a better excuse.

Tilly set her purse down on the table by the door. "Yeah. I heard you broke ya wrist. I'm so sorry, honey," she said kindly.

"I fell skating," said Emily, feeling relieved. She'd always liked Tilly.

"So you did. Your grandma was real bothered by all that...Well, come on down, and let's make us some hot chocolate. Maybe that'll make you feel better," she said, waving Emily toward the back of the house. "Freezin' cold out there today, ain't it?"

Emily followed her down the hall and into the big kitchen—it was big enough for two kitchens. But it was her favorite part of her grandmother's house. It was always full of goodies. The cupboards in the service pantry were stuffed with all kinds of cookies, chips—her Grandfather loved his bad snacks. She wondered why she'd never heard her dad say anything to him about how his teeth were going to rot from junk food—and she wondered if anyone ever spanked Grandfather Smithson for eating candy when he was a kid.

Tilly looked at her curiously, as she took the milk out of the refrigerator, and reached for the cocoa. "Yo grandparents had a *business* emergency—on a *Sunday?*" she asked.

Emily nodded.

"Hmm. Seems like some folks just don't much respect the Lord's Day anymore..." Tilly said, staring at her.

"I guess it must have been really important," Emily suggested, feeling a little defensive. It wasn't her fault that they had to work—and even if they'd lied about what they were doing, she'd had no control over that, either. Sometimes she was a part of this family, but sometimes, she didn't want to be…and she felt bad about thinking that way.

"Um hum," Tilly said, acting like she knew something that Emily didn't.

Emily's was curious about what Tilly might know. "Do you know where they went?"

Tilly seemed surprised at Emily's question, and although she shrugged, Tilly looked like she *did* know.

"I heard talk. Maybe it was somethin' to do with the damn police brutality that's been goin' on," Tilly continued slowly, "It's a dangerous world out there, young'un. *Everybody's* walkin' around on thin ice these days." She paused and shook her head. "Yeah. All you can do is keep ya head down, act nice, stay safe—and don't ask too many questions."

Emily watched Tilly as she slowly moved around the kitchen. Tilly seemed really tired, and very sad.

"Tilly, why is there so much fighting—about race?"

Tilly looked at her with a surprised smile. She looked up at the ceiling and took a long time to answer.

"It's all about fear, baby girl. People, they get afraid of what they don't understand." She shook her head. "The thing is, people are all the same—on the inside. But some folks—when they see a person with skin that's a different color, they get scared…and then they never find out what's really goin' on—on the inside."

Emily thought about that. Tilly was right. She'd been afraid of Jaheen—just because she looked different—Jaheen's skin was very black. But her mother wasn't afraid of colored people. Her mom believed all people were the same, just like Tilly said. And, Emily realized, ever since she'd gotten to know Jaheen a little better, she hadn't been afraid of her… She'd actually started to *like* Jaheen. She was pretty smart—and funny.

Emily shifed around in her chair at the counter as she thought about the way her dad and her grandparents thought that there was something wrong with colored people.

"God made all the people on earth, right?"

"Yep, honey, he sure did." Tilly said firmly.

"Well, then why didn't he make everybody the same color?"

Tilly grinned and shook her head. "That's a *real good* question, honey!" She chuckled. "I have *no* idea why some people are colored...but when I walk through those pearly gates, and meet my sweet Lord Jesus, he's gonna tell me why—cause, yeah, I'm sure to be asking him that same question!" Then, Tilly's face turned sad again, and she said, "But, until then, *everybody's* sufferin'...And until then, we just got to try and survive all the hate in the world...Like I told ya, baby, I jus' keep my head down, and act—"

The hot chocolate bubbled to the top of the pan. Tilly hurried to the stove, and turned off the gas flame. As Emily watched her pour the thick, dark milk into two large, shiny cups, a sick feeling of dread was creeping over her. Instead of making her feel better, Tilly's answers had seemed like some kind of a warning, and suddenly, she shivered.

* * *

The phone rang somewhere in the dark hospital room. Abe felt like he was lying at the bottom of a deep, dark well, and he couldn't reach up high enough to pick up the receiver.

Suddenly, he heard Georgie's voice. "He's asleep. What do you want?" Georgie snapped. "Daisy, *who*?" She paused. "Oh, you're *that* Daisy. Let me see if he can talk."

Peeking through a swollen eye, he could see Georgie holding the phone against her bulging breasts. She was sending him an impatient look. "Can you talk to *Daisy*, or d'ya want her to call back another time?" she asked him, her voice dripping with sarcasm.

He slowly reached out on hand for the phone. "I can talk," he said. His voice was hoarse, so he took a sip from a cup of ice chips to wet his parched and swollen lips. Georgie handed him the receiver.

"Hi Daisy," he whispered quietly into the phone, coughing.

"Abe, how *are* you?" Daisy asked, with serious concern in her voice.

"I've been better," he answered, his voice more like a frog's croak.

"What's the damage?" Daisy asked. Tact was not one of her strong points, Abe thought. He failed at trying to smile under his ice pack.

"I'll live," he tried to smile again, but most of his face hurt, and he winced. "A few bones cracked. Slight concussion. Should be fine in a couple of days."

Georgie rolled her eyes, and added a swing of her entire head, at his answer, and she looked toward the window. "Try a few *weeks*," she mouthed, shaking her head as if he was a delinquent teenager.

"Daisy, I'll be back for next Tuesday's session," he assured her as loudly as he could.

"Don't push it, Abe," Daisy warned.

"I won't."

Georgie looked disgusted with him, and marched out of the room.

"What the hell were you trying to do? Scare up some publicity? That's my job!" Daisy was saying. She never held back, he grumbled to himself, even now, with him lying here, with a smashed-up face…He had to laugh. What else could he do?

He tried to smile again, but the results were the same: it hurt. He pushed his ice pack back up, over his shattered cheekbone, and he closed his eyes. "I was...we were...trying to work out...to some cool soul vibes. You know, just to loosen up."

"Abe—"

"Okay, yeah, we were trespassing, but Daisy—" he paused. He sounded drunk, even to himself. "Somethin' *really* came through for us!"

"You could have been killed, Abe...and Anna—"

"I know, and I'm really sorry. I didn't think..."

"No you didn't think. *No more thinking!* From now on, let me handle your training, the dances you do in public, the news people—everything—okay? *I'm* your trainer—remember?" There was a long pause. "And...Abe?"

"Yeah, Daisy..." he said, feeling dizzy; the pain pills were making him so sleepy that he couldn't hold the phone, and it dropped onto his chest.

She must have hung up, and he must have passed out, because when he heard the dial humming from the receiver, it woke him up.

He'd been dreaming about jumping off a steep cliff. In the dream, he had been holding Anna's hand, and he'd pulled her over the edge with him. Falling on top of her, he hit his face on some sharp rocks. He realized that Anna had saved him from dying, but she had died—because of him. He felt like he was going to throw up.

Had he really been dreaming?

Chapter 27 ❁ Jaheen

Today, her father was coming home from the hospital, and Jaheen couldn't wait to see him. She'd missed him a lot, and she'd been really worried about him. She hadn't been allowed to visit—stupid hospital rules—she was too young, they said.

When she'd talked to him on the phone, he hadn't sounded like himself at all. But it made her feel better, when he'd told that her he loved her, and that he'd be okay.

Her mother was really mad about the cops, and was working on getting a lawyer from the Civil Rights Center to sue the city. Jaheen wanted to know more details, but her mother didn't want to talk about whatever had happened on the day her dad had been arrested.

Jaheen had called Emily, who'd filled her in on some of the details. The rest she'd figured out on her own, from watching the news, and reading the paper. Jaheen knew that her dad and Emily's mom had been practicing their new dance routine, on roller skates, in some old empty building downtown, and the cops had caught them trespassing on private property. One of the cops had hurt her father while they were taking Emily's mom and her dad to jail.

The good part was that Emily's family knew the owner of the building, and so Mrs. Smithson was released right away, but they weren't going to let her dad go—

something about *public lootness.* Jaheen and Emily hadn't understood that part.

Then, Emily's mom had refused to leave the jail unless the charges were dropped against her father, too. Jaheen felt good that Mrs. Smithson had stood up to the man—and she'd helped her dad to get out of jail. Jaheen had even started to wonder if she and Emily were starting to be…kind of…like friends?

Poor dad, Jaheen thought. He's such a nice guy, but people always picked on him. He was just starting to stand up for himself a little more lately, and then this had to happen to him! Jaheen watched out of her window for her mother's car. They would be home soon—any minute now.

There was a knock on the front door. She looked out on the empty Saturday morning street. Maybe her parents had driven up, and she somehow hadn't seen them? She ran downstairs, and opened the door. A package fell in on her, onto her bare foot, and she jumped back in pain.

"Ouch! What the…" she cried out.

She picked up the white paper-wrapped package. It had "Whitey Lover" written on the outside of it in pencil. It was at least a foot long, and about six inches wide. It was solid, and felt rigid, like a big, heavy book.

The string was loosely wrapped around it, and had fallen half off, so she opened the package all the way. Her eyes grew large as she read the words that had been carved in large letters, cut deeply into the wood: "Stay away from whites or death."

She looked up and down the street. No one was there. She stepped back into the house, and slammed the front door, feeling scared, she locked the dead bolt. She threw the board on the floor, as if it were on fire.

Chapter 28 ❋ Anna

Anna slid the tuna casserole into the oven and set the temperature. The house was quiet. She'd lost her desire to play the radio. She liked it quiet lately, so she could think. So much had happened...

At first, she'd thought about packing a suitcase, and running away from everything...but where would she go?

And, for sure, she couldn't leave Em alone with Bill.

No, she knew she had to face her problems.

But did she have the strength to do that?

Leaning against the kitchen counter, watching the sun setting over the neighbor's rooftop, she felt a hundred years old. Until the arrest, she'd *started* to feel stronger. She'd found some hope for a better life. But now, she felt old, and discouraged.

Was she going to turn bitter and angry—like her father?

She was beginning understand why her dad had been depressed and down-hearted about everything—and maybe that was why he'd drank so much. Life was hard—and people were even harder to figure out.

Why couldn't people just get along? Why was there so much hate in the world?

She supposed it was time to drag out the Christmas stuff, and start decorating the house for the holidays, but her heart wasn't in it. Maybe things would change—and maybe they might get worse.

How much worse could things get?

Emily was more withdrawn than ever, her husband wasn't speaking to her, Abe was in the hospital, his family was receiving death threats...

And the idea of skating—something she had enjoyed so much, for so long—triggered a new kind of fear in her that was beyond her old dread of making mistakes in a competition. Now she, Abe—and their families—could really be in danger, just because some hate-filled bigot might see them together.

When she thought of the times that she and Abe skated like they were dancing in heaven, she had to block them out of her memory. Abe was lucky to be alive, but he could have died, and she would have been at least partially to blame. He was a married man, and he needed his family to help him recover. He needed to go back to living his teacher's life, where he would be safe.

She remembered reading in a magazine about how a person could be permanently changed—and become afraid of living everyday life—after they were violently attacked. And, although she had not been physically hurt in the arrest, the horrible images of Abe falling—of being pushed—seemed to be seared into her brain. It felt like a hole had been ripped in her own face, whenever she thought of Abe's suffering.

At night, lying alone in her new bedroom—she'd moved her things into the guest room—she couldn't sleep, and when she finally did, she had terrible nightmares. Sometimes, she would wake up crying, and when she really got angry, she just wanted to find that jerk cop and punch him in his ugly, snarling face—just like her deal old father would have done.

It had been over a week since the arrest. Bill was out of town. He was in Miami—probably with some new girlfriend. She and Emily spent quiet days and evenings together at home. Emily watched a lot of TV, while Anna continued her workouts, just to wear herself out, so she could sleep at night.

Anna was losing weight, and she was becoming physically fit and strong, but she didn't care about how she looked. She ate at breakfast, and again, at dinnertime, in order to be a good role model for Emily. She made meals that were full of fresh vegetables, and she made healthy desserts from fresh fruit.

She kept up a smiling face, as much as she could—for Emily's sake. She cleaned the house like mad, just to keep busy during the day, while Em was in school.

Today, she was volunteering to help with Em's Christmas play, and now she was putting the finishing touches of paint on the pine tree scenery for the set.

Steph's mother stood next to her, and asked, "Anna, can I talk to you for a minute?"

Anna put down her brush, and wiped her hands on her jeans. Pleasantly surprised, Anna put on her best, school-mom smile. "Sure…Jean, it's Jean, right?" Anna was embarrassed that she had to ask the name of the mother of Em's best friend.

Jean returned her smile warmly, "Yes, yes, that's right. Could we talk over there?"

"Okay," Anna said, and followed Jean behind the curtain at the back of the stage.

Jean looked around, as if making sure no one else was listening.

"Anna, I'm very worried…about Emily."

"About *Emily*?" Anna wasn't expecting to hear that. She'd expected Jean to share something about how Stephanie had been causing problems at school, or at home, or something like that. She was a very outspoken child.

"Yes," said Jane flatly. "Look, I don't mean to interfere. Our daughters are very close friends, and...well, Emily tells Stephanie things—personal things—about you, and ah, about some of the problems that you and your husband are having. And of course, there was that terrible incident on the news about you and..."

Anna felt attacked. She lifted her chin, and stared at Jean with a look that dared her to trespass into her private life—or criticize her. "And?"

Jean touched her forearm gently. "It's okay, Anna. I know how it feels to have problems at home. Believe me, I am not judging you. I'm just trying to help...And I think you need to know that Emily is seriously thinking of running away..."

It took some time for Anna to grasp what Jean had said. "What?" Anna said blankly. "Emily told Stephanie she planned to run away...*from home?*"

Jean nodded. "Yes. Stephanie told me, because she's very concerned about Emily's safety. She gave me permission to share this with you—which tells me how worried Stephanie has been..." Anna felt Jean watching her closely. Jean looked embarrassed, and then she added, as if to lighten her message, "You know how teenagers are, about telling their parents anything..."

Anna looked down, feeling ashamed. The last thing she ever wanted was for Emily to be so unhappy. And it was her fault for being a terrible mother...

Anna had decided in the last week that she could be miserable forever; that she could stay in her unhappy marriage for stability, safety and security, for Emily's sake. But her daughter...her beautiful, sweet little girl deserved the best out of life.

But she understood why Emily wanted to run away. Anna had had to lock her own suitcase in a closet, to keep herself from packing it…

Anna looked at Jean. Tears burned her eyes, and she said, "Thank you so much for telling me, Jean. I know it wasn't an easy thing to do. I'll talk to her…*and* I'm going to have to make some changes—to make sure this never happens again."

"Look, if there's anything I can do to help, please call me. Anytime…Maybe come over for coffee next week?" Jane smiled warmly.

Anna nodded. "I'd like that. And…thanks again."

Turning to walk away, Jean stopped and added, "You know my husband Mike is an attorney. He does divorces. I'm prejudiced, of course, but I think he's the best…"

Anna felt her back go stiff, and she caught her breath in surprise. Divorce? Emily running away? Tears filled her eyes. More failures. More disappointments. What kind of a parent was she? How could she fix her broken life?

"Call me, Anna," said Jean.

Anna nodded, and, to hide her tears, she turned away.

Chapter 29 ❋ Abe

Abe paced around the bedroom. He didn't need to take any more time off from work. He was feeling better, but everyone said he looked like hell. His substitute had been contracted to cover his classes until winter break. All his papers were graded. He had nothing to do, but to sit at home…and to think.

He regretted having sex with Georgie the other night. It had been terrible for him, and probably for her, too, he guessed. Even though she'd said his arrest and injuries were awful, she seemed more interested in suing the cops, and "that whitey slumlord," than she cared about touching him——and kissing his smashed-up face.

She hadn't wanted to kiss his swollen lips, or touch his bruises, or even look at him, in his bloodshot eyes. She'd asked him hurry up, so it had been, for him, like making love to a blow-up doll.

He had tried kissing her, just to see if he could really mean it, but he felt nothing. They had kept on anyway, petting and rubbing one another, silently and quickly. The only way he could get hard was to think about Anna. Georgie had her eyes closed the whole time. Once inside her, and they both finished, he realized that their attempt at lovemaking had meant nothing to him.

Their sex had been a purely physical act, he realized; something that they had repeated a couple of times each year, like some ritual of obligation. He'd known that the fire had gone out of their relationship. Why had he tried to look for it again?

From the first time that Georgie had called him "Uncle Tom," Georgie had crushed him, and his self-respect, the way she ground out her fancy lady cigarettes in her crystal ash trays...And she'd kept doing it, over and over, for years, until his respect and desire for her was as cold as the frost on the window next to his bed.

And he'd let it all happen. To keep a home for Jaheen. And maybe because he was afraid to change his life...

Staring out the window at the lifeless tree tops in front of his house, his thoughts drifted to Anna. Remembering her sparkling green eyes—smiling at him, her joking and her teasing, her laugh, and the way she had pulled him in close...And the way she was afraid to face her fears, too. He squeezed his eyes closed, and the muscles in his face jumped into a painful spasm.

He reached for the ice pack. It was the thing that had brought him comfort when he was alone—the soft blue bag of ice. It had been like a friend to him from his first painful moments in the hospital, to now, almost two weeks later. He held the pack in his hands, and the cold helped distract him from longing for a woman that he had no right to even speak to, ever again.

* * *

The knocking on the front door wouldn't stop. The banging blended into Anna's dream, where she was slapping the mean face of the short cop, over and over...

Anna pulled herself up off of the fainting couch. She stretched as she stumbled toward the front door, trying to shake off the nightmare.

"This is what I get for taking a nap in the afternoon," she mumbled out loud, to the empty house. Restless and sleepless nights had taken their toll on her moods. Passing the hall mirror, she saw a frightening image: a sorry-looking, skinny woman in stained old kitty-cat pajamas. Her short haircut had started to grow out into her old, familiar spikes and lumps. *I need a serious hospital beauty parlor visit…but who cares*, she thought.

"Yes? Who is it?" She said to the person pounding on the other side of the door.

"It's me, Daisy, Anna, open up!"

Anna hesitated. Daisy was on Bill's "no talk to" list.

She shook her head, even though no one could see her, and said, "Daisy, I can't…"

"You can too, Anna. Let me in," Daisy insisted.

Knowing she was alone, and Bill was at work, Anna figured she could risk it, just for a couple of minutes. Daze had been so kind, to her—and to Abe…

She unlocked the door, and opening it only part way, she looked at Daisy though the crack.

Daisy stared at her in amazement, and she pushed the door open.

"My God, Anna! You're a *mess!*" Daisy said as she stepped through the door.

Anna stepped back, but Daisy reached out and held onto Anna's upper arm. "We need to talk." She squeezed Anna's arm. "Hum…thin… Honey, how are you?"

Anna shut the door, looking down at the floor. "I've lost my craving for sweets these days…But, yeah, I do your workouts—to keep from going crazy…."

"Oh, Anna…come here." Daisy reached out and hugged her. Anna wasn't prepared for it. She felt whatever defenses she had melt away, and she started to cry, laying her face down onto the top of Daisy's soft gray head. Her tears exploded, and she couldn't stop them. Not since her father died—and when she'd first realized that she'd become an orphan—had Anna cried so hard.

193

Daisy held her until her sobbing stopped enough for Anna to catch her breath. She guided Anna into a chair in the living room, as if Anna didn't know which way to go in her own house.

"Daisy, I don't know what to do! You're right. My life *is* a mess," Anna choked. "Bill hates me, my in-laws hate me...My daughter wants to run away...Abe...I've failed him, too...and you...everyone...I'm a terrible mother, a terrible person..."

"Wait, wait, Anna. No one hates you!" Daisy looked worried. "Emily wants to run away?"

"That's what Steph's mother told me today. I hope she's not really serious, but...I can't blame her. I want to run away myself! Who wants to be around—*this house?* It's not a home, it's...it's just a showplace, a shell...a jail."

Anna looked around the room, and then at Daisy. Daisy reached for a nearby chair, and pulled it front of Anna's. She took Anna's hands in hers, and her eyes were soft, but her expression was very serious. "Look, Anna, you've got to get a grip...You need to take charge of your *own life.* That's what's wrong with Emily...and with everything in your life. Don't you *see?*" she paused. Anna watched her as if she was hypnotized, soaking up all of Daisy's words, like a dry sponge falling into dishwater. "Anna, what did you tell me your father used to say, about living your life?"

"I don't know anymore." Anna sniffled, reaching for a tissue from the box next to her. "He said not to lie...something about lying to myself is like lying to God."

"Yes...and how have you lying to yourself?"

Anna stopped to think, and bit her lip. "I don't care about the truth. The truth hurts too much, Daze."

"Yes, the truth can be painful, honey," Daisy said softly. "But, without telling the truth, how can you know what you really want in life?"

Anna wiped her eyes.

Daisy continued. "In order to be happy, we have to make changes our lives…"

Anna shook her head. "I'm tired of change. Of hurting people—of people getting hurt…all because of the *stupid truth*…"

Daisy leaned back in her chair, still holding Anna's hands.

Anna didn't want her to go. It felt good to talk. "You want to hear the truth, Daze? I let Bill tell me what to do. I ignored his cheating on me…but, what is the *real* truth? Maybe God wants me to stay with him, no matter what—and keep our family together…you know, we promised until death…and all that?"

Daisy shook her head slowly, her tiny lips were pressed together into a thin line. She let go of Anna, and rubbed her own neck with both hands. She looked frustrated. "Anna, do you really think that God wants you to be unhappy?—to live like this?"

Anna looked around the room, and she shrugged.

"Doesn't God want you to use the special gifts you've been given?" Daisy asked.

"I don't know, Daisy. I'm confused about that. I've thought about it and thought about it, believe me. It's easy to say, 'be happy' and 'be true to yourself' but, what the hell does all that mean?"

"I don't have the answers for you, honey…" she smiled. "But how will you find the answers, *if you stop looking for them?*"

Anna was listening, and she felt the impact of Daisy's question in her heart.

Daisy continued on, in such a kind way, that Anna wanted to hug her again. "Sure, you made some mistakes. We all have. But how can we learn from them—from living, unless we make mistakes?"

"I know," Anna whispered with a small smile. "If that's true, I've sure been learning a lot lately...I've made some pretty big mistakes, as you well know..."

"That's all right. Mistakes are a part of life, Anna. Isn't that what you tell Emily?"

Anna nodded, and smiled. "Yes."

Daisy smiled. "Okay, then. Now it's time to move on. It's time to forgive yourself...and to move on..."

"You're right. But I guess I just don't know how to move on..."

"He wants you to come back," Daisy said quietly.

Anna looked at her, rubbing her eyes.

"I don't know, Daisy. Bill has forbidden it. He calls Abe 'that criminal.' Emily's in the middle. She's worried that I'll get hurt—like Abe did...and I don't want Abe's family to be in any more danger..."

Daisy nodded slowly, and she sighed, as if the weight of the world were on her shoulders.

"Anna, we all make choices in life. Some are easy, and some take a great deal of courage. I can't tell you what to do. I wouldn't dare. But, honey, I want you to take a look in that mirror," she pointed to the tall, golden-framed wall mirror in the hallway, and she continued, in serious tone, "Check out what you see in there. If you don't see happiness in those eyes, then you'd better look again at the choices you're making in your life...Because when you make the right choices, you'll know it...You'll see the love—you'll see God—right there, shinin' in your own, pretty Irish eyes..."

She hugged Daisy, and she started to cry again, but the tears felt different this time. They were tears of gratitude for her friend. She remembered Abe saying that God sent people who helped you to change your life.

Now, Anna couldn't wait to take another long look in that mirror. She wanted to see—longed to fine the love that Daisy promised she could find there.

There was nothing she wanted to do or to see more than that.

Chapter 30 ❀ Emily

"Hi…anybody home?" Emily called into the open foyer, hoping not to hear anyone answer. She liked to listen her voice echo up to the balcony—when her parents weren't there. She turned to Steph, who'd followed her into the house, and signaled a thumbs-up to her friend, telling her that the coast was clear.

Emily knew her mother was still at school, helping Steph's mom with the Christmas play, so Emily had invited Steph to come in for a quick snack—and for some girl talk. Her father didn't want Steph in the house; Steph, he'd said, asked him too many questions, and she wasn't polite enough, so she had to sneak Steph in, when no one was home.

Her mom was fine with Steph's visiting, especially now, that her mom and Steph's mom were friends, but Emily didn't want to get her mom into any more trouble with her dad—any more trouble than her mom was already in, because of the police, and the news about her mother's arrest. Emily hadn't seen the article in the paper. Her dad had strictly forbidden her to read it, but Steph had read it to Emily over the phone…and Emily had felt really sorry about Jaheen's dad's injuries.

"What's for snack? Something cool?" Steph asked boldly. Emily admired the way her friend was always took charge, wherever she went.

They dropped their books on the floor near the door, and headed for the kitchen. "Mom made some apple crisp last night. It's pretty good. Want that?"

"Ya, that's cool," said Steph, using her new favorite word again.

The girls collected plates and forks, and took the dessert out of the refrigerator. Emily heard the front door open. She looked at Steph, and started to worry.

"Ah, you're home early, *Mom?*" Emily called out, hoping it really was her mother.

There was no answer. They waited, hardly breathing. Both girls jumped when Emily's father walked into the kitchen.

"Well, *hello* girls," he said, in stern and unfriendly voice. "How are you…*Stephanie?* Right? It's been awhile since you've been here, hasn't it?"

Emily spoke up quickly, trying to think up as many excuses as she could. "Steph just—stopped over—for a minute—on her way home, and…since she was hungry, I invited her in, for a quick snack." Feeling guilty, and afraid of what her father might say or do next, she glanced at Steph nervously, and back to her father.

He didn't smile. He was looking at Steph like she'd done something wrong, and Emily didn't like that. It was her fault that she broke her father's rules, not Steph's.

"I see." He continued slowly. "And does your mother know that you have company…here in the house?" he asked, sounding like a policeman or something.

"Oh no!" Emily said quickly, ready to defend her mother. "She's still at my—our school—helping Steph's mom and the teachers with the Christmas play."

"Well, I got to get going now, Em," said Steph hurriedly. "Bye, Mister Smithson. See ya tomorrow, Em." She practically ran out of the kitchen.

After the front door had slammed shut, Emily's father walked toward her. Emily backed away from him. He looked very angry. "Emily, I'm going to put you on restriction. You're mother thinks you are too old to spank, but you deserve it. How many times must you be told that any visitors must be scheduled, in advance, with either myself, or your mother?"

Emily hung her head. Her hands were cold, but, at the same time, she had the urge to stick out her tongue at him, and tell him how mean he'd been to her very best friend. But that wouldn't be polite, so she just stood there, fuming inside, trying to hold her feelings inside, by swallowing hard, and holding her breath.

"Yes, Dad," she managed to answer, in between gulps. "May I go up to my room now?"

"After you clean up your mess here. And...no TV or phone for a week, young lady," he barked, slamming his briefcase down on the kitchen table, sending dishes crashing onto the floor.

* * *

"Steph, I just can't take it anymore," Emily whispered into the phone. "My dad is—like you said, a *tyrant*—like that mean king we learned about in social studies class. He's hardly ever home, but when he is, he bosses me and mom around *all the time*..."

"I know, Em. He is *so uncool.*"

"What should I do? You said that running away is a bad idea...and it probably is...but, I don't know. I mean, things around here got better for a while, when mom was standing up to him. Then...you-know-what happened, and she caved...Maybe she's afraid of him—like I am?"

"I dunno, Em. Talk to your mom—she told my mom she's doing something about all the bad stuff going on in your house."

Emily just listened, and thought about what Steph was saying. She hoped that her mother was trying to make things better...

"I know it's been bad. Your mom got arrested... and your dad—well, my mom says something's not right with him. But give your mom some time to work things out, Em, so don't run away, *please?*"

There was a click on the extension. Oh no, was that Dad listening on the phone?

"Gotta go now, Steph. Bye."

When she heard footsteps on the stairs, her worst fears were confirmed. Her dad *had* been listening on the other line. Oh, God. She was *really* in for it now.

Chapter 31 ❋ Anna

Anna came in the front door, her arms loaded down with costumes to alter for the school play. The house was quiet. She was surprised that Bill's car was in the driveway. He was never home this early on his day off. The top was up, so she knew he was in for the night, and the thought of him in the house instantly crashed her good mood. She had enjoyed meeting Jean for coffee this afternoon. She'd actually laughed with her new friend...

She looked around the corner into the living room, and there he was, sitting in front of the fire, reading the paper.

"Hello," she called coldly. Passing the big mirror in the hall, she noticed her sorry reflection. It reminded her of what she'd seen in that mirror, on the day Daisy came to visit her. The unhappiness that she'd found there, in her own eyes, had been haunting her ever since.

She immediately headed for the stairs. She would rather skip dinner, than talk to Bill.

"I'm going to work on these costumes for Emily's play," she told him as she stopped on one of the steps.

Without looking at her, he said, using his slowest, most irritating southern drawl; that tone, she knew, usually meant some kind of trouble: "What kind of mother are you, that you can't you control your daughter?"

"What are you talking about?" She stopped on the stairs and gripped the railing. Now what? She wondered.

Her neck and shoulder muscles tightened up, and she bit her lip.

"Your daughter allowed that little uncouth friend of hers to come here, into our home, after school today—*without permission*, I am assuming…"

Anna did some quick thinking, trying to find a way to protect Emily and Steph—and herself, too, so she asked, "Did she say she didn't have permission?"

"You gave her *permission*? You know how I feel about that girl."

Anna decided not to answer him, to see if he'd just drop the subject.

"I see," he said. Shaking his paper, he added, "Well, since you learned to *lie* so well—in jail—and you can't handle Emily, I took care of the situation for you."

Anna's eyes automatically looked up toward Emily's room. She dropped the costumes on the steps, her heart beating fast, she bounded up the rest of the stairs.

Emily's door was partially closed, and the light was off. Her radio was playing quietly. She pushed the door open, and tiptoed in.

"Em?" she asked.

"Mama" Emily said from the darkened bed. "Mama, Daddy spanked me," she said with a sad whimper.

Anna found the bed in the dark, and hugged her daughter. She said, kissing the top of her head, "I'm so sorry, honey. Are you okay? Did he hurt you?"

"He used his belt, but I'm okay, Mommy. I was bad…and I deserved it."

The fury she'd felt toward the policeman who had attacked Abe had been the greatest anger that Anna had ever experienced, but now, the rage she felt toward Bill far exceeded even that…

She rocked Em like a baby, holding her in her arms. "As God is my witness, baby girl," she swore, meaning every word. "That will *never, ever* happen to you again."

* * *

"Daisy, I'm back," Anna said into the phone the next morning. She was still trying to shake the anger, but her newly discovered determination burned inside of her like fire. "You were right. My mirror told me what I wanted to do—what I needed to do. I just wasn't ready to listen until Em…"

"Until what?"

"Ah, nothing. Never mind…But I've decided—I'm going to move on—make big changes in my life. I want to be happy, Daze…And I want that for Em, too."

"You deserve to be happy, Anna. Everyone does. And I think that your daughter will be a lot happier, when *you* are. You're her example—her role model."

"Well, I haven't been a very good one, but I plan to get better at it—and fast…So, for starters, I want to train with you—and Abe—again. That is, if you—and Abe—think it's safe enough to…"

Daisy sounded grim. "Anna, there are no guarantees in life. You know that. The decision to continue skating together is yours—and Abe's—to make. But I'll be happy to coach the two of you, if you want me to."

"Daze, you've been so wonderful—"

Daisy cut her off. "Yes, well…okay…So, are evenings good for you?"

"Ah, no. I can't train at night, Daze. I…I've got to be home…to be around here…for Emily. Can you—and Abe—do any mornings?"

"I think he can. At least until his classes start in January. Any time's fine with me. So, we'll go early—maybe try for nine…when?

"Tomorrow?"

"Tomorrow it is. I'll call him, and let him know. Anna, he'll be thrilled—he misses you."

There was an awkward silence.

Daisy said slowly: "You know, hon, I didn't want to push you—or pry into your personal life, but I'm glad you've finally decided to..." Anna pictured Daisy tilting her head to one side, the way she did, whenever she searched for just the right word, and Anna's heart warmed with the idea that she'd be with her—and Abe—again. "...to make the choices that'll make you happy. You and Abe, when you're together, amazing things happen...and, I may be prejudiced, but I think the whole world should see it."

"We do have...something special...And you're special, too, Daze. We—I—couldn't have done—anything—without you," Anna said, tears coming now. "And, Daisy...?"

"Yes, I know...you're very welcome!"

Hanging up, Anna didn't need a mirror to tell her that her eyes were smiling right now, beneath some tears of relief that were flowing down her face.

Get a grip, she told herself. There were important phone calls to make, and lots to do for herself— and for Emily...*starting now!*

Chapter 32 ❀ Jaheen

Jaheen couldn't remember when her father had been more excited about anything. Seeing him so happy made her feel good, too. They were in his car, driving to her last day of school before the holiday break. She'd been trying to talk him into letting her miss her morning classes, so she could go with him to his training session today. There was nothing she'd rather do than watch him work with Daisy French.

"Sorry, girl," he said. He looked serious because he couldn't smile much yet—because of his injuries. He was concentrating on his driving, going extra slow because the roads were wet. The sun was just coming through the clouds now, and she noticed the bruises on his face were glowing a purple color in the morning light. She didn't like to be reminded of what happened to him. It upset her stomach, and made her mad. She turned to watch the cars ahead of them to distract herself.

"Your education is the most important thing right now—even though you probably don't believe it," he said, his eyes focused on the traffic. She glanced over at him. He looked strange without his glasses. They had been broken when he fell, and he hadn't gotten new ones. Instead, he had gone to the eye doctor and gotten contact lenses. He blinked his eyes a lot—he said that he was still trying to get used to wearing them.

"I know, I know, Dad...," she said, laughing. She wasn't worried about school. She was getting better at math...and he'd help her, when she needed it. She had gotten even closer to her dad since he'd been hurt, and he'd been home all the time.

She was feeling more confident about herself, too. She even had Em—a white girl—for a friend. And, best of all, she would go to the Olympics *and* go to college—if she really wanted to.

"Ah-hah," he sighed. "I thought I knew a lot at your age, too—and until very recently—I thought I knew how to live." He rubbed the side of his face with one hand. "Turns out, I didn't know a whole helluva lot about life."

"You mean because you got hurt by the cops?" she asked, confused.

He took some time to think. "Yeah, that...and well, about loving people you care about...letting them know how you feel. What they mean to you." He looked at her. "I love you, J."

"I love you, too Dad."

He kept rubbing his face. "I learned that you can't waste time. You gotta do what makes you happy. It took me a long time to figure that out. I hope one day you'll understand that, without having to get hurt—or cause other people to get hurt."

She nodded. She understood more about life—about his life—and her own—than anybody knew she did. Life was simple, she'd decided. You made choices—and then you acted on them. You had to take risks. Otherwise, nothing ever changed—and you didn't get what you wanted in life.

Chapter 33 ✻ *Abe*

Abe looked over at his daughter. He was almost overwhelmed with a need to protect her—to care for her, to ensure her future. She was so bright, so smart, and so full of promise. He slowed the car down to a near-crawl. He wanted to make sure that she arrived at school safely. He might be late to the rink, but that was okay.

She smiled at him, with a wise, knowing look that seemed beyond her teenage years. She was growing up—becoming a fine young woman, and, until this last week, he hadn't appreciated the level of her maturity. During his ordeal with the police and his time in the hospital, she'd showered him with love and concern...drawing him get-well cards, writing him notes with smiling faces, bringing him ice, and snacks, when he was bedridden with the concussion. They had talked, and played cards and board games together, and he'd helped her with her homework.

But most of all, he was impressed by her loyalty when he'd been in trouble. She'd tried to protect him. She'd called Emily, and she'd asked Em for help. She'd taken his side against Georgie, defending him, and his passion for skating.

He felt the need to tell her how he was feeling now, but he was having difficulty finding the right way to put it into words. "J, I really want to thank you for helping me—for being there for me. Knowing that you cared..." He shook his head. "It means so much. You helped me make it through a really tough time..."

"You don't have to thank me—you're my dad," she said, watching the road. "You're a great guy. You deserve to be happy."

He smiled at the depth of her compassion. How much of this kind of closeness had he missed with his daughter? He'd spent too much time avoiding Georgie—reading and working on new courses at home, and in the process, he'd missed valuable father-daughter time.

He grimaced, and feelings of regret gripped his face. His cheek and nose were hurting; he'd stopped the powerful pain pills; he took only an aspirin every few hours. He'd wanted to be clear-headed, to drive safely...and to be at his best today, for Daisy and for—

"Is Emily's mom going to be there today?" asked Jaheen, as if she had read his mind.

"Yes, I believe she is," he answered, starting to feel tense. "Why do you ask?"

"Emily told me that she and her mother may be moving away," he saw Jaheen look at him out of the corner of her eye, as if she was wondering how he'd react.

Abe stared straight ahead, trying to act calm, but feeling just the opposite.

"Really?" he said, as casually as he could.

"Yeah. Emily's father is a real *jerk*. She told me he hit her with his belt. Then Mrs. Smithson came unglued when she found out. She reported him to somebody—the police, I think, and then she told him she wanted a divorce," Jaheen spoke with conviction, like someone who knew important secrets. "Emily heard her say it—a divorce," she added, emphatically.

Abe slowed the car down even more, as he was now finding it difficult to concentrate, and to absorb this new information. He was relieved to see the school parking lot up ahead. The line of cars seemed endless, as they creeped alongside the busses and the student drop-off spot, and it was all he could do to hold back from asking Jaheen more details. His mind was reeling, but he said nothing.

A divorce? The police? How was Anna feeling? What would she be like today?

He sighed, and when he hugged Jaheen goodbye as she got out of the car, he thought of something else: now that their two daughters had become friends, what Jaheen had told Emily about him, and Georgie?

Chapter 34 ❀ Anna

Anna was warming up in the big rink, when she saw Abe walk into the arena. He went straight over to Daisy, who was waiting for him by the door. She hadn't seen him since the afternoon of their arrest. She didn't know how she'd feel, when she saw him again.

Managing her feelings about him, and what had happened to them, had been like riding a roller coaster. She'd felt extreme lows of terrible sadness about his horrible injuries, and then she'd fought her anger and outrage; he had put her in a risky situation by taking her to the warehouse, without her knowledge, or her informed consent—but he'd wanted them learn to dance together better—and his had certainly worked…

She saw that his movements were slower, and very deliberate. He looked different: older, and thinner. His hair was trimmed short, his face was clean-shaven—and—his glasses were gone! How was he going to see anything without those coke-bottle-bottom lenses?

She looked away, and she kept moving. It felt great to stretch her legs and skate fast again. Daisy had promised that they would only be working out on the ice, and Anna was glad about that.

She saw Abe sit down and take off his shoes out of the corner of her vision. Daisy was skating towards her, head down, waving one hand. Anna veered to meet up her, and stopped in front of Daisy, waiting for her to speak.

"He's really upset, Anna. He's afraid that you can't forgive him." Daisy said, looking over at Abe, who was looking down, lacing up his skates.

Anna nodded slowly. Her feelings tumbled around inside of her, like clothes in a dryer. She really couldn't sort them all out, as much as she wanted to. She looked at Daisy, and then at Abe. She saw him looked up at her from across the arena. He looked so different...like a stranger.

"I think—if you want my opinion—" Daisy offered. "He hasn't forgiven *himself.*"

Anna nodded, locking eyes with Daisy. She hadn't thought about that. "Okay. Let me talk to him, just for a minute?" Anna asked.

"Tell him to spend some time in front of the mirror," Daisy said, smiling.

She watched Daisy tilt her head to one side, and Anna knew that more important advice was coming. Daisy reached for Anna's hand, and she whispered softly: "In the meantime, Anna, honey, maybe *you* could be his mirror?"

Anna looked at Daisy and nodded. She understood. Abe had been trying to find his own kind of happiness, and do what he loved to do. Maybe he'd made mistakes, but she'd made lots of them, too. They were human beings, and making mistakes was the way that people learned about life she reminded herself.

But you had to keep on trying—keep looking in the mirrors. That was the way to find what you loved...and to find love...

Chapter 35 ❀ Abe

Abraham Lincoln Brown stood up to face his training partner as she approached him. He thought of his full name now, because, he knew, that this moment would probably be *his* moment. He'd been named him for President Lincoln, and his grandma had said he would do something that would change history; this moment would—one way or another—change *his* history.

When he'd first decided to learn to skate like a professional, he'd envisioned his moment as one in which he was recognized for his skills as a skater—he'd win an award from white people, who would recognize what he could do on the ice. His name would be called out to an applauding crowd, and he accepted a prize, and a bouquet of flowers.

But that was before. Things had changed.

Recovering from his injuries, and having hours of time alone to think, he'd discovered that he wanted—he needed—something more than prizes and flowers or personal recognition. The pain and conflict he'd been through in the past few weeks, had caused him to ask a lot of important questions about what he wanted from life— and what he could give back to the world.

The answers he found, he realized, had been mostly taught to him by the women in his life. Real success was about living life in a way that really mattered, as his grandma had said. He'd learned about single-minded focus from Georgie. He'd learned from Anna about standing up for what you believed in. And, Jaheen—in spite of her tough, know-it-all shell—was *still* teaching him about helping the people that you loved, and allowing them to help you, too.

Anna was nearly in front of him now, sliding to a stop on her skates. He could almost reach out and touch her, like he wanted to do so very badly. He wanted to hug her, hold her, to let her know how painful the last couple of weeks had been without her. He wanted to explain all that he had learned...and to thank her for all that she had taught him.

But, he didn't.

He stood in front of her, wondering if she would even speak to him at all.

Chapter 36 ❀ Anna

Anna almost slid into Abe. She stopped and steadied herself by grabbing each of his forearms with both her hands.

Her eyes scanned him with a fierce intensity. She saw the bruises, and reached for his face. He didn't flinch. She gently stroked his swollen cheek, and lightly ran her finger around his dented brow bone.

Tears burned from behind her eyes, as she gazed into his soft brown ones. It was as if she was putting pieces of a broken puzzle back together—and making a whole new picture; he looked like a different person in some ways, and yet, the feeling in her heart told her that nothing had changed between them. Whatever magical energy erupted when they were together was still alive and well—and maybe even growing.

"Oh, Abe," she whispered. "*My God.*"

There seemed to be no more need for words. She didn't know whether he moved to hug her first, or she'd started to hug him first. It didn't matter. They stood together, in a tight embrace that rocked her soul more than any love song that she could remember.

"Anna, I'm so sorry—"Abe began.

"Okay, you two!" yelled Daisy from the center of the arena. "Break it up! Get back to work!"

Anna looked up at him. Her grin felt so big, and her joy was so great, she wasn't sure that her face could contain it all. She saw her feelings mirrored in Abe's face. If this was what Daisy meant about getting Abe in front of a mirror, then she was more than happy to be his reflection.

They broke away, and skated together toward Daisy, holding hands.

Chapter 37 ❄ Abe

Abe couldn't believe how light and free he felt. His skates hardly touched the ice during his warm-up rounds. But that didn't last long. The pain in his face, and flashbacks of his attack started to distract him, and he had to fight to keep control of his body. His forehead and his palms were wet with sweat, and his sweatshirt was beginning to feel hot.

Daisy and Anna looked at him with concern.

"Take it slow, Abe," Daisy cautioned.

"I'm fine—really," he said to their doubting faces.

"Let's just do some footwork, and call it a day," Daisy said. "You're both doing all right…for being off the ice for a while. It'll take a couple of days to get back…"

Anna nodded, and looked at Abe, giving him a short smile that he returned to her.

Daisy showed them a new sequence. They copied her, as she counted out loud for them. She guided them through it a second time, but he was too tired, and he tripped twice. Daisy seemed to know that it was time to stop, and he was relieved when she sent them home with practice instructions: At least an hour a day, in addition to their regular fitness workouts. In spite of the women's concerns for him, he insisted that he was up for more sessions, every morning, except on Sundays, over the holidays.

Abe was exhausted, but he was sure that he'd never felt happier. He wanted to spend more time talking with Anna, to tell her about everything that he'd been thinking about, and to thank her for what she'd done for him, but she had left in a hurry, without much of an explanation.

He assumed, from her hug, and by her sweet and tender smiles, that she had forgiven him—or at least understood that he was sorry—but he wished that they could have talked things over. There was so much that he wanted to explain…and to ask about. Her moving away? And a divorce?

But Daisy was right, he needed to go home and rest, and rebuild his stamina. There would be time enough for clearing the air with Anna…once he felt a little stronger, and he was sure of what he was planning to do about his own life…

Chapter 38 ❋ Emily

Emily didn't completely understand everything that was going on in her house, but she knew a lot more than her parents thought she did. They were taking about getting a divorce, and, thanks to Steph, she understood what that really meant.

Emily had paid attention to other kids in her who class had parents who were divorced. Most of them didn't seem too happy about the whole thing. But one girl had said her father wouldn't pay her mother for food and rent after the divorce. That worried Emily because her mother didn't work. How would they buy food if her dad didn't give them any money?

But the idea of a divorce in her own life was still making her sick to her stomach. Her mom took her to the doctor, but he'd said she was fine—that there was nothing wrong with her stomach. He did say that she had something that sounded like "sichosomic," so, at least her tummy aches had a name—even though there was nothing the doctor could do about it. He'd told her to eat lots of small snacks, all day long—anything she wanted—which was, like Steph said: very cool.

She'd overheard her mother talking on the phone with Steph's mom about finding another place to live. Her mother was living into the guest bedroom since she had been arrested, and Steph had been right again: it was a sign that divorce was coming.

She'd heard her father telling Grandfather Smithson that he was going to "end this, once and for all," so she figured that her father would be the one getting the divorce.

After answering the phone for her mother from an agency called social-something, she'd heard her mother ask if there was anything they could do about her father's spanking her with a belt. It didn't sound like there was. Just as well, Emily thought. She wanted to forget about that night. Her father told her if she was good, she'd never need another spanking. But she was mad at him for hurting her, and treating her like a little kid.

Steph and Jaheen told her that their fathers didn't hit them. Why couldn't her own dad be more like them? Emily didn't like being afraid of her own father, and sometimes lately, as much as she wanted a happy family, she thought that maybe it would be better, if the divorce happened.

But Christmas was coming. Emily wondered what the holidays would be like in her house this year. There weren't any decorations up yet. All the stores downtown were full of bright lights and tinsel, and she wished her house was, too. She and her mother had always "decked all their halls" they used to say to each other. She remembered how they'd laughed together, shopping like crazy, icing tons of holiday cookies in the big kitchen, and then eating them warm, just out of the oven, in front of the fireplace. Her mother loved sweets; Emily did too, and it was one of the few, special times every year that her father allowed them to eat cookies...but mom never told him how many they'd really had eaten, or he would have blown his top.

What would it be like to not see her mom every day? To have her mom around to dance, shop, and eat cookies with? Steph told her that sometimes divorced kids had to live with each parent, for a part of the year. It depended on what the judge said. The thought turned her stomach sour again. Living with her dad wouldn't be fun at all. He didn't let her do anything fun. He still refused to let her skate. He'd bought her a violin instead, and he'd arranged for her to start music lessons in January.

Her mother came in through the side door with a two bags full of food from the grocery store deli. She had not been much cooking lately. She came home from her training sessions, and usually had a long bath. She took a lot of naps, too, but she looked tired most of the time.

"Hi Mom," Emily greeted her with a quick hug.

"Hi Sweetie," her mother smiled down at her, then frowned.

"Did you eat anything this morning?"

"Yeah, I did. I had a peanut butter sandwich. I'm fine."

"For *breakfast?* Emily…"

Emily didn't want to talk about food, so she changed the subject. "How was your lesson?"

"Oh honey, it was *so great* today!" her mother said, her face lighting up like a flashbulb on a camera. She stopped putting food away to look at Emily, leaving the fridge door wide open. "Daisy let us pick the music, and we did our free-dance! You know, like I like to do…And we were— oh, it was—*really* fabulous! Even Daisy said so."

Emily smiled at her mother's bubbling enthusiasm. This was the only time that her mom seemed really happy—when she was dancing or skating to her music—or talking about it.

After all of the trouble with the police, Emily began to understand how important her mom's friendship with Jaheen's father really was. Jaheen had explained that her mother had risked her own freedom and safety, just to get him get out of jail, and Emily respected her for that. *Her mother had actually refused to leave the jail without Mr. Brown!* That was a brave thing for her to do, Jaheen had said on the phone.

But yesterday, Steph had asked if her mom and Mr. Brown were becoming more than friends, and Emily got upset. She didn't want to think that about her mother. Her mother was *still married*, and so was Mr. Brown.

"That's cool, Mom!" Emily said. She paused, and trying to be strong like Jaheen, she asked: "Are you and daddy going to get a divorce—for sure?"

Her mother stopped pouring orange juice into a glass. Her eyes were tight and wrinkled, and she rubbed them with her fingers, and she was biting her lip.

"Let's sit down and talk about that, OK? Do you want some juice?"

Emily shook her head, and followed her mother to the kitchen table.

Her mother took a long drink of orange juice. She set her glass down in front of them, and they both stared at it.

"Em, I think it's best that I tell you the truth. Yes. I've been talking with Steph's father. You know, he's a divorce attorney, and…your father an' I, well, we just can't seem to get along anymore."

Emily stared into her mother's face, and saw the worry there. It made her feel sad. The happy look that was there, when her mom had come home, had disappeared.

"What…" Emily had about a million questions spinning around in her mind, so she couldn't pick just one to ask about.

"Aye, I know, my sweet, girl. There's so much to talk about, and lots to plan for. But, for now, I want you to understand some things." Her mother reached out and held her chin up by her thumb. "Me and your dad, we love you, and none of this has to do with you. You've done nothing wrong—but you can't fix things between your father and me. Do you *know* all that, Em?"

Emily nodded.

"Ah, come here, my sweet little lass," her mother said, blinking back tears, reaching out to hug her. Emily stood up, and fell into her mother's arms, and they hugged for a long time. Emily felt better—relieved—and she decided then that she knew too much about her parents' problems already. She really didn't want to know more details right then—so she didn't ask any more questions.

Chapter 39 ❀ Jaheen

Jaheen was alone in the house. Her mother was out showing real estate property, and her father hadn't returned from his practice session at the rink.

She was restless and bored with her homework.

She went downstairs and flipped on the big stereo. It was one of her dad's favorite soul group songs, the one he liked on when he did his practices at home. The music filled the house. She liked the vibes, and cranked it up, almost as loud is it would go.

She remembered some of the moves that she'd seen him do, and she copied them. She added some dips and turns of her own. And then, getting lost in the rhythm, she sang with the words of the chorus. She began to feel too hot, so she slipped off her sweatshirt, dancing in her bra and jeans. She closed her eyes and envisioned having a tall, handsome partner dance with her, hold her, and spin her around the ice.

Wow, did this feel good, she thought. Was this what her dad had been doing with Em's mom when the police caught them? The music filled her. The beat shook her insides. She was totally into the lyrics. When she finished her last spin, she ran both her hands slowly up her chest, she opened her eyes and jumped back.

Her father was standing in the doorway of the living room, his hands on his hips. Embarrassed, she grabbed her sweatshirt to cover her chest, and reached over to snap off the music as fast as she could.

"Ah...sorry, Dad...I..."

He just stared at her, as if he was frozen to the floor. He shook his head as if to clear it.

"J...I don't know what to say," he rubbed the bruised side of his face.

"I was just practicing. I thought nobody was home. I door's locked and..."

He nodded, but still seemed to be thinking over what he'd seen her doing. She re-adjusted her sweatshirt for more coverage.

"Honey, you can *really* dance," he finally said with a small smile. He seemed a little embarrassed. "You *do* have a gift—talent, J. I—had no idea..."

Jaheen relaxed, still breathing hard. "Thanks. But I've been telling you! I want to be a pro skater—like you. And, I think I'm way good..."

His mouth was in a thin line, and she knew he was doing some more deep thinking.

"Yeah, you're good...but, you know, it takes more than just talent," he said. "If there's anything I've learned, it's that you need a good teacher, lots and lots of hard work...and you have to believe in yourself."

"I *know*, Dad. Why do you think I've been asking to work with Daisy? If I could work with her, I *promise*..."

He nodded, "Promises....are easy, honey—they're so easy to make. But the hard part is living up to them." He was shaking his head.

"Like you and Ma?" she said, cringing, wishing she hadn't said that.

He looked startled, and his eyes bored down, into hers.

"I forget that you're growing up. So fast...Too fast." he said, evading her remark.

She decided to be quiet, and just wait—to see what more he would say about the way things were changing in their house. Her mother was being nicer to him lately; she even cooked chili for them yesterday—shock! But her father seemed to be pulling away from her mother, now, more than ever.

"I *am* grown up, Dad. I know a lot...You forget that I can see a lot more than you guys think I can," she said to him, as he sat down heavily in his big lounge chair.

He rolled his eyes up to hers. "Put on your shirt," he said. "Next time you go dancing topless, make sure the curtains are closed." With that, he picked up the newspaper, and she knew he was finished talking.

She had mixed feelings as she turned away from him and pulled on her sweatshirt. A part of her wanted to know more about what was going on with her parents, and the other part didn't.

But it was enough, for now, that at least her dad appreciated her talent. The problems between her parents would work out, one way or the other, and, she figured, it was up to them to decide what they were going to do next. She'd have to go just along with whatever choices they made...

Chapter 40 ❀ *Anna*

It was Christmas Eve, and Anna had slept in. It was after ten, and she still wasn't ready to get out of bed yet. She ached all over. Daisy had been working them super hard every day, and, *thank God*, she thought, today she could lie there under the covers for as long as she wanted. Every joint was sore, and every muscle fiber felt as tight as the strings on Emily's new violin.

Her feet were blistered, too. She wiggled her toes under the weird wraps and plasters that Daisy had recommended she use on her feet, but she still felt every sore spot.

Her eyes were heavy. She closed them, and listened to the wind blowing a new storm in from the north. Gusts rattled the panes of the windows in the guest room—her room—for good—for now, until the divorce was final.

Yes, she was getting a divorce, and there were no more hiding the truth about that.

She pulled the covers up around her chin, soaking in the warmth of the heavy down quilt, and listening to the Christmas carols that played softly from her radio on the bedside stand. A divorce. This would be her last holiday in this house.

This was turning out to be a very strange Christmas, she thought. But she was surprised that it was sort of okay. She was scared—but better. Every morning after Daisy's demanding workouts, Anna would look forward to stretching out in the big bed, and taking a long nap. She still wasn't sleeping that much at night.

Fatigue and stress had slowed down the sexual energy that used to flare up for her whenever she and Abe danced close together. It had been so long—over two years—since Bill had been intimate with her. She remembered how aggressive he'd been, and how quick he came. No caressing, no romancing. But when *was* the last time she and Bill shared any kind of romance or honest emotion? When was there romantic dinners, kissing, hand-holding? Even in the beginning, they were both so inexperienced, so pressured by school, hang-ups…and then there was the pregnancy, Bill's angry parents, grief over the loss of her father, her quitting school. What a nightmare their marriage had been, from the very start!

It had taken a lot of painful honesty and mirror-gazing for Anna to admit that she and Bill shared the responsibility for mistakes that were made in their marriage—and to start to try to forgive everything and everyone. She had Daisy to thank for that.

She thought about her breakfast with Daze that morning. She and Daze had lingered over coffee, watching the holiday crowds doing last-minute shopping, she'd said, "Daze, I have to tell you something."

"What's that, honey?"

"It was you—and your idea about looking into the mirror, had really helped me to turn my life around."

Daisy had patted her hand, like the mother that Anna always wished that she still had.

"I'm serious. Seeing the misery right there—in front of me—in my very own eyes, well, that helped me to find out something important about myself."

"What's that, dear?"

"That I don't deserve to look that sad—that unhappy. Nobody does."

"That's what I believe, too. But I know it's been a long, hard road for you—to come to that conclusion."

"It was Emily, too, you know…"

"I understand. You're her mother. She wanted her family to stay together. So, you wanted to make her happy, even at the expense of your own happiness."

Anna nodded, rearranging the leftover pieces of toast on her plate.

"I can't ever live with Bill, as his wife, again, Daze. I've filed for a divorce."

Daisy hadn't seemed surprised. "I see. I assume you have a good lawyer?"

"Yes."

"Hmm. And you want me to tell Abe?"

"How did you…?"

"Honey, it is so clear that you have feelings for him. I know you both too well. I will let him know, and I'll keep him updated about what you're doing."

"Thanks, Daze. I shouldn't be seen with him—or with any man—until the divorce is final."

Through it all, Daze had been terrific, she thought.

Steph's mother, Jean, had been her friend, too.

Jean and Mike had warned Anna to be cautious about meeting with men alone—in public, or in private—especially married ones, until the divorce was final, so Anna hadn't spent any time with Abe—before or after their practice sessions; they'd had no more meetings at the college library.

Bill's lawyers had proposed the separation of their assets. She'd been surprised at the large amount of money they'd offered at first, but when she'd fought them about Emily, the tone of the negotiations had quickly changed.

She'd insisted on custody, and she didn't back down. Her father would have been proud. Money meant nothing to her. Being with her daughter—and keeping her from the poisonous Smithson family—was everything that mattered.

Anna was grateful to Stephanie's father. Mike not only made sure that Anna received her fair share, he'd won Bill's agreement to give Anna school-year custody, with weekend and summer visits to be arranged between them. But Bill had given in, only after Mike had threatened to make his affairs public. Anna had given Mike all the written proof—the hotel bills, the dinner receipts—that he'd needed.

Now that the papers had been signed, and the waiting period for the divorce decree was well under way, Anna found herself still adjusting to the reality of it. There were decisions to be made about what she should do with her new life as a single woman.

She planned to start house-hunting after the holidays. Her goal was to keep Em in the same school, but that, she knew, would be difficult. Most houses in her neighborhood were very expensive, and way over her budget. Maybe she would go back to school—and become a college history teacher, like Abe.

She thought about Abe. She missed him. She missed their talks. He seemed to understand her feelings. Their connection went far beyond their skating act. Thinking about his face, and the touch of his soft hands created sensations in her that she felt all over her body. Lying there in her bed, thinking about him, she felt the same warm glow that she felt whenever they were together.

Did he feel it, too?

But Abe was married. He had a wife and a nice family—unlike her own, she thought, feeling ashamed of her failures, and feeling bad about acting in sexual ways with Abe. She had no right.

230

Her own family had fallen apart. And she had contributed to the mess. She was a terrible wife. She figured that she'd probably be alone, paying for her mistakes for the rest of her life.

What did the future hold for her? She didn't know. The old year was ending soon. What would the new year bring—for her—and for her daughter?

If only her own father were here with her now, she wished. In the darkness of her memory, she saw him grinning, and heard his laughing brogue, drunk, singing old Irish Christmas songs by the tree on Christmas Eve, and she drifted into a deep sleep that bordered on exhaustion.

* * *

Abe, Georgie and Jaheen sat around a tall, silver metal tree, opening their gifts. Jaheen screamed with excitement as she ripped the wrapping from around a brand new gold patent leather skate bag.

"Gold—for your medal!" Abe said to his smiling daughter.

"Oh...Thank you, Daddy!"

"That bag should take you all the way to the Olympics," he replied, sipping his holiday drink of Jack Daniels that Georgie had given him. He raised his glass to Georgie in appreciation.

"Yeah, you got that right. That bag's gotta be made of real gold, if ya'll can go by that big price tag," Georgie said sarcastically. He was disappointed to see that she'd left the store sales tag, with the hundred and ten dollar price on it, attached to Jaheen's gift.

Georgie took a big gulp from her own glass of whiskey, and looked at the tree. He watched her stare at the turning light that projected colors onto the sparkling silver tree. It seemed to calm her, as if she was being hypnotized by the booze.

He appreciated the fact that Georgie had been trying to be pleasant toward him. She'd toned down her critical remarks, after he had that serious talk with her about the way her negativity was affecting Jaheen. When he'd asked Georgie how she felt about him, she'd stopped short, and had no answer.

He didn't know what Georgie was really thinking—or doing with her time, for that matter. Her walls were thick with rhetoric about her causes, but he was past the point of worrying about understanding her anymore. She spent a lot of time with Joe, her colleague at the Center. He wondered about the extent of their relationship sometimes.

But there was one thing he did know: Georgie had no use for ice skating. To ask for support for his and Jaheen's passion for the sport was too big of a stretch. She tolerated it. Although Abe didn't want or need Georgie's approval, he felt sad for Jaheen, whose face fell after hearing her mother put down something she loved to do, more than anything in the world.

Now, he felt the need to cheer up Jaheen. "Hey, J, check out this one last gift back here that Santa must have left for you," Abe said with his best cheerful voice. He handed her a large heavy box wrapped in gold paper. "Look! More gold!" he said.

Jaheen's eyes grew big, as she took the box from him.

"You stop it with the 'J' stuff, Abraham...Her name is *Jaheen*. I named her right—with a boy's name, so she could get *someplace* in this world..." He wished she'd stop, but Georgie seemed to be unable to resist digging at him, "and there you go...keep fillin' her head with all of that nonsense about winnin' gold medals...Ain't no black girl gonna—"

"Georgie..." Abe interrupted

"Ma, I like to be called 'J.' And, Olympic skating's really cool..." Jaheen's eyes immediately held tears.

Abe thought his heart might break, watching his daughter need her mother's understanding, and getting nothing but shit from Georgie—who was drinking too much to notice. He felt his anger changing into rage toward Georgie. He swallowed hard. He took another gulp of his drink. His tongue burned, and he knew it wasn't the smooth whiskey that was stinging his throat.

"Baby, go ahead and open your gift," he choked, and coughed on purpose, allowing him to take some deep breaths, and giving him time to calm himself down.

It was *Christmas Eve*, he reminded himself. *This* was the family he had helped to create, and, by God, he was gonna keep it together. Jaheen looked to him to be in control...He*had* to act his role of the good father.

So he put on his best mask, and pushed his new brown-rimmed glasses higher up onto his nose with all the determination he could find. He'd keep trying to please Georgie. But nothing seemed to please her. He'd stopped wearing his new contacts around her. But she'd never let him forget how his old glasses had gotten broken during his arrest, and how*dumb* it was that his skating coach made him waste good money on contact lenses.

Jaheen was slowly opening her last present. A large shoe box slipped easily out of the shiny wrapping. When she lifted the lid, her eyes opened wide—as big as he'd ever seen them, and they sparkled with excitement. As if she was afraid to pick them up, Jaheen gently stroked the gleaming pair of bright white figure skates where they lay, nestled in their box, like they were another one of her pet cats.

Abe grinned. He had spent his entire text book return money on them—over three hundred dollars; Daisy had helped him select the perfect ones, and she'd purchased them for him, from her wholesale supplier. Georgie's mouth hung wide open. She was, he thought, for one rare moment, completely speechless.

Jaheen jumped up into his lap, whooping with joy, covering his neck and face with frantic hugs and kisses, knocking his glasses off onto the floor. His cheek hurt, but a surge of happiness washed his pain away, and he felt a giant smile rip through whatever was left of his mask.

Still hugging Jaheen, he looked over at Georgie. Her face was contorted, into a forced smile, but he could see resentment in the way she sat back stiffly in her chair and gripped her glass. She quietly took another drink of whiskey, and, without another comment, she started to gather up the scraps of holiday gift wrap off of their living room floor, stomping around in the fuzzy white slippers he'd given her.

Happy Christmas to you, too, Georgie, he thought. His heart felt sad, but his soul—his soul was gone—gone missing from his body—his soul was somewhere else40

Chapter 41 ❉ Anna

Anna breathed in the rich smells of incense and burning candles. The massive old church glowed with hundreds of flickering lights. Music and song from the holiday choir and the orchestra echoed from the stone floor to high above them in the soaring, wood-beamed ceiling.

The Christmas Eve service reminded Anna of her early childhood visits to a small Irish Catholic church, where the mass was said in a strange language. And even though she hadn't understood the words, she remembered sensing that something important was happening there.

Distant memories of her parents sitting next to her on a hard wooden bench like this one came to her like wispy shadows too faint to see, but she could feel their love. She'd been three years old when her mother had passed away. Anna was sorry that her father's grief had blocked his ability to forgive God for taking his wife from him. Her father had suffered with unhappiness, just like she had suffered, but friends had come into her life, and had helped her to forgive—and to find hope for a better future.

Anna looked down at Emily. Em smiled up at her. The midnight service was crowded, so they were squeezed together into a pew near the back of the church. A cold draft circled around her legs whenever people came and went, but Anna felt cozy, relaxed, and—happy? Happier than she'd been in a very long time...

And she was finally feeling the spirit of the holidays. She and Em had feasted on the delicious turkey buffet dinner in the church foyer before the service. Emily had even finished two helpings of turkey and gravy!

Em leaned her soft brown curls against Anna's shoulder. She'd probably stayed up all night at Steph's, Anna guessed, putting her arm around her daughter, and giving her a hug. Steph's family were wonderful people; their friendship had been such a gift, to both of them, in so many ways...It was too bad that Bill couldn't seem to understand what real friendship was all about. His relationships were always with women at the office—and they had seemed to always turn sexual. Mike had said that Bill had some kind of mental illness, and, Anna had agreed with him.

When the red-robed minister invited everyone to say silent prayers, Anna closed her eyes. She wanted to pray, but she didn't know exactly what to say. What did God want? The truth? Well, okay, this was the truth, and she hoped that God would understand: She'd been a failure as a wife, but Bill had failed her as a husband, too. She'd been trying to be honest—stopping the bad lying, and pretending...And she was grateful, too, for custody of Emily, friendships with Daisy and Jane, the end of having to worry about Bill's cheating and bad moods, the divorce settlement, financial security, music, and skating, and, of course, meeting the most wonderful person she had ever known: she was thankful for Abe. There. That was it. That was the best, most honest prayer she could come up with.

Her heart felt lighter. When she opened her eyes, Emily was looking at her again, smiling gently, but her eyes were begging for sleep. "Let's go home, Ma," she said softly, as people were starting to get up for the communion.

"OK, honey," Anna whispered. "We can go."

They stepped into the aisle, and headed toward the exit. Emily led the way. Anna felt a light tap on her shoulder. Thinking she'd cut off someone's progress in line, she whispered, "Sorry."

Then Anna felt an object being pressed into her hand, and a very familiar, very deep voice say, "Merry Christmas." She turned and saw the top of a quickly retreating brown head of hair that she instantly recognized. Abe? How did he know where to find her? There were lots churches, and so many had midnight services...Daisy!

She looked down at the little package she was holding—and a surge of warmth came over her. Just as quickly, she felt bad about not giving Abe a gift. She certainly would have—but she'd had to be very careful, because Anna had been warned, often enough, that, until her decree was final, improper conduct on her part could affect the divorce.

* * *

Home again, in her guest bedroom, Anna snuggled down under the covers. Emily had fallen asleep in the car, and had barely made it up the stairs. Now, Em was, she assumed, sleeping and probably dreaming of the things that most young girls dreamed about, on Christmas eve...like she herself had wished for at Em's age—a happy-ever-after life.

Anna remembered her own teenage dreams of meeting and marrying a tall handsome guy. Her life with Bill had been nothing like her fantasies—not even from the beginning. All she'd ever wanted to do was to build a family and feel loved, but she hadn't been enough for Bill. She was too...too fat, too Irish, not pretty—and he'd said she smothered him.

But real life wasn't about dreams. She would soon be a single mother. That was the truth, and she had to accept what was happening, and go on…like it or not, she just had to go on.

She sighed, and looked at the small, unopened package still in her hand. She thought about Abe, and how he had taken another big chance, to go out and find her on Christmas Eve, to give her this gift.

Why had he gone to all that trouble?

She shook her head. Her he tall, handsome stranger was married to someone else.

She turned the little, gold foil-wrapped present over and over in her hand, and she felt Abe's kindness radiating from it. Just thinking about him touching it warmed her. It didn't make sense that her feelings for Abe, Emily, Jane, and Daisy—and even God—seemed to cause the same kind of warm feelings in her heart. How could that be?

Maybe she'd talk with Daisy or Jane about that. Talking with friends. How grateful she was for the people in her life!

She started to unwrap Abe's gift, and the phone rang. It was a little after midnight. Now, it was also Christmas morning. She shivered. Who could be calling her at that hour? Should she answer it, or not?

Her curiosity got the better of her.

"Hello?" she asked, with hesitation.

"Anna, it's me, Daisy. Are you still awake?"

"Aye, I am, Daze. What's wrong?"

"Oh, honey, nothing's wrong…And everything's right!"

"What…are you talking about? Have you been drinking too much egg nog?"

"No, honey. I'm as sober as a judge. But I couldn't wait to tell you the news."

"What news?"

"Well, I just got home from a party with—anyway, I found this phone message waiting for me on my machine. It was from a promoter friend of mine—up in Canada. He runs ice shows. I'd run into him a couple of weeks ago—long story—but I'd told him about you guys—and your, um, how should I say—your *unusual* act..."

Anna smiled. She'd suspected that Daisy, liked their spicy free-dancing a lot more than she let on.

"Go on..."

"Anna, he wants you and Abe to go up to Montreal, and fill an open spot in his show over New Year's—just three performances. His 'talent'—that's what he calls his ice dancers—both fell today. Badly. Broken bones, and all—so they're down for the count." Daisy sounded excited, and she added, "He's really in a jam—and he's willing to pay big money to have you guys work for him, at the last minute."

"But...but, he hasn't even seen us skate," said Anna, immediately shying away from the idea of a public performance. No one had really seen her and Abe skating together—except Daisy—and their daughters. That had been Anna's requirement.

"He trusts my judgment," Daisy said simply.

"But...if we take money, we'll lose our amateur status, right?"

"*Anna*...when were you were planning to skate in the Olympics?"

"Ah, well...of course not...we weren't..."

"I didn't think so. This is an exhibition, Anna. A chance to show an audience what you two can do...and get paid for it—very well paid, I might add. All expenses. Travel, hotel, meals, plus ten thousand." She paused, and added, "Abe could use the money."

239

"You've already asked him about this, haven't you?"

"Yes, I have," Daisy was probably grinning now, Anna could hear it in her voice.

"And he said 'yes'?"

"He did."

Anna took a deep breath, her head was swimming with more possible excuses and objections. But Abe needed the money...

"Oh, wait...I can't go...I can't leave Em....You know, Bill's in New York...and..."

"Emily's going with us. So is Jaheen. I've arranged all that with Earl, my man there. Em's trip's a bonus. All expenses paid, Anna...Merry Christmas!"

Chapter 42 ❄ Anna

Extra practice sessions, and the last-minute preparations for the trip to Montreal helped to slow down Anna's preoccupation with performing, but it certainly didn't stop it. She was doing this for Abe, she kept reminding herself. He needed the money. After what he'd been through…it was the least she could do for him.

And how bad could it be: skating in another country? They were going to do a modified version of their "dance thing" as Daisy called it, so wouldn't it be…shouldn't it be…kind of *fun*? All she had to do was focus, let go—and let it happen, Daze had said.

But, like vampires, her fears came out in the dark, at night, when she tried to sleep. She tried reading a good book by her favorite mystery writer. Sometimes she watched TV until it went off the air. Hot baths helped a little, but sleep only came in the near-dawn hours.

Jean had even given her a crazy Christmas present— one of those "female companion" vibrating devices to try, but she was so embarrassed by the idea, she'd tossed it in a trash can at the grocery store, where Em couldn't find it.

Now, blinking her tired eyes, she packed a few snacks for Emily into her carry-on bag. Next, she grabbed her paper checklist for securing the house for the four days they would be away.

As she headed for the thermostat, she passed the hall mirror, and she stopped in front of it. She hardly recognized the tense face with the red and puffy eyes that she saw in there. Her hair had grown out again, and it fanned out like red flames out of its hairband and made her face look extra-pale. Yuk! *I look terrible,* she thought.

Then she looked down at her throat, and, for the thousandth time, she held the tiny gold skate that hung from a delicate gold chain between her fingers—it was her precious Christmas gift from Abe. It reminded her of him, and how he'd helped her when she'd fallen—on that very first day they'd met—the day her life started to change…for the better.

Abe's gift also reminded her of Christmas Eve, when she'd thanked God for the good things in her life…and when Abe had delivered his gift to her, in person—going to the trouble of finding her in the crowded church.

She and Abe had only been speaking to one another other during practices. Sometimes he would whisper a funny joke or a quick, wise-ass comment while they were posing for a sequence. Sometimes she'd catch him watching her with those intense, golden eyes of his. She'd feel a surge of feelings, and the hot flashes would fill her whole body. She'd act aloof, like she didn't care. She felt bad about lying to him, and to everyone—but it was a *good* lie. He was a married man. God understood that.

She also felt gratitude for the change in Bill's attitude, although she didn't really trust him. But he'd surprised her, when he'd let Emily go to Montreal. She never expected him to agree, but he was going to the Bahamas—doing some kind of business there—and he'd be gone, for couple of weeks, so taking Emily with her was okay with him.

"Mom, is this sweater warm enough for the plane?" Emily asked. It wasn't her first plane ride, but Em hadn't flown since she was seven—when the three of them had gone to Miami for the holidays—the last time they'd gone anywhere as a family. Em seemed nervous, and excited. Her new blue suitcase, heavy with winter outfits—a gift from her grandmother—was packed and ready by the door.

How pretty she looked, Anna thought as she watched her now-teenaged girl locking her train case. Em was dressed in a new blue suit that Anna helped her to choose for the trip. Her hair was pushed back with a matching blue headband. She was even wearing a smear of lip gloss. My little girl is growing up, Anna thought, tears threatening to make an appearance.

"Yep, I think so, sweetie," Anna replied. Taking a deep breath, Anna began to read her checklist out loud. "Okay…the back door's locked. Garage locked. Hall light's on. Heat down to 65. Note for mailman, in the box…All checked, and ready to go!"

The airport taxi would be arriving soon, Anna guessed. She took one final look around the empty house. The floors, walls and furniture were gleaming with polish—she'd spent a lot of nervous energy over the past week, scrubbing and cleaning after their extra-long sessions with Daisy.

But nagging worries were Anna's constant companions. What if she fumbled, or fell, or forgot a sequence, failing Abe and Daisy—in front of *hundreds of people*? What if people *hated* them, like they did here in Atlanta, for being black and white? What if the Canadian audience didn't *get* American soul music?

A loud knock at the door interrupted even more scenes of imagined performance disasters. Anna opened the door wide, and was hit in the face by a blast of cold air. It felt good, and it woke her up to reality: They were really going to Canada—*now, today!*

She and Emily handed their bags to the friendly driver. She was proud of the way Em introduced herself, and offered to help load their luggage. Emily was becoming a young lady. This trip, Anna realized, would be something that she and Emily would never forget—one way or another, no matter how she performed—neither one of them would always remember this adventure.

They were starting a new phase of life together. Anna felt a sense of growing anticipation, and as she slammed and locked the front door, she knew that there was no turning back now.

Chapter 43 ❄ Jaheen

Jaheen could hardly contain her excitement. She paced back in forth in front of the tall airport windows, sometimes doing a skating step, sometimes a dance. She strained her eyes, staring through the glass, looking into the sunset for the lights of the arriving airplanes, wondering which one was hers.

Two ladies in gray uniforms that showed off their chests and hips stood behind the ticket desk. They were watching her. Jaheen didn't care. She was as close to pure happiness as she had ever been in her life. She was going to a *foreign country* to see *professional ice skaters...* and watch her very own father on the ice for his first *public appearance!* She still couldn't believe her mother had agreed to let her go so fast, but she had been prepared to push her to the limit about it. She wouldn't have missed this trip for anything!

Her father was reading his newspaper, in the corner of the waiting room. Daisy was off somewhere, getting coffee.

Where was Emily? And her mom? They were late! What if they missed the plane? That just couldn't happen...If they did, she and her dad would have to just go without them.

"This your first trip on a plane, honey?" asked the colored girl in the gray uniform. She spoke slowly, and sweetly, and a soft, southern voice. Her name tag had the name "Patty" on it.

"Ah, yeah…well, no, I *did* fly when I was a kid once, to see my grandma." Jaheen said seriously, making sure she was being truthful—and polite, like her father told her she had to do for the whole trip.

Her mom had said, "*be honest*", and dad had said, "*be nice*". She figured there had to be a way to do both.

"But I don't remember much about it." She grinned at Patty, stretching her left leg up to her chest, and then the right one, as Daisy had just taught her to do, a few minutes ago, while they were waiting. I'm doing professional skating warm-ups, Jaheen thought proudly, to herself.

"Where you going?" The other attendant asked. She was a white woman with a pinched nose, and bright red lipstick—and not friendly, like Patty.

"Canada. We're going to Montreal. My dad is a famous ice dancer." She looked over at her father, and pointing vaguely to the waiting area.

Patty and the other attendant looked around the room with interest. And back at Jaheen, with disbelief in their faces.

"Where, honey?" asked Patty. "I don't see him."

Jaheen pointed directly at her father, who looked up from his paper, and nodded to her; he was too far away to hear them talking.

"Oh! How…how very nice," said the white lady coldly, frowning her red lips at Jaheen.

Patty smiled, and lowered her eyes to her desk, shuffling some papers. She looked back up at Jaheen, Her smile got bigger. "Your father is…he's an *ice skater?*"

"Oh yeah…he and this white wom…There she is now, that's his skating partner." Jaheen pointed to Anna and Emily, who had just arrived, and were setting down their coats and bags around her father's chair.

Jaheen looked at Patty, and then to the other attendant, who was staring at her father, with her ugly mouth turned down at the corners. Patty gave Jaheen a look of concern, and Jaheen, suddenly realized how unusual—and maybe dangerous—that her father's situation really was. In the eyes of people who didn't know him, he was being judged—even hated—for the color of his skin.

Her anger started growing in her body, and she had to work hard to calm down. She took deep breaths, and starting counting numbers, like her dad had taught her to do.

"Are you okay little girl?" asked the sour red lips.

"Yes…Yes,   I   am…See,   ya'll   don't understand…we *love to skate* and…well, some people don't really care about what color we…" she told them, knowing how lame she must be sounding. She shrugged, and looked at Patty for understanding.

"Good luck, honey." Patty said, with a small smile, and Jaheen saw a sad look in her dark, eye-liner made-up eyes. Patty's kind look disappeared when she glanced at the woman with the red lips. Patty stood up tall, and changed her voice, speaking in a white-lady voice, she said to Jaheen: "Have a pleasant journey, Miss. I have to go prepare the ramp for the arriving flight now."

Patty turned and left, leaving Jaheen alone with the pouting red lipped woman, who shook her head, and stared at her. Jaheen stared back for a long time, and then, deciding it wasn't worth the risk, or her time, she walked away.

* * *

"Sorry about the red-eye," Daisy apologized, leaning in toward Anna from her window seat.

Abe was sitting on the other side of Anna; his long legs were stretched far out into the aisle.

"It was all I could get. We were lucky to get this flight at all—because of the holidays." Daisy added.

Anna nodded. She unbuckled her seat belt, wanting to make a trip to the ladies' room. They were in the last two rows of seats in the back of the narrow jet. "It's fine, Daze. I'm so tired, I think I'll be able to sleep, now that we're in the air. We change planes in Boston, right?"

"Yes. And on the next one, we'll have first class seats, so hang in there. This'll be the worst part of the trip— we're in the damn smoking section, too. Abe...you have enough room over there?"

"I'm fine, Daisy, thank you," he said, shifting his weight to the other hip, obviously uncomfortable in the small seat.

"Liar," Anna whispered to him, as she squeezed passed him, grinning.

He looked up at her, and he smiled. "Better check on those noisy young ladies behind us, while you're up. Don't want any trouble back there," he said, loudly, in an exaggerated, teasing tone that Jaheen could hear from her seat, which was directly behind him.

"Don't worry, Dad," Jaheen laughed. The seat between the girls was empty; Emily was sitting by the window.

"Thanks for letting Em have the window seat, Jaheen," Anna said to her as she passed by them.

"We're taking turns," said Jaheen.

"Ah. Good." Anna smiled at them. The girls were setting up a board game in between them on the empty seat, giggling when the turbulence shook some of the pieces onto the floor.

Anna paused to watch them, holding onto Abe's seat back, to steady herself. She couldn't quite believe what she was seeing. Gratitude—like the kind she'd felt in the church on Christmas Eve—flooded her. The girls were getting along so well....like real friends!

Amazed, she watched them for as long as she dared, and then she continued down the aisle. They were both good girls—lucky girls. They had parents who loved them—parents who were trying to do their best, and still live lives that held meaning for them. It wasn't easy being a parent, and, it certainly wasn't easy to know which choices were the right ones—for everyone concerned, she thought with a sigh.

As she closed and locked the bathroom door, she gripped the handle to steady herself; she knew it was not just the turbulent airplane that was causing her to feel like the whole world was shifting under her feet.

Chapter 44 ❀ *Abe*

Abe was happy. Anna was leaning on his shoulder, and Jaheen was whispering and giggling with Emily in the seats behind them—and life felt good.

Abe figured it must be around midnight. He needed to go to the toilet, but he would rather suffer with a full bladder, than to move Anna off of his shoulder. Anna was snoring lightly, like a children do, when they have a cold. He'd heard that sound during the many, times he'd sat by Jaheen's crib or at her bedside during baby and childhood illnesses.

Georgie? The image of her face shot though him like a jolt. She had always been too busy or too gone. Her projects, the selling and buying houses, took all her time, having none left to care for her husband and their daughter, the way she should have. He could taste the resentment in his throat. He'd had been on thin ice with his department for calling in sick, canceling classes, or, when Jaheen had the measles and chicken pox, asking for a long-term substitute teacher.

He looked down at Anna, hoping he hadn't disturbed her. He was relieved to see that she was still sleeping, and breathing more quietly now. His arm ached—not from her weight, but from wanting to pull her closer, into his chest.

But something was bothering him. He felt a little guilty, but that really wasn't it. He hadn't actually done anything wrong. He thought about that last time that he and Georgie had sex, and how there was no fire there. Nothing. He didn't blame Georgie. He hadn't wanted to touch her, either. That night was a mistake. Okay, he'd been fantasizing about Anna, and he'd been out of his mind with thoughts about holding her, kissing her...Even at the second he came, it was like Anna's lips were on his.

Anna? Daisy told him that Anna wanted honesty in her new life. No more lying. Ha! What a joke! How could he tell Anna the truth about the way he was feeling about her?

He was pretty sure that Georgie was in awe—and probably in lust—with her guy, Joe. The dude was her friend, and her business partner at the center, and now he was going to be her campaign manager, too. He was aggressive—and a loud mouth, really—just the opposite of Abe. They were a great match, Abe thought. Go for it, Georgie. He's what you want. And...just maybe, she'd already gone for him?

More truth: He and Georgie were staying together Jaheen's sake.

And, the worst truth of all: he, Abraham Lincoln Brown, must have had some sick need for someone to put him down.

Abe shook his head in disgust. Maybe he'd had a need to be treated badly, because that's what he'd put up with for most of his life, but that need was *gone!*

He let that thought sink in, and his anger at Georgie changed. The anger wasn't gone; he felt the rage turn toward himself. Emotions jumped from his head to his gut, and the plane's bumpy descent into the blustery Boston airport agitated him even more.

Honesty? Okay. Georgie was probably with Joe this very minute. Maybe she was doing it with him, right now.

That was probably the reason she hadn't objected to his taking Jaheen on this trip.

If all that was true, then, yes, he'd feel betrayed—his manhood would be bruised. But if he was honest with himself months ago, he would have left the marriage when he'd first met Anna. From the day he picked her up off the ice, he'd been infected with that spark in her green eyes, and his feelings for her had never stopped...

Total honesty? His desire for Anna was growing deeper...and it was not going to go away.

"We're landing, aren't we?" Anna asked, sleepily. Stretching and pulling herself into a sitting position, she gripped the arm rests. The turbulence was getting stronger, and the plane was pitching from side to side.

Anna looked at Daisy, the experienced world traveler, who was fast asleep, leaning against the window, an eye pillow covering most of her tiny face.

"How can she sleep through all of this shaking?" Anna asked him.

He patted her arm. "We'll be down soon. Just hold on, lady."

Anna gave him a worried look. She turned around, and peeked through the space between the seats at their daughters.

"How are they doin' back there?" He asked her.

"Looks like they're finally sleeping. But their belts are on," she whispered in a low voice. She slipped her arm under his, and held onto him as the plane rocked, dipped and then turned for the approach to Logan airport.

He couldn't wait any longer. He unbuckled his seat belt, hoping to make a quick trip to the bathroom before they landed.

"Sir, you'll have to keep your seat," a uniformed stewardess said sharply as she passed by them. "We're landing now."

He flashed her his best apologetic look. "I'm sorry, but it's kind of an emergency," he said, putting on his best "be nice, no matter how rude people are to you" mask.

She looked at Anna's arm resting on his with obvious disapproval, and she rolled her eyes. She spoke to him as if he were a child who was misbehaving. "Well, I'm sorry, *sir*, if you're having some kind of a *problem*, but you'll have to wait until we touch down."

He felt Anna's body react. She unsnapped her belt and was leaning forward, starting to stand up. He knew she was about to say something to the departing woman. Abe squeezed her arm firmly, and nudged her back into her seat.

"It's not worth it" he said. "I'll be fine. I can wait."

Chapter 45 ❋ Emily

Barely able to open her eyes enough to keep looking for her pajama bottoms, Emily rummaged through her suitcase.

"J, I can't find my..." and then she found them, rolled up, under a sweater. Steph had told her that packing clothes in a ball made more room. Emily wished that Steph had come, too. They would have had fun. But, she admitted, J was really great company. J made jokes about everything—and, well, sometimes they were a little bit rude and maybe even crude, but J was fun to be around.

On the plane, Jaheen had told Emily all about her plans to train for the Olympics. It sounded like a lot of hard work, and Emily had started to wonder if skating was the right sport for her. Maybe next semester she would try to learn the violin.

J was already sleeping in the other big bed. She and J had insisted on sharing a room together, but they'd only gotten their way because Daisy had agreed to take the room next to them, the room that shared a door with theirs—"just in case..." her mother had said.

In case of what? Emily didn't understand. What could go wrong, here, in a fancy hotel downtown, in Montreal? She remembered the threats to her mother and Abe because he was colored back in Atlanta, and she shivered. How could people be so mean? Abe was a very nice man. She was glad that they were far away from there, and they were safe now. People were nicer here in Canada.

Emily yawned, and snuggled under the fluffy white hotel blankets. Tomorrow would be a wonderful day…eating a big, yummy breakfast in the hotel, hanging out with J in the afternoon, and then watching her mother in her first ice show! She was so glad her father was a million miles away, in New York City.

Chapter 46 ❊ Abe

Abe stepped into the marble-walled shower. As tired as he was, he wanted to feel hot water wash over his sore cheek, and soothe his cramped muscles. Holding in his emotions, and sitting so close to Anna in the small seat for so long, had worn him out. He needed to get a good night's sleep—and he doubted that would be a problem tonight.

Scenes of their arrival in Montreal flashed through his mind. The expansive array of lighted city buildings that he'd seen from the limousine window seemed like two American cities put together. Many of the buildings were a century or more old.

He'd never been to Europe, but he'd always wanted to go. There was so much history to experience by touring foreign cultures. But Georgie didn't want—He stopped himself. No more thinking about her, or his marriage now. He planned to take care of that in the morning. Tomorrow was honesty day. He would call her, say his piece, and he would end it. His marriage was over.

He looked down at his soft penis, watching the soap and water dripping down from it. How had he used his dick? For pride? Power? Out of guilt? He was ashamed about the way he'd acted with women in the past—and about staying with Georgie, long past the time when his feelings for her had gone.

He wanted a different future. He vowed that the next time he shared himself with a woman, it would be something special, and he would wait—for as long as it took—to find the love that he craved.

Stepping out of the shower, he wrapped his body in a huge monogrammed bath towel, and walked through the living room, to the windows. He felt like an emperor, surveying his empire, as he stood, looking down at the sleeping city below. It took his breath away. Lights blinked in shop windows. Churches and buildings glowed from colorful ground lighting. The massive scale of it all made him feel small and humble, and suddenly, he felt very much alone. He wanted to share this amazing view with…

His eyes went, almost automatically, to the door that adjoined his suite with Anna's. He could hear her bathtub running. He was glad the passage was locked from both sides, because he didn't trust himself right now. He heard her humming, and all he could think about was her, in the bathtub…the water lapping against her freckled skin, caressing every part of her body…

But she needed him to be strong right now. She didn't need him to upset her any more than she already was. He understood her fear of performing tomorrow night, and, truth be told, he was starting to feel some doubts about it, too.

Were they as crazy now, as they were the day they'd met? Could they really pull off professional performances for the next three nights?

He wasn't worried about the opening number—where all of the skaters performed together, like an Olympic opening ceremony—at the beginning of each show. He *was*

257

concerned about their dance act, where they would have six minutes on the ice—alone, in front of a sold-out crowd of nearly a thousand people.

Daisy had reassured them that they were ready. He hoped Daze knew what she was talking about. He and Anna were still having some problems with parts of their act. Some practices had seemed to go great, and others just didn't flow…Their best performances, in his opinion—and Anna's—were when Daisy allowed them to choose their own music, and "do their thing," as Daisy said, whenever she turned them loose after an hour of classical work.

But he was grateful to Daisy. She was a top-notch coach, and she'd become a good friend, too. But friendship aside, she demanded a lot from them, and both he and Anna had grown into strong, skilled skaters under her expert instruction. He looked in the mirror as he pulled on his pajamas, and he slapped his gut. He'd never been so fit and trim before.

Anna looked terrific, too; she was slender, and all muscled up, but no one could tell, because she still always wore baggy clothes. And when she was tired, she made mistakes, and when she was anxious, she *really* lost her concentration. He was afraid that she was facing both of her biggest challenges tomorrow. She was both tired and anxious, and that was a worrisome combination.

How could he help her? He wondered.

Chapter 47 ❈ Anna

Someone was banging on her door. Anna knew it was Bill.

Go away!

The pounding continued. She sat up in bed, her head swimming with confusion. She had no idea what time it was, or even where she was. She knew she was awake, but the knocking continued, and then she realized what was happening: She'd been dreaming. This was her first day in Montreal—and—rehearsal! Oh no! What time was it?

She ran to the door, and opened it to find Daisy and the girls waiting in the hall.

"Am I late?" she asked in a panic.

"No, dear, but you did miss a wonderful breakfast," Daisy said, ushering the girls into Anna's room. "It's only eleven. We need to be out on the ice by noon, though, so, it's time to get cracking."

Anna gave Emily a quick hug and a kiss, and she sent a smile and a wave to Jaheen. Daisy walked to the window and threw the full length curtains wide open.

"Do you want me to order you something from room service?"

"Um, no. Thanks. I'll grab something downstairs. Is Abe up yet?"

"Haven't seen him, either. But I'd better get him going, too. I'll bring you a bagel."

The girls ran over to the window, and Anna followed behind them. Snow was falling outside, and the scene below them was like a picture from a book of fairy tales.

"Wow!" the girls said together, and looked at one another, laughing at the coincidence.

"It's magical, isn't it?" said Anna.

They stood quietly, staring at the snow-covered buildings. There was a church with a round stained glass window, and many old buildings of varying heights. Many were made of gray stone. A few modern shaped-structures rose up between them. The city followed a river, which seemed to expand into the horizon, without an end in sight.

"It looks like a giant snow globe," Emily whispered.

"Yeah," said Jaheen. "It doesn't look real."

Anna put her arms around both girls.

"I couldn't be happier, sharing all this—this trip—with you girls."

"Happy new year, mom."

"Thanks, sweetie!" she squeezed Em tightly with one arm.

"Ah, happy new year…from me too," said Jaheen shyly.

And Anna squeezed Jaheen into a light hug with her other arm. It felt good, hugging Abe's daughter. It made her feel closer to him, and, she thought with surprise, that she was really starting to like her. She was quite outspoken, and maybe a little over-confident, but she was bright, and witty—and probably a good match for shy little Emily.

"Thanks, J. I wish that all of our dreams come true this year!" Anna said smiling.

Chapter 48 ❀ Abe

A man answered. Did he dial the wrong number?

"Ah...Hello. I was looking for..." he took a breath. "Is Georgie Brown there?"

"Yeah. Hold on."

He recognized Georgie's voice in the background, and then there was talking, between Georgie and the man who had answered the phone, but Abe couldn't understand what they were saying. He was pretty sure that the guy was Joe.

"This is Georgie Brown. How can I help you?"

"It's me," Abe said.

"Abraham!" He could tell she was more than a little surprised. "Is Jaheen...?"

"J's fine. Who's there with you?"

"Ah, it's just Joe. You know, Joe—Joe Johnson—my campaign manager."

"And your lover, too. Am I right?"

Georgie was silent. He could almost see shock on her face. He waited, thinking about angry things he could say: Guess what, Georgie? It's your good old hubby Abe—you know, your wimpy-ass husband who never stands up for himself? The one who never talks to you about what's really going on? Well, that guy is history...He's quitting the bitch-wife and her boyfriend forever...

"Georgie, it's over. I'm done." He said simply.

"Abraham—"

"Tell Mr. Johnson congratulations. He's got you all to himself now."

"Ab—"

"Georgie. Get a lawyer."

And he hung up the phone.

There was a knock at the door. He ignored it. The knocking wouldn't stop. He went to the door. Still fuming, he almost shouted. "Who's there?"

"It's me, Abe. Your trainer? Open up."

He unlocked the dead bolt, and Daisy pushed her way in, and he moved aside.

Her strength and her determination, for such a little lady, always amazed him.

"You only have a few minutes to get ready. Here." She handed him a brown bag. "Still in pajamas?"

"Yeah, well…I—"

"We've got a lot to do today, Abe. Rehearsals, costume fittings, make-up…Get dressed."

He looked at her, holding the brown bag. He was still feeling wild inside, almost light-headed. He'd just ended it with Georgie—the wife from hell! He was free! It was exhilarating. Daisy looked at him like he was nuts, and he didn't blame her.

"Abe? Are you—" she said, backing up, a look of alarm on her face.

He laughed, and grabbed her into a hug.

"I'm free, Daze!"

"Yeah. That happened a hundred and fifty years ago, Abe."

"No! I just told Georgie that I wanted out—I'm getting a divorce!"

"You're kidding."

"Oh no. I'm dead serious. I'm done with her, and I can't tell you how many times I've wanted to tell her to go to hell."

"So you pick today—the most important day of your skating career, to divorce your wife?"

That set him back. He hadn't thought about that. Not good planning on his part.

"Terrible timing, Abe. I wish you would let me know about these kinds of things. Do you know how stressful it is to end a marriage?" She was tense when she came in, but now she was visibly upset. He knew she was just trying to help. He cared a lot about Daisy, and he was sorry he was doing this to her. She was under a lot of pressure, too, he suddenly realized.

"You're right, Daze. I should have picked a better time."

"Damn straight." She shook her head. "But…what's done is done. Now, can you put your *divorce* on the back burner, and get your ass ready for a practice session in an hour?"

"Sure thing. I'll be ready. Meet you in the lobby in fifteen minutes."

She looked at him with a grim smile, as she stopped before opening the door. "Abe, I'm really glad that you're doing something that's gonna make you happy. But I'm serious. Don't even *think* about this again until Sunday night—after we're finished here."

He nodded.

"And one more thing. Don't tell Anna. She's got enough on her mind. Okay?"

He nodded again, and she was gone.

263

Chapter 49 ❅ Jaheen

Jaheen and Emily sat in box seats that were reserved, just for them. Daisy's name was taped to each chair. The expo center arena had been converted to the biggest ice rink that Jaheen had ever seen. It was very cold in the building, like it was everywhere else in Montreal. Just sitting there thrilled her so much that she was shaking with excitement—and to keep warm.

"Look at that!" Emily screeched, pointing to the towers and poles of metal riggings that were being erected to hold the stage lights. "This place feels like heaven on earth."

"Hmm." Jaheen didn't know anything about heaven, but she agreed, "Yeah, wow!"

"And would you look at all of those seats, J?" Emily breathed, as she waved her arms up around at the huge open ceiling. "The last rows are so high, I can't believe people can see *anything* from up there!"

"Daisy said they're all sold out—mostly to see the featured solo skater, I think. She's from Canada, and she's been in the Olympics. Daisy knows her trainer," Jaheen said feeling proud to know Daisy. She added, "People will pay to see me skate someday, too."

"They will, J." said Emily. "You're really good. You're in the best in our class." Jaheen liked that Emily listened to her, and she didn't argue with everything she said—like Emily's friend Steph did. Emily was easygoing, but she was smart, and nice, too, Jaheen thought. She liked that she and Em were friends now.

"Thanks" Jaheen said. As she looked over to smile at Em, she noticed Emily was frowning, and staring at her mother.

"What's wrong?"

"My mom looks really nervous. I'm kinda worried about—"

Jaheen cut her off, and touched her arm. "Worrying doesn't help, Em. My dad will help her out. He's the greatest. They'll do fine."

Chapter 50 ❄ Abe

Abe and Anna waited in the dress rehearsal line-up with all the rest of the skaters in the show. Everyone wore the special long white tunics that had been given to them by the show managers for the opening number. Colorful flags from each skaters' home country were sewn on the backs of them.

Coaches were standing along the barrier in the warm-up area, watching, as their skaters stood at attention, ready to enter at the signal—which was the first musical strains of the Canadian National Anthem.

The show choreographers had passed out maps of the arena that indicated where skaters would stand, wait, and then perform a short routine together. Abe held their set of instructions in his hands carefully, and he reviewed them one more time, just to be sure of everything they had to do. He was as in awe of the event as Anna appeared to be, and he had to work hard, to concentrate.

The music started and he stuffed the papers down inside his sweater. He took Anna's hand, and they followed along behind a much younger looking couple, who were so thin and supple, they seemed like a set of joined pipe cleaners. Abe was feeling his age. He was sure he was one of the oldest members of the show.

Abe pulled Anna toward him, to slow her down, and they did a quick spin together.

"Hey, relax!" he said to her. "You feel like a piece of wood!"

"Sorry," she said mouthed to him quietly, but her eyes were as wide as dinner plates. She was worrying him.

The music made it hard to hear, or to say, much of anything at all. Someone was yelling through a bullhorn at a group of children carrying a banner, and the overhead speakers squawked with electronic sounds. The loud word: "testing" blasted into the song, causing Anna to jump whenever it happened.

Abe spun her around again, grabbing her waist and guiding her into a few warm up steps and turns, which seemed to calm her down a little, but her face was still frozen in concentration.

"Hey, this is Canada...where are the Mounties?" he yelled, grinning down at her, hoping to tease her into relaxing. She gave him an eye roll.

The entire production had halted while the sound system was being repaired. He was still trying to coax some life out of Anna when the slender pair approached them.

"Allo!" said the young man with a smile. "Da two yu skate—togeder—here?" he asked, his French probably far better than his English, Abe guessed.

"Yes, we do a dance number. We're sixth—after you, I think," Abe answered.

"Ah, yes," the man said. He reached out his hand to Abe, and again to Anna. "Goot! We welcome you! Deez is Johanna. I am Jon," They shook hands all around.

"Best luck!" Johanna said.

"Yes...or as the English say: break the leg! No?" Jon added, grinning, as they skated back to their spot.

Abe smiled. He felt accepted by this couple—feelings that were new to him at a white event. He was enjoying mixing with people from all over the world. He was accepted here, in spite of his color. He was pleased about his good-bye call to Georgie. He was holding Anna's hand. Everything was going his way, and he was sure that he must be the happiest guy in town.

He couldn't wait to tell Anna his news about getting divorced. Forget what Daisy said, he didn't think he could make it through the weekend if he couldn't share his excitement with his friend…with his…Anna.

Chapter 51 ❀ *Anna*

Anna was in awe of the level of composure that she'd seen in the other performers during the rehearsal earlier. She pulled Daisy aside after Abe had left to take the girls out for a snack. Anna had been too nervous to even think about eating anything.

"Daze, how the hell do these people stay so calm? Look at them! Everybody is just walking and talking, like they were—they were at home, in their own backyard!"

Daisy had smiled at her with her usual wise expression, and she said, "They're more nervous than they look—believe me. They're acting cool, most of them, but everybody's keyed up before a performance, Anna, you can bet on that."

"I would think that's so, Daze...It's good to be jazzed up before you go out there, isn't it?"

"Of course." Daisy nodded. "But being too jazzed up is a problem, too—."

"Don't I know it," Anna interrupted.

Daisy touched her arm. "Anna, dear. What have I been telling you about pre-performance thinking?"

"You say to 'visualize' the dance by running it completely through, in my head, one time, and then trust my body—and give myself over to the music."

"Perfect. So what's your question?"

Anna just shook her head. "I have no more questions. Thanks, Daze. See you later."

"Okay. But be back for your make-up and costume fitting session at four, okay?" Daisy called to her as she walked away. "And drink some water!"

Anna waved at Daisy, and kept walking. She checked her watch. It was two thirty. She had to move. In two hours, she would be stuffed into some stupid costume, and they would do stuff to her hair and face. Ridiculous. Bill was right. This was stupid.

Why had she agreed to try to do this crazy thing—in front of so many people?

She wandered through the endless halls of the expo hall. She couldn't stop or sit down. She sipped her water, and listened to coaches and skaters as she passed by them. They were talking about simple, fun things, like seeing the sights in Montreal, and going to the after-party.

She weaved through the tunnels, and came out on the other side of the rink. From there, she saw the children practicing on the ice. Even the kids were acting like they skated in these kinds of shows all the time.

What was wrong with her?

She felt so very different from everyone here, and so out of place. Not one person seemed to be as nervous as she was. And now, it was nearly time to get into a costume—like a performing circus animal.

She returned to the staging area, and waiting for her appointment with a make-up "consultant" near the dressing rooms. Women and children milled around, and everyone—except Anna—seemed to have something funny to say to someone else. She felt all alone, sitting there, waiting…

"Anna Smithson."

Finally! Thank God! Anna had been seriously considering asking Daisy to take her to the nearest emergency room. She was growing so close to full-blown panic, she'd thought she'd faint. At the hospital they could admit her as a mental patient, and send her to the nut ward, where the only way to cure her would be to forbid her to skate—ever again!

"Hello, Anna!" said a beautiful young woman with flaming red hair and glowing green eyes. "I'm Colleen. Glad to know ya," she said, in a strong Irish brogue.

Some of Anna's anxiety started to melt into curiosity. "Hello," Anna replied.

"Well now, ar ya ready for yer transformation?" There wasn't a hint of sarcasm in Colleen's soothing voice, and Anna found that just being around her was calming her down. The woman pointed to a barber's chair at a nearby make-up table that was partially hidden behind a curtain. When Anna didn't move, Colleen took her by the hand, and Anna followed her, feeling like a little girl going to see the dentist for the first time.

Anna sat in the chair, and Colleen pulled the curtain around them. Anna watched her move confidently and make a professional appraisal, running her fingers through Anna's hair, and examining her face with her eyes. Anna watched in the mirror, her hands gripping the side of the chair.

Anna nodded, sending up a weak smile. "My father was Irish...and so am I. You're..."

"Yep, I hail from the Emerald Isle, I do...from the North," she said, extending her hand. "Aye, Daisy sent ya ta me. Said I would be the best one to help ya. I have the same kinda wig!" She laughed and pulled at her own curls.

Anna smile grew a little more confident, but her embarrassment at having her appearance being evaluated by a professional nagged at her. It must have shown in her face.

"Donya worry, lass. They're *all* a bunch a ducklin's out there, but tonight, *they'll all be swans*—thanks ta the likes of us!" She giggled, and waved her arm toward the rink.

"I really appreciate you being so patient with me, Colleen....It's very nice to meet you. It's me—you know, I just don't have a lot of—" Anna's voice trailed off, but Colleen seemed to know what she meant, and the woman's kindness was starting to melt her resistance a little more.

"So, now, let's take a serious look *tagether*, 'n see what we can do...okay?"

"Okay...go ahead, and do whatever you can. I'll trust your judgment," Anna shook her head, feeling more like an ugly duckling being sent to a slaughterhouse.

"Darlin,' me an the Lord, we kin work miracles. Besides, you're a pretty girl, so don be sellin yerself sa short!"

"I could use a miracle," said Anna chuckled, biting her lip. But in spite of herself, and she started to feel better. She leaned back into the chair, looked away from the mirror, and she surrendered to whatever might lie ahead for her—for her makeover, and for her first public performance.

Chapter 52 ❋ Abe

Abe paced around the folding chairs that lined the door to the women's dressing rooms, waiting for Anna to emerge. What the *hell* could be taking so long? He had been dressed and ready in *twenty minutes*. Anna had been in there for almost *two hours*! He hoped that she was all right…and she hadn't gotten sick or something.

He wasn't the only man who was standing around, looking impatient, but he'd seen at least three couples come and go while he'd been there. Daisy had taken the girls back to the hotel, and to help them get dressed up for the evening performance.

Performance? Their first public *trial* was more like it. His nerves were getting to him, and he tried everything he could remember to do to loosen up that Daisy had taught him. He tried picturing the performance in his head. He couldn't concentrate enough to do that. Damn! He knew if he couldn't focus better than that, they would both go down in flames tonight.

He saw another woman walking out. She reminded him of Anna. Same hair color, but…

"Holy sh…" Abe said out loud, without thinking. He was stunned. "Anna?"

Anna smiled at him meekly, twisting her lip to one side, and biting it like she always did, when she was feeling shy and insecure.

"Well?" she asked him with a grin.

"Damnation, woman…" Abe stared at her, trying to find Anna's real face under the heavy make-up, and to absorb how downright beautiful she looked—like some TV actress. Her eyes were lined with black pencil, and, what was that…? False eyelashes? Her pretty green eyes, shadowed with sparkling purple colors, seemed to pop right out of her face. Her hair had been cut again, even shorter this time, and each curl was plastered into place, like a wig. Was that glitter on her cheeks, too? Wow!

His eyes moved up and down her body. Her all-white, form-fitting costume looked like a sexy bathing suit with a short skirt. Her shapely, muscled legs filled the white tights. The white top had tiny diamonds on it that caught the light, whenever she moved. And the long silky sleeves showed off her long arms, making her look like—a kind of beautiful ballerina.

Abe almost needed to sit down; his knees were shaky. "You look—you look *fabulous!*"

"Thanks you!" She bowed. "So do *you*! Look at you— you're so much the handsome one!" she smiled, looking him over. She raised her perfectly outlined eyebrows at his tuxedo-tights that flared out at the bottom over his skates, and she whistled at him.

Maybe it was the make-up, or the outfit, but she seemed a lot more confident and much happier than she was just two hours ago. What the *hell* did they *do* to women in there? He chuckled at the idea that Canadians used some kind of magic wand on Americans who wanted makeovers.

He stifled an impulse to grab her and hug her, but he just wanted to stand back, and keep looking at her. This was big change from the jeans and big sweaters he'd always seen her wearing. Once again, she reminded him of the doll on his Grandma's mantle. But Anna was far more beautiful…

"Well, now that we *look* like professional skaters, all we have to do is *act* like we are!" He was happy to hear her joking. That was a very good sign, he thought.

But his own nerves were nibbling at his gut. Like that glass doll, Anna was fragile, and he knew it. He had to have only one purpose now: he had to help her, and protect her from breaking tonight. He checked the clock overhead. "Need a snack, or a drink before we warm up?" He asked her, collecting himself, putting on his parent mask.

"I drank all of my waters. But, no, for once, I am *not* hungry," she said with a grin.

"Me neither. Daisy said to start warming up at seven, and it's about six-fifty. Are you ready?"

"No."

"Anna, I'm not kidding…are you *really* okay? Before you were…"

"I'm fine. Really. I'm fine now…and I'm with you. Together—we can do this!"

He looked at her, her big eyes full of trust and hope—and willingness." He couldn't let her down…and he hoped that he wouldn't let her down—now, or ever…

Chapter 53 ❀ *Jaheen*

Jaheen's heart was beating in her throat. There he was! Her father! Out there, in front of the *whole world*!

Their seats were only two rows behind the rink's barrier, so she could see the smiles on the skaters' faces. She'd watched each one as they went by, during the opening ceremonies. Her dad was the only Negro man in the show! He looked tall and strong in his long black skating pants, and the big American flag on top of his tuxedo jacket.

She was fascinated by the group of mostly Asian children who were the first to enter the rink. They were from a skating club in Montreal, the program said, and they were carrying banners for the opening, and then they would be collecting the flowers that the audience threw on the ice after each of the skaters performed. There were two dark-skinned boys in the group, too, she noticed. One who could have been…maybe Spanish? They made another round. No way! One boy was a *Negro!*

"Em, Em, look! That boy's black!"

"Really? Where?"

"Look, there he is!"

Emily's eyes followed Jaheen's outstretched arm.

"Wow…He is! That's great!" Emily said with surprise.

She smiled wide. Just seeing the boy, she instantly felt like she was a part of something…like she wasn't a total outsider…She wanted to tell Emily about how good she felt, but she didn't know how. Emily would never know how it felt to be so different. Maybe she would try to talk about it later, when they were alone, in their room. They'd shared some stuff about family life on the plane, and Emily seemed to hate it when her parents argued, too, so maybe...

Jaheen had been so busy analyzing the boy skater—and tracking her father—that she hadn't looked very closely at Emily's mother. On the second time around the arena, they slid to a stop, nearly in front of their box. Who was with her dad? That *couldn't* be Em's mom!

But it was. Mrs. Smithson's wild red hair was cut and fixed into a pretty style—with glitter in it! She always dressed in clothes that were too big for her, so Jaheen had no idea she had such a slim figure—and very pretty legs, too. Real skater's legs! Jaheen stared at her father holding Em's mom's hand, and she poked Em in the ribs.

"Look at your mom!" she said excitedly, "she looks *really cool—like a dancer!*"

The music had finished and the skaters turned toward the center of the rink.

"I know...it doesn't even look like her..." Emily whispered.

"Yeah." Jaheen glanced at Emily, wondering how to help her friend get over the shock of seeing her parent as a person—just like she was doing. Seeing her father out there brought up so many feelings—Jaheen was afraid for him, and proud for him at the same time.

"Well, I can't believe that's my dad, either. He looks like—like a penguin in that outfit!" Emily giggled a little at that, and Jaheen felt glad. She laughed nervously, too. Daisy arrived, and sat down next to them.

"It's really something to see—and to remember, isn't it girls?" Daisy said to them.

Jaheen nodded, not taking her eyes off of her dad.

"You should be proud of your parents," Daisy added, her tone was serious, and, turning toward the arena, she said. "I am. They've worked hard for this moment."

Suddenly the house lights went off, and the spotlight lit the Canadian flag, following it as it rose high up in the air. It was followed by flags from several other countries, including the United States' flag.

Jaheen felt a thrill ripple through her, at the sight of her American flag. She, Emily and Daisy stood up together in the dark, and that same sense of belonging to something bigger than just herself, her family, and even her country, came over her again. She wondered if this was what the Olympics would be like—people joining together for the love of their sport, no matter what country you were from, and no matter what color your skin was.

Chapter 54 ❀ Anna

Anna stood next to Abe on "deck," in the ally leading to the entrance gate of the main arena. They were the next pair to perform. She tried to follow Daisy's advice, and focus on picturing the sequences of their dance number, but her mind would stop whenever she thought about the crowd watching her.

Daisy had come down from the stands to direct their warm-up, and she'd focused on going over a couple of tricky spots. They hadn't gone through the whole thing since yesterday, and that had been done without the music. Anna needed music, and she'd felt awkward without it. She'd even tripped and fallen during the warm-up, and her right knee was starting to swell a little. She hid it now, behind her left leg, so Abe wouldn't see, but the soreness was getting worse, and the muscle tension was creeping up into her thigh.

Daisy's final hug and encouraging words were slipping away...Instead, the critical voices in her head were starting to take over. They teased her—sounding like her father and his friends, taunting her, telling her that she couldn't skate good enough...that she wasn't tough enough...

She tried talking to herself like she would talk to Em. *The opening session had gone fine, so this dance part will go fine, too.* But, the critical voices said that she'd been sharing the rink with other skaters, and no one had been looking at *just her*...like they would be now.

Then she distracted herself by watching their new friends, the pair from France, who were still performing in the arena to the theme from the ballet, *Swan Lake*. She heard a rippling of applause as the couple completed a long, low spiral under the muted blue spotlights.

Anna immediately compared the French couple were doing with the snappy dance moves that she and Abe were planning, and she felt sick inside. Why had she agreed to do this? What had she been thinking? She wondered how the audience was going to react to their choice of pop song— covered by a famous black American female soul artist. She started to regret not taking Daisy's advice; she should have chosen Daze's classical music! And it was too late now to change it!

She felt Abe squeeze her hand. She looked up at him, and instantly knew why she was doing this. Electricity flowed from his warm eyes and energized hers. Even in the darkness, she felt his care and concern for her. He smiled at her and shrugged, but kept hold of her hand, rubbing it gently with his free hand.

"Are you okay?" he whispered.

She held his eyes with hers, as she smiled, and nodded slightly.

"It's not too late to cancel, if you're not ready…" He said it with such intensity, that she knew he meant every word.

"No…I'm fine," she said, and squeezed his hand. "Ready—*Ice Man?*"

His grin grew, and he winced, and she could tell his still-healing cheek bone hurt him. His grip tightened around both her hands, "Yep, Ice Lady…let's dance!"

Chapter 55 ❀ Abe

The house lights came on. Abe heard the announcer thanking the previous skaters, and then he and Anna were immediately introduced, in the way that they had wanted to be, in honor of Anna's mother, and to recognize Abe's full name: "...the American pair of ice dancers from Atlanta, Georgia, Abraham Lincoln Brown, and Anna Margaret Smithson."

The spotlight nearly blinded him, as he led Anna out on the ice, waving his free arm in response to the welcoming applause. Anna did the same, but he felt her moving a little more slowly than usual, so he adjusted his speed to accommodate her.

They reached their center mark, and waited in the silence, standing as still as statues, while the child skaters finished collecting the flowers that had been tossed on the ice for the last pair. The delay seemed like one of the longest moments of his life. He didn't dare look down at Anna. He just squeezed her hand, and kept his eyes focused, as Daisy had taught him to do, high above the crowds.

As the children passed out of the rink in a single file, one of them slipped fell on the ice, and the "oohs" echoed from the spectators. The child scrambled onto his feet, and the crowd roared and applauded. He could feel Anna glance over at him, but he didn't move a muscle.

The lights dimmed, and the intense bright spot hit them again, as the musical introduction to their song began. He moved out too quickly, pulling Anna off balance, and he had to strong-arm her, to keep her from falling. He apologized to her in his mind.

They began the first part of their dance with a simple backward-forward-facing samba, and he felt himself start to relax into the rhythm of the beat. Anna seemed to be doing all right. She was following his lead, but she was moving very deliberately, and with some hesitation, as if she was afraid to fall. He knew he was moving with less speed and energy than he would have liked to do, but he decided to take his cues from Anna, to play it safe.

He also began to realize that they would not remain in sync with the song if they slowed down too much, so he began to calculate what moves he could cut short. He tried to catch Anna's attention, but she seemed to be concentrating very hard, following some sort of inner map, and she wasn't looking at him. At one point during their sit-and-spin sequence, he saw her counting with her lips moving.

Anna seemed afraid to feel the music. He wasn't sure what the problem was; her timing was off, but she was still holding her own. He took the lead for each and every segment, and she followed him, mechanically, and shadow-like. He knew that he was doing most of the work, but that was all right with him. As they neared the final chorus—he relaxed, knowing that they were just about home free. The song was almost over. He could finish any time now, and they would be okay.

The final notes of the song ended, and they halted with a slow turn very nearly on their center mark. Not too bad, he thought, hearing the applause erupt and echo into the air. It was far from thunderous, but it was strong!

They both took their bows, making a full circle, in order to thank each section of seats. He was smiling, and swallowing big gulps of air. He raised Anna's hand, and pointed to her, and the applause increased in volume, just a little. He saw that she looked pale, and that she was breathing heavily, too...but she was smiling. And he was too. *She'd made it through her first performance!*

As they skated toward the gate, a feeling of pure joy washed over him when he saw Jaheen and Emily jumping up and down in the box, waving and calling to them. Anna was looking up at them, too, and waving at their girls. *Their girls*, he thought happily.

The child skaters sped past them, collecting the flowers—not nearly as many as they'd gathered for the last pair, maybe, but they were for just him—and Anna—and Abe was grateful for each and every one. As he pulled Anna through the access gate, Daisy grabbed them into a long, tear-filled bear-hug.

The black child on skates approached them, and handed Abe an armful of flowers. Abe shook the boy's hand, and thanked him. Abe realized that this was the first time anyone had ever given him flowers. He thought about the little black boy, and he was especially moved, because this child, like himself, probably loved to skate—and he would probably have a long road ahead of him, just because of his skin color.

Abe hugged Daisy and Anna. And, as they whispered congratulations to one another, Abe felt someone tugging at his tux. The little black boy stood next to him again, gripping a rolled-up program in his small hand. When he asked Abe to autograph it, Abe felt his public mask melt away. His act was finally over, and he could no longer hold back the tears.

Chapter 56 ❄ Emily

During their fancy Italian dinner in the elegant hotel dining room, Emily had been stealing peeks at her mother between bites of the best ravioli she'd ever tasted. Emily's curiosity was driving her crazy.

How could make-up change anyone *that much*?

She was absolutely fascinated by the difference that the make-up had made in her mother's appearance. Maybe it was because all of her freckles were covered over. Emily wasn't sure that she liked that part, but the way her mom looked made her want to try some make-up on herself.

On the plane, she and Jaheen had talked about trying to wear mascara and lipstick, and now, after seeing how pretty her mom's eyes were, she decided that she wanted to try some eyeshadow, too.

Her mother gave her "the look" that mothers gave kids, when they were going to ask: "What?" So Emily knew it was coming.

"Okay, now, Em. Out with it. Why are you looking at me like that?"

"Mom, that make-up—it makes you look so...*different!*"

Her mother laughed, rubbing her cheeks. "I tried to scrub the stuff off, but I think they used paint, or a special glue, or something..."

Everybody laughed, and Daisy said, "Honey, I said it before, and I'll say it again, now: you looked *stunning*. My friend Colleen is one of the best make-up artists I know."

Daisy looked at Emily, and said, "Make-up is just part of the show, sweetie—just like the costumes and the music. Skaters are kind of like actors, really. People come to see the acts—the spectacle...the glamor...and the skaters have to dress up, to give the audience what they paid to see."

"That's right," Abe added. "Some of those folks spent a hundred dollars or more, for a ticket."

Emily felt her eyes go wide in surprise. "A hundred dollars?"

"Yep," he nodded, biting into a breadstick, and smiling at her. Emily thought that Abe had the whitest teeth of any man she'd ever seen when he smiled. She watched J lean her face in close to her father's. "So where's *your* make-up dad?" J teased, giggling.

Her father laughed again. "It's still there, right here. Can't you see it?" he pointed to his nose. "I'll scrub it off later, secretly at night, like I always do. Didn't you know that I'm really a different color, underneath all this brown stuff?"

Emily saw her mother smile at him. Her mother never smiled like that at her father. Emily felt a little upset about that. She wasn't sure why she felt that way, because Abe was a very nice person—much nicer than her father was.

"Well I think it's silly," Emily announced suddenly, in a too-loud voice, her stomach feeling queasy.

Everyone stopped laughing, and looked at her.

"What I mean is...people should be looking at the skills of the skaters, and not treat ice skating like a fashion show." She felt everyone's eyes on her, and her cheeks got warm.

285

Daisy came to her rescue with her kind, southern accent. "Sweetie, you are so *right!* It would be *great* if that were the case, wouldn't it?" Daisy scanned everyone around the table. "Perhaps you youngsters will see that kind of change come to pass in your lifetime—I know it won't happen in *mine*," Daisy reached out and patted Emily's hand. "Maybe you—and J—and your generation—will be the ones who'll help to make ice skating more of a sport, and less of a fashion show."

Abe said, "I agree, Daze, but knowing history the way I do, I've learned that social change happens very slowly...it can take many generations sometimes...so don't get your hopes up too high, girls."

"Uh huh," her mother nodded in agreement, finishing a bite of tortellini. "You know, it's true...what we did today felt more like acting in a play, than a sports performance." She reached for her water, and took a drink.

Emily wondered why her mom looked more sad than happy.

Abe shook his head. "Ah, but professionals—such as yours truly—and the honorable Mrs. Smithson here—make it look easy...People don't realize that exhibition skating takes a lot of mental concentration and physical conditioning. It's a lot tougher out there than it looks..."

"You can say that again, Abe," said Daisy. She looked at Abe, and stopped him with a raised hand, laughing. "Ah...don't say that again, Abe..."

The waiter interrupted the joking, and cheesecake desserts were passed around the table. Emily watched the adults stir cream into their coffees, while she and Jaheen dug into their desserts.

"There was a black boy in the skating club, wasn't there?" asked J, between bites.

Abe smiled. "Yeah! He even asked me for my autograph!"

"Wow, isn't that *great?* You're a big time role model for him now, Dad. I mean, I hope…in the future, more Negroes will decide to be professional skaters—just because of *you!*" J said, looking at her father with admiration.

"I think so, too, J." Emily's mom agreed. "Having people who believe in you, and help you—encourage you—we all need that sometimes," she said quietly, looking at Daisy, and then at Abe. "That's what got me here, tonight—."

Her mother looked around the table, and she raised her water glass for a toast. "And, speaking of tonight, I want to thank each of you—for helping me to get through my first public performance—such as it was…"

Everyone cheered and clapped.

Emily watched her mother's eyes tear up as she smiled at her, but when her mom looked at Abe, her mother's eyes shined with a brighter light, as if she was sending him some special kind of thanks.

Chapter 57 ❄ Anna

As soon as everyone had said goodnight, and had gone to their rooms, Anna ran down to the lobby gift shop, and bought a scented candle. She was surprised at the variety of items that the hotel carried—from clothing and towels, to alcoholic beverages and snacks. The clerk looked at her oddly, and Anna realized she was still wearing the heavy stage make-up. She'd have to find a way to get the stuff off her face, and the sooner, the better, she thought.

She ran up the back stairs, so no one would see her looking like a clown. Back in her room, she lit the candle, and turned off all the lights in her suite. She filled the tub, and not waiting for the water to reach the top, she slipped her tired body and aching knee into the hot water.

She was sorry that she'd run up five floors' worth of steps. It was just one more thing that she didn't do right today...

Watching the candlelight dance on the white tiles, she replayed her performance over and over in her mind. Abe had done a wonderful job, but what had happened to her?

She had skated like a rag doll. Okay, she had a sore knee, but that hadn't been enough to turn her dance act into—what—a beginner's skating lesson?

To be fair to herself, she *had* actually gone through with it. She'd performed in public, and she hadn't made a *total* fool of herself. But she knew that Abe had saved her ass out there. He'd done all the work, and she'd just followed him around, like a puppy dog tagging along after its mother...

Her face felt flushed, and it wasn't just the hot bath water; she felt *plain stupid*. She should just go tell Abe to find another partner—someone who would make his amazing performances *more amazing*—not *ruin* them.

He didn't need a partner who rode along on the coat tails of his tuxedo—which looked *magnificent* on him—by the way. She was ashamed of the way she'd skated today...and she was ashamed now, because whenever she pictured how attractive he looked, she been feeling hot tingles—down there...

Chapter 58 ❋ Abe

Abe was annoyed with the constant tapping that was coming from the hot water pipes in the wall. Even though the hotel was very elegant, it was very old. If that noise didn't quit, he'd have to call the front desk.

He rolled over and turned up the volume on the bedside radio. The station was playing some of his favorite jazz songs from the forties.

He'd been trying to write a review of textbook for his spring class, but he couldn't concentrate. He kept mulling over tonight's performance.

Something had been very wrong.

It was great that Anna had gone through with performing in public with him. But in all honesty, tonight, she'd only *gone through the motions* of performing.

She'd been able to overcome, what she believed to be, her biggest fear, and that was cool. But why hadn't she been unbelievably happy afterward?

It confused him that she hadn't acted like she'd overcome much of anything tonight. She seemed almost down about her accomplishment...and after all they'd been through together, he'd learned that, if she was not happy, then he wasn't happy, either.

What could he do or say that would encourage her—and help her to realize her success?

The audience seemed to accept them. They had applauded. They had thrown flowers. People here in

Canada seemed to be much more open-minded—compared to people in Atlanta. Daisy had been right. Montreal had been a good place to make their first public appearance...and he had done a terrific job out there.

He should be on top of the world.

So why was he feeling so alone, and so dissatisfied?

He closed his book, and then the answer hit him. It hit him as hard as the floor that had smashed his face in that abandoned warehouse the day they were arrested: Skating was a fantastic thing to do, and he loved it, but skating wasn't everything he wanted. Without Anna, his life wasn't—and would never be—complete. But did she felt the same way about him, too?

He had to find out.

This was not the time, or the place, but soon. He just had to know how she felt about him. And not just as a skating partner, and not just as a friend...

The tapping was growing louder, and, when he turned down the radio, he noticed that the sound was coming from the adjoining door—the door that led to Anna's room.

Chapter 59 ❋ Anna

Anna stood at Abe's door, knocking softly hoping he wasn't asleep. Finally, his side of the door opened, and she saw his look of total surprise.

Always polite and respectful, she noticed that he hadn't looked down at her pajamas. Before she'd knocked, she hadn't stopped to think about how she might look…but now, standing there, in front of him, face-to-face, she was suddenly embarrassed. She was wearing her old, worn-out, two sizes too big pajamas with the faded cat pictures on them.

She backed away, starting to close the door. "Hi, Abe…Ah, I'm sorry…I didn't mean to bother you—"

"Anna, hi," Abe cut her off, moving forward, toward her. "Don't go. You're not bothering me—not at all. Come in"

"Well, okay. I just wanted to talk to you, just for a minute. I know you're tired."

He opened the door wider, and he waved her through it. "I'm fine. Come, sit down." He walked toward the sofa, gesturing for her to follow him, and she did.

She sat down, and he joined her—a full seat cushion away.

"Hey…where's my manners? Would like something to drink—or to eat?"

"Um, no. Thanks. I'm pretty full from dinner. It was very good—didn't you think?"

"It was great. The hotel has great food, but, tomorrow night, I was thinking that maybe we could branch out a little—you know, try one of the French restaurants that Montreal is so famous for."

She could tell that he noticed that her somber mood, and she really wasn't listening.

"What's wrong, Anna?"

He could read her, like a book, she thought.

"I couldn't sleep…"

"Me neither."

"I'm sorry…"

"Don't be. I'll just keep reading that boring history book and…"

"I mean, I'm sorry about tonight, Abe—about the dance. I lost it."

"Hon…Anna, *no!*" he shook his head for emphasis, moving closer to her. "Do *not* apologize to me for tonight. It was a—a triumph—for you, and for me—for Daisy, too. You faced your fear of performing in public, and you…"

"I *blew it*, Abraham, and you know it… I just…followed you around out there. You kept it all together. You led the whole time. If you hadn't, it would have been a total disaster."

He leaned back, and took a deep breath.

She sat back, too, and scratched at one of the cat's ears on her pant leg.

"Anna…It was your *first time!* You had a bad case of stage fright." He took another breath. "And you fell during the warm-up. I know that your knee was sore…I saw you trying to hide it." He spoke gently and quietly, his eyes following her hand that was now rubbing her sore knee.

She wanted to look at him, but she couldn't. They both stared at her knee.

293

She felt in his kindness; it was like medicine she needed. He soothed her nerves and made her feel better, like he always did. Ever since they'd met—ever since the day he picked her up off of the ice, he had been there for her, she thought. But what had she given back? Nothing but a sad performance tonight—a bad acting job. It wasn't fair to him. She'd decided in the tub that she couldn't keep taking from him. It just wasn't right.

"Abe, I quit. You have to find another partner."

He sighed, bit his lip, and looked up at the carvings on the ceiling. "Why, Anna?"

"You have…*tremendous* talent. Daisy says so. Anybody can see it. You could go single. I'm just holding you back." She looked down at one of the cats on her pants, took its whole head in her hand, and squeezed it tightly into her fist.

He was silent for a long time. Then he reached out, and touched the little skate on the necklace he'd given her. She sat still, her shoulders rigid, not knowing what to expect. She wasn't afraid of him. He had her total trust. He held the charm between his fingers and then let it drop. He moved both his hands onto his own knees, gripping them tightly, through his striped pajama bottoms.

"Anna, I have to tell you something" He said slowly, staring at the floor. "I owe you the truth."

She looked at him.

"What?"

"I'm in love with you, Anna" he looked at her, and he repeated, "I'm in love with you, and I have been…for some time…maybe since I first saw you, I don't know…I don't know exactly when it happened…"

She swallowed hard, and she stared into his deep brown eyes. She knew, she had known, and yet, hearing him say the words thrilled her in a new way, as if she'd never thought them before…What he had just said—about loving her—was slowly becoming more real, and joy began to rise in her chest, like a bird flapping its wings, ready to fly out of a cage.

"Oh, Abe…" she said, reaching out to touch his cheek. He didn't move. Her fingers lightly stroked the spots—now covered with make-up—where the bruises and pain he'd suffered were still healing beneath his skin. Injuries and hurt that he'd endured, because of her.

"I love you, too," she said.

Chapter 60 ✳ Abe

"I know you love me, Anna," He shook his head. "But I want you to understand something. I'm *in love* with you."

Anna looked at him, feeling confusion fill her face. "Well now, what's the difference? Love is *love*."

He smiled, and took a deep breath. He knew the difference. But did she? How the *hell* was he going to explain being in love?

He leaned back into the soft cushions, and put one arm around her shoulders.

"Okay…I'll try to explain. You love Emily. I love Jaheen. We both love Daisy, right?"

She bobbed her head in agreement, and she watched him intently. He noticed the dark circles of mascara under her eyes, and against her pale skin, she looked a little ghost-like.

"All right…" he stopped to think. He wanted to be accurate, and precise. It was important that she understood what he was about to explain—or try to explain.

After a long pause, he watched her reactions as he continued, "The kind of love we have for our children will always be there, but when they leave—when leave home and start living their own lives, we're okay with that. Right?"

"Yes," Anna said.

"And the same thing goes for our friends," he said as if he was teaching a child. "They leave us sometimes. Maybe they move away…and we expect that, because they have their own lives to live…"

"I understand. But what has that got to do with the way *I* feel about *you*?"

"I'm getting to that, honey." He liked the sound of his own voice calling her "honey." It was the first time, and he hoped she liked it, too. She was smiling, and that was a good sign.

He took a deeper breath. He was about to take the biggest risk of his life. If she didn't get this part…if she rejected him after she'd heard the whole truth, the truth that had been in his heart so long, he didn't know if he could stand it.

"Being in love—for me is—different. The way I feel about you—it's not like the love I feel for J—or Daisy. I mean, it is, and it isn't. It's different. When I'm with you, *I'm* different. I'm who I *really am*. I'm not acting. I'm not pretending. When you're with me, I never want you to go…" he looked at the ceiling again, he closed his eyes.

He never saw it coming. And when it came, he was taken completely by surprise. He was so used to her grabbing at him, and falling into him, when they skated, that it took a few seconds for him to realize what was really happening.

He felt her strong arms slide behind his shoulders. Just as quickly, she leaned her upper body into his, and she pulled him toward her. She pressed her lips against his with such pressure, he couldn't say a word—or even take a breath. Her mouth was on his, like a tight seal. When he realized what was happening, he opened his mouth, and his tongue slipped naturally into hers. Her grip on his arms lightened, and her lips softened. Her mouth and tongue began to relax, and his hunger for more of her grew inside of him.

They both took deep breaths, taking in air in gasps whenever they could. He held her against him, and tasted the inside of her lips, exploring her mouth, as if he was starving for her, discovering, and savoring her sweet and salty flavors.

The lower half of his body had not yet had time to respond. He didn't care. Only their mouths and her kisses existed, and he had no idea how long they spent kissing. But the emotional and physical demands of their day started to take their toll, and they started to melt down together, nearly exhausted, folding into each other's arms, and leaning against the back of the couch.

He and kissed the top of her fuzzy curls. They smelled of the chemical sprays and the perfumed stuff that women used on their hair. When he could finally talk, he chuckled. "I never expected *that*…Ice Woman, but boy, I'm sure glad—that you—"

She looked up at him, her head on his chest. She was grinning in that sly way he knew and loved so well—the way her eyes crinkled up, and signaled for him to get ready, because she was about to tease him with some corny joke.

"Well, teacher, I just thought that you could—umm, use a little illustration—with your love lesson. So I thought I'd help you out. I may be a *little* inexperienced, but…"

"Ah, well," he laughed, "I *really* liked the way you explain things, lady. I couldn't have said that better myself."

"I *do* love you Abe," she said, slowly and sadly, leaning away from him now, and trying to sit up. "But…you're a married man, and I need to respect that…You know, I've had to act like I was just your friend for so long. It isn't—hasn't been easy…"

"No. It hasn't been easy for me, either—all the acting, the pretending...God, it's been so hard to not tell you how I feel about you." He held onto her, rubbing her arm through the pajama top, and kissed the top of her head again, brushing his good cheek against her hair.

"I'm glad I've been honest—with myself—and with you. But now—now we have to do what's right, and just forget that all of this happened, and go back to the way it was—" She looked up at him again, tears in her eyes, she tried to pull herself away.

"No, we don't. Anna, my marriage is over," he said with conviction. "And I didn't just decide that tonight. I've known it for a while. Georgie's and I have lost whatever it was we had, years ago...And she's with another man now—her manager..."

"What?" Anna glared at him in shock. "She's with...when did you find that out? Did she tell you?"

"She didn't have to tell me. I knew. I didn't want to admit it, I guess. I don't know. But I've...I been with a lot of women, when I was a kid—a teenager—and in my twenties. I know the signs when a woman's been with other guys...but, it's not something I wanted to talk about—or to face. Like you and Bill. It takes time to figure it all out..."

"I know all about that part," Anna nodded.

He reached for her face, and held it to his. "Anna, I want you to know that I've asked her for a divorce. I was going to wait until after we were done here to tell you. You've had enough on your mind...But now..."

Anna was looking at him, staring at him, listening to what he was saying, trying to take in all that he was telling her. "Gee. Abe. My God. Wow..."

He waited. He'd decided that she would have to make the next move. She leaned over and kissed his chin, and

299

then she slumped back onto his chest. She squeezed him tightly. "Oh, Abe." she sighed deeply.

He could tell she was exhausted, and even though he was worn out, too, he didn't want this time with her to end. He wanted to pull her into his bed, and wrap himself around her, and never let her get away from him again.

Chapter 61 ❀ Anna

Anna looked up at Abe. In the half-light, his features were soft with sleep. His warm breath rustled through her hair, and she had never felt so close to any man—to any person—in her life before.

She looked at the clock over the TV. It was almost four in the morning. Her back was sore from lying in one position for so long. Their legs were twisted together. Luckily, she thought, the couch was a wide one.

She hated to wake him, but she was worried his back and legs would cramp up, and that he wouldn't have rested enough, which could hurt his performance—their performance—again—today? Tonight? She groaned. They were going to have to skate again in about twelve hours.

She lightly played with his hair. "Abe, honey...we should get to bed."

"Hmm?" He stirred slightly, and then he jumped, his eyes fully open, but he looked confused, as if he was dreaming.

"I think we need to go to bed—and get some sleep," Anna repeated. "I'm going back to my room."

"Oh. Yeah. What time is it?"

"Around four. Daisy and I can take the girls down for breakfast in a couple of hours, but I'll tell them you have a headache, and then you can sleep in."

"No, you won't."

"What?"

"No more lying, Anna. No more acting and pretending...remember?"

"We'll talk about that later. About what we'll say—what we'll do—about everything. Now, go! Go get some *real* sleep. We have a performance to do tonight—I mean today."

He pulled her mouth onto his. She could feel his smile melting into her own. She relaxed into him, and held him tight. His mouth was warm and soft, and she felt a surge of desire that drove her to want to pull him into her, just as close to her as she could.

"You're not going anywhere," he whispered between kisses.

"Nope," she breathed. "I'm not."

"You'll always be my Ice Woman?" he asked, licking her lips.

"You still want me to stay here, then?"

He rolled his hip and thigh onto hers, and she guessed she had her answer.

Chapter 62 ❀ Emily

Emily thought it was strange that her mother had been so tired this morning, even though she'd slept in so late she'd missed breakfast again. But Daisy had explained that emotions could be draining, and her mother needed extra sleep—to recharge her batteries—and to be ready for tonight's performance.

Emily knew how nervous her mother was about performing, so it made sense that her mom needed more rest. Emily liked Daisy a lot. She was so much nicer than her grandmother, who was about the same age. Why were some old ladies so sweet and understanding, and others, so mean? She'd have to talk *that* over with J, when they had another wild pajama party in their room later.

As she walked along the river with Daisy and J, she thought about how much fun she was having. Last night had been a blast! She and J had stayed up talking and laughing until after midnight, eating the ice cream sundaes that Daisy had sent them from room service. It probably was because of all the sugar, like her dad always said, but they couldn't sleep until Daisy had knocked on their door at one in the morning, and reminded them that they needed to get some rest for their day of sightseeing.

After watching the late morning training session with their parents, Daisy had taken she and J to a pizza lunch, and then they'd went to an amazing art museum in the afternoon. Emily had loved the paintings, and she was now seriously considering becoming a famous artist. The French painter, Paul Gauguin, was by far her favorite. He'd painted tropical scenes with birds and colorfully dressed women from the Pacific Islands. The canvases were so big, they looked like small billboards. With her spending money, she'd bought a poster of his work.

J had enthusiastically approved of her taste in art, agreeing that it was cool that the people in the paintings were not all fat white ladies in old fashioned hats and long dresses.

Now, she, J, and Daisy were walking all the way back, through a park on the river, so they could see more of the city. The store windows were filled with the newest fashions, and were decorated with Christmas trees and holiday lights.

J was chatting about the elegant—and crazy—outfits.

"Look at that cool dress, Em!" J teased, pointing at a red, low-cut cocktail dress on a mannequin. "How would that cute guy in your math class like that one?"

"Ah, no, J, I think that's more *your* style!" She gave J a poke in the ribs, and an exaggerated eye roll in the direction of J's well-developed chest.

"You girls!" said Daisy, pretending to disapprove. But Emily knew Daisy was kidding, and she seemed really pleased with how well the two of them were getting along.

Emily glanced at Daisy, hoping she wouldn't remember J's remark about the boy in her class. She knew her mother and Daisy shared a lot of personal stuff, and she didn't want her mother to know she had become very interested in boys lately.

The wind was coming up, and it was getting colder, so they walked faster, staying together as best they could. They were bumped and squeezed by busy city people who were dressed in long coats, cold weather boots and warm hats.

Emily's nose felt like it was frozen solid. She was happy to see the big electric marquee flashing the times for tonight's show. The front entrance was built from huge slabs of marble stones that had been carved and curved to fit around the high windows. Big flakes of white snow were falling now, and it stuck on the roofs and window sills, like powdered sugar, and it looked like a storybook castle.

The grand entrance hall was beautiful, too. The high wooden beams and hanging lights reminded her of her church, back home in Atlanta. Daisy seemed to notice that she was feeling overwhelmed by everything—and maybe a little homesick—because she reached out and put her arm around her, and hugged her.

"Awesome, isn't it?" Daisy asked.

"How did they ever build a place like this?" Emily asked, as she looked up at the ceiling. Colored flags from different countries hung from the rafters.

Daisy smiled. "The craftsmanship needed to construct these buildings came from European settlers. The French colonized this area—of course, they ran the native Indians off their land—but they brought their culture, and their fine building skills with them."

J asked, "What did they do to the Indians?"

"Ah, that's a dark part of history for most of North America—"

J looked like she was ready to start lecturing them about how people of color were abused—one of the topics that upset her, and really got her talking—but Daisy cut her short. "Time to get up to our seats, girls. I've got to run, and help your folks get ready."

She led them up the ramp to their box, and left them there. Emily sat down, and scanned the warm-up area for her mother. She thought about what Daisy had said about how nervous her mother had been, and she hoped her mom was doing okay.

She was not very concerned about tonight's performance, though, because the second night was supposed to be the same as the first one. All her mom had to do was to repeat last night's performance. People had seemed to like it okay...

But tomorrow night—the third night—was the grand finale. And that *was* going to be very different from the first two shows. Emily figured, that the last night was probably worrying her mom because during the final night's performance, Daisy said that the performers were going to be shown on live television—and there would be ice skating experts commenting on the skaters' performances for the TV audience.

"Won't that be really distracting to the skaters—the idea that people are watching them on TV?" J had asked Daisy.

"You bet it could." Daisy had answered. "But don't worry. We coaches were allowed to supply the details about their programs—so the announcers will use my information. And...your parents are doing very well, so far. By tomorrow night, they'll have their routine down pat. There will be no surprises. They'll do just fine."

Emily wasn't so sure. It sounded awfully scary, knowing that people were talking about you while you were skating—and while you were on TV, too.

"Will we get to see the TV program, Daisy?" she'd asked.

"Oh, yes. There'll be a private screening of the taping after the show for all the skaters and coaches—and their families—right here, in the press room."

Chapter 63 ❋ Anna

Anna was ready. Tonight would be better. She knew what to expect. She was prepared for the shifts in lighting. she understood how spotlights could blind a skater. There were dark spots on the ice, too, where the lights didn't keep up fast enough…and the idea that people were watching her didn't seem as frightening as it had been yesterday—only yesterday? She shook her head. A lot had happened since yesterday! Now, she and Abe were a real pair!

She bent her knee. It still felt tight, and a little sore. Daisy had wrapped it with special tape that wouldn't show through her skin-colored tights. But her knee was the least of her problems. Her thighs ached from lying on the couch all night, twisted around Abe. The thought of them acting like teenagers making out in the back seat of a car made her giggle. It was their big secret, and pretending that nothing had changed between them wasn't easy. She wanted to tell everyone. She was in love. In love with Abraham Lincoln Brown. She felt the pressure of his lips on hers whenever she thought about him, and it sent chills all over her body.

Daisy had noticed something. She was just too damn smart, as Abe had said, after their warm-up. Daisy didn't miss much. Not that they wouldn't tell her, of course, but she and Abe had agreed that this was not the time to discuss their relationship with anyone, so they'd done their best to avoid looking at one another when Daisy, or the girls, were around.

Waiting in their place in line at the gate, Abe leaned toward her and said, "Just keep looking over my shoulder...don't look at my eyes." He cracked a small grin. "And I won't look at you, either. Nothing personal—by the way...you look *terrific!*" His breath on her ear caused her heart to jump.

They shared a last look, and then, as Abe suggested, Anna stared at the sparkles on the collar of his black topcoat.

"Ready?" she asked.

"As ready as I can be—for somebody who slept on the damn couch all night."

She wanted to kiss him right then and there, in front of everyone. But she didn't. She squeezed his hand instead. She took slow, deep breaths, as Daisy had taught her, and she felt herself slip into the still uncomfortable role of a professional performer. Acting like she and Abe were all about the work, and nothing more, she prayed that she wouldn't fail him on the ice tonight. And afterward? She fought her nagging thoughts about that...

The grand entrance fanfare began, and they followed the skaters in front of them, as everyone filed into the rink on cue. The parade was alive with smiling, waving skaters wearing flags.

Anna felt proud to be holding hands with the most handsome, wonderful man she'd ever known. Slowly, she felt herself allowing Abe's feelings for her—and hers for him to sink deeper into her heart. She wondered, as he led her around the arena, how the simple act of kissing could make the idea of love feel so solid, so much more real...And then, determined to not let him down tonight, she went to work.

Chapter 64 ✿ Abe

Abe was beyond happy. He was just about on cloud nine. Confidence flowed through him like a kind of electricity. He had kissed her! And, she had *kissed him first*! What had he done to deserve this—this astounding turn of events?

He stood, as still as stone, next to her, his Ice Woman, holding her hand, in front of a thousand people, waiting for the opening notes to their dance number. Anna was posed in her starting position. She was much more relaxed tonight, he could tell. Her energy level was way higher than it had been last night, even though her knee was still bothering her, and causing her to shorten her stride sometimes.

He felt a twinge from the angry muscles in his back. He knew the pain had come from lying crooked on the sofa for so long. He didn't care. It had been worth every minute.

The strong samba beat began, and they kicked off into slow spins under the spotlight. Even though they were repeating the same program that they had done the night before, he immediately felt a change in the energy between them.

Anna was moving with enthusiasm tonight. She met his leads more quickly. He smiled at the idea that they were a different kind of team now. She was his partner, in every way...

When the lyrics began, he was ready to dance—with his Anna. The song was about love. It was generic, but love themes were all he heard in the upbeat lyrics. It was as if the words were flowing through his blood, pumping from his heart. A few people in the audience were clapping in time with the music. Daisy had been right. This pop song was a pretty good crowd-pleaser, even though it hadn't been his and Anna's first choice.

Anna was looking over his shoulder, but he wanted to look at her. Just one quick look. He couldn't help himself. And when her eyes met his, and he saw her become uncomfortable, and that one second was all it took. He lost his balance, and he tripped. He went down on his right knee, and it hurt like hell.

She helped him up by pulling him around from the side, and he recovered quickly, but not before he heard some "oohs" rumble through the audience. The clapping had stopped, and only the music continued.

The pain in his knee was sharp enough to get, and keep, his attention. He grabbed her waist, and he focused on the sheer mechanics of completing their routine. He kept his facial expression neutral, which, for him was fairly easy. After years of hiding his feelings behind his mask, he was thankful that his acting skills had automatically kicked in to save him.

But he was hurting, and he could tell Anna knew it, too. He allowed her to take over the lead for the final chorus. She compensated for him, and for his loss of power. She pulled him through with her powerful strides, flashing a quick smile at the crowd. She added some extra footwork sequences, and then threw in a few ballet moves, all on her own, just holding onto one of his hands for support.

He was so grateful to her—and proud of her, too.

They finished on time, spinning together slowly, ending simultaneously with the final bars of the music. Falling into each other's arms, they gulped for air.

They bowed to the audience, and they smiled because Daisy had trained them well, and that was how skaters were supposed to end a performance—no matter what had happened.

He knew he'd messed up tonight, and the applause that they were receiving was a gift. But none of that mattered. He knew that the real gift was right there, standing beside him, waving at the crowd, and squeezing his hand, with a smile on her face that was brighter than any spotlight he'd ever seen.

Chapter 65 ❀ Jaheen

The smells of the French restaurant were so delicious, Jaheen thought that they'd used garlic butter to paint the dark wooden walls. Everything glowed with candlelight. The waiters were dressed like penguins, and the kids' menus didn't have prices on them.

Emily was trying to eat French onion soup, but the cheese was sticking to her spoon. Jaheen watched her using a butter knife to try and scoop it off. "I'm gonna have to learn to eat this, if I'm going to live in Paris," Emily laughed.

Everyone chuckled.

Jaheen was enjoying being with these people. She didn't know when it had first started, but she felt that they were becoming like a family—a very weird kind of a family, but they had a fun together, and she wanted this trip to go on forever.

She missed her mother sometimes, but she talked to her every night on the phone. Her mother had seemed a little upset. Maybe she'd felt left out. Jaheen wouldn't blame her if she did—especially since she and her father was having such a good time.

Jaheen thought about the decisions that she and Emily had made on this trip: Emily had decided that she was going to be an artist—go to art school, and live in France. And, Jaheen was determined to live here, in Canada. She couldn't believe that there had been people of different races and colors and cultures skating in the exhibition. She wanted to be a part of a place like that—and not be the only colored skater in Carol's class. She'd felt so alone at the all-white skating club in Atlanta. Now, at least she'd have Em for a friend there...

"Dad, someday I want to skate—and train—here, in Montreal."

Her father looked at her across the bright white table cloth and the shining water goblets, and he smiled. She noticed he was doing that a lot lately—smiling—like he was *really* happy. She liked the change in him.

"I can understand that. It's a beautiful place." He laughed, and took a bite of his cheesecake.

"Oh, Dad! It would be *so cool* to be able to skate with kids—kids that are like me. We could live here, and you would be safe here too, you know, from—"

Her father nodded, and his face turned really serious. "I know, baby. Back home, well, I know it's been hard for you at the skate club. It is for me too, sometimes..." He looked around the table. "And we *are* different—you and I—we look different, and that scares people. But we can't run away and hide all the time. When we came here, we— Daisy, Em's mom—and me—we made the decision to take a chance, and not let fear run our lives.

"There are bigots here too, right here in Montreal, I'm sad to say," Daisy agreed.

Her dad looked at Emily's mom. She looked serious, too, and she said, "It's true, J. People seem more open minded here, and it's been a relief from—you know—the horrible violence that we've seen, and heard about, at home...but, I'm sorry to say, hatred is everywhere..."

Jaheen thought Mrs. Smithson was right. Jaheen noticed that she looked sort of pretty tonight, with the sparkles still in her hair. Her heavy make-up was gone.

Daisy had given her a special cream for removing stage paint.

Her dad said, "J, I'm sorry that we can't stay here, in Canada, honey, but I do have some news that might make you happy." Jaheen saw everyone at the table turn in his direction. "Daisy has agreed to take you on, as her private student."

"What? Oh, wow…really?" Jaheen screeched with excitement. She got up, and hugged her father. "Thank you *so much*, Dad!" Then she looked at Daisy, who had been quietly eating her salad, and Daisy was grinning now. She held out her arms, inviting a hug. Jaheen ran around the table, and wrapped her arms around the little woman—her new, world-class skating coach!

As Jaheen walked back and sat down in her chair, she looked around and her kind-of-new-family, and her heart was glowing like the candle that was burning in the middle of them all. This group of special people shared a love for her sport, and they cared about her, and her future—and she cared about them all, too.

"That's really cool news, J! I'm really happy for you!" Em said.

Em's mother looked like she was going to cry. "That's wonderful news!" she said.

"Thanks—everybody!" Jaheen said.

Emily said quietly, "I…I think it's sad that people are mean to other people, just because of a little thing like skin color."

"Yeah, it's gay," Jaheen agreed.

"You know, I'm gay," said Daisy, and everyone around the table stopped eating. Her father almost choked on his water, and Em's mother's eyes were big.

"I'm gay," Daisy repeated. "So that's not a good word to use for something that's bad, J." She took a sip of her red wine. "Being gay's a good thing—at least, for me."

Em looked confused. "Doesn't gay mean, 'happy'?"

"Sweetie, Gay also means I prefer being with a woman, and not marrying a man. It's no big deal. Carol and I have…" Daisy stopped herself.

Jaheen had noticed that Daisy'd had and extra glass of wine tonight—just to celebrate. Jaheen knew that people who drank too much sometimes said things they didn't mean to say. Her mother did that sometimes…and then Jaheen gasped. She'd just figured out what Daisy was saying. Daisy and *Carol?* Whoops! Jaheen had to stifle a giggle. She'd never guessed that Daisy and Carol were a couple!

"Well, if…" Em still seemed confused.

"I'll explain it to ya later, Em," Jaheen whispered to her.

Jaheen saw funny looks pass between her father, Em's mother, and Daisy.

Daisy said, proudly, "You see, girls—I'm different, too. Everybody is different, really— in their own way." She looked at each of them, and back to Jaheen, and added. "So I'm not a stranger to feeling like I don't fit in! I have to act like I'm straight—or I might lose students."

Jaheen nodded, trying to be cool. "I understand."

"Thanks for being so honest with us, Daze." Emily's mother said slowly.

Her father nodded, but Jaheen saw a look on his face that told her he was probably still in shock.

"I trust you all, so much, or I wouldn't have told you," Daisy said, taking another sip of her wine.

Chapter 66 ❋ Abe

Abe pushed Anna's door open. He assumed it was his invitation to enter her room. He heard the water splashing in the bathtub. Her suite smelled like roses. Candlelight flickered from under the bathroom door.

Daisy was gay. Daisy was gay. Man. He'd have to think about. He never would have guessed...Daisy was one hell of an actress, he thought. But, then, he knew from first-hand experience, that people had their secrets.

He sat down on the floor in Anna's room, doing some stretches. His pajama bottoms were still damp in the seat; he'd washed them out in his bathroom sink this morning. He'd only packed one pair of pajamas, and hadn't had the time to go out and buy new ones. Sometime during the night, last night, on the couch, in all of the excitement, he'd lost control and he'd come in his pants, but hadn't told Anna.

The weird thing was, he thought, she hadn't even seemed to notice. She was the most sexually uneducated women he'd ever met. He smiled to himself. He wanted to be her teacher. She could be his star student...He knew that she was a quick study...

Anna walked out of the bathroom. Her tall, thin figure was wrapped in one of the long, flowing white hotel towels. She didn't seem surprised to see him there. He looked at her, and raised his arms up, toward her.

"Come down here, Ice Woman, and keep me company," he said, grinning.

Keeping the towel snugly wrapped around herself, she sat down next to him, and she leaned over, onto his chest. Her make-up was gone, and he saw all of the familiar freckles that dotted her nose, cheeks, and her shoulders. Her hair was still damp and it smelled like flowers.

His heart started racing now, as he pulled her smiling face next his. He could smell her body. Roses. Memories of her soft lips came flooding back from the night before, and he was hungry to taste her mouth again.

They kissed for a long time. He was getting excited, and didn't know what he should do, or say. He wanted her. All of her. Right now. But...

As often happened, she said what he'd been thinking, "Make love to me, Abe."

He sat up.

"I can't."

"Why not?"

"I'm not...ready."

"What do you mean?"

"I'm *not ready*. You're not ready, either. I'm still married...And I have to get—tested."

"Tested? For what?"

"Ha." He rolled onto his back, looking up at the ceiling, trying to decide how to tell her. "Honey, I told you...yesterday...that Georgie's been with another man. I know that for a fact. I talked with him on the phone..."

He caught her nod out of the corner of his eye. She readjusted her towel, pulling it tight around herself.

"Oh. You mean for—diseases?"

"Yes. I've got to be sure I didn't catch something from her. I need to get tested."

"Ah...I see. Okay."

317

He rolled back onto his side, and saw her worried expression. "It's not serious. Probably nothing. But, I'm sorry...It's all my fault. I shouldn't have slept with her a few weeks ago. And then I should've gone to the doctor...but we've been so busy—"

"And you didn't want to admit that she was cheating on you," she finished for him.

How could she read him so well?

She said softly, "I know what it's like—to not want to face the truth, about a bad marriage." She smiled at him. "Sometimes it hurts too much, and it's easier to just ignore everything...and hope things will get better—for the sake of your child..."

He took her hand. "I love you." He kissed her hand. "I *will* take care of everything. No more lying—between the two of us, right?"

She nodded, and she said, almost to herself: "Right. So I have something I should tell you..."

"What's that, baby?" he said, his eyes searching hers.

She sighed, looking down at his hand. "I haven't been totally honest with you—about being afraid—of you."

"Afraid...of *me?*"

"Abe, I haven't been with my husband—you know—that way—for more than *two years*. And he was the only man I've ever slept with—had sex with. You've probably had so many women. I...I don't know if I—"

He thought about what he could say to reassure her. This was something he hadn't prepared himself for. All the women he'd been with—and there had been many—had known plenty about sex. Hell, he'd learned from *them!* And how could Anna act so sexy, and dance—she was so hot when she danced—and not know what all those moves were for?

"Are you're worried that you won't be—enough for me?" He asked her.

"Well, yes. Maybe…" She looked miserable. She rocked back and forth, pulling her knees under her chin, holding onto her towel. "I mean, you know, I watch TV, I go to the movies. I've even read books about it…I can *dance* it—even *skate* it. But I've never really…*enjoyed* it—you know, *real sex*—with a *real person* before."

She was blowing him away. He was beginning to feel excited about rising to the challenge of being her teacher—her sex coach.

He took a long, deep breath. "Look, Anna, it's true that I've been with lots of women. But…but I've never been in love like this—like I am with you. *This*—the way you and I jam together—it's kind of new for me, too."

He reached for her hand. She still didn't look at him.

"But, hey," he couldn't stop a sly smile from coming, and he said "I'll be happy to teach you—all that I know—when the time is right. We can go as slow as you want…"

She glanced up into his eyes, and he saw tiny tears forming in hers. He took her face in his hands, and gave her a slow, tender kiss that quickly exploded into a passionate exploration of her tongue and teeth with his own.

"We'll start your lessons," he said between breaths, "right here, right now—with the student's permission…"

And she gave him her permission by reaching for his shoulders, and gripping them hard, with both her hands. He eased her back onto the floor, and kissed and licked her neck. He nibbled on her chin, and raked her hair with his fingers. When he blew into her ear, and whispered her name, she started to moan and to call out his name.

He opened her towel, just enough to expose her breasts, and he worked his tongue toward each of her rigid

319

pink nipples. He noticed how pale she was, and that her freckles were everywhere. They were a part of her that he had fallen in love with, and he kissed them with his eyes half-closed, licking and touching each one.

He wanted to know every inch of her. It might take him years to learn her, but that was just fine with him. The idea of spending years with her caused him to feel a kind of happiness that he'd never known existed.

Chapter 67 ❀ Anna

"Why...why did you stop?" Anna asked him, confused, trying to catch her breath.

"You're not ready, either," he said with a small smile.

"What do you mean?"

He slid his hand down to her waist, and played with the elastic top of her panties.

"You're not ready yet, honey."

"Why, because I *forgot*? Just because I *forgot* to take off my..."

"You didn't *forget* to take off your underwear, Anna." He laughed. "You just got out of the bathtub. You *knew* I was coming over. You left the door open for me...but it's *okay*, baby! Hey...let's face it, you're *just not ready* yet...and neither am I."

He kissed her mouth, and she returned his kiss with a wave of desire that she'd never felt in her body before. He was trying to sit up, but she tried to keep him locked in her arms. He slowly and gently broke away from her.

She felt a surge of disappointment as she gathered herself into her towel again, smoothing it, like she was removing wrinkles from a rumpled dress.

"I'm not sure I like this total honesty business," she laughed, peeking up at him.

He grinned, and reached for her face. He held her cheeks in his hands, and he leaned down to touch his forehead to hers. "I love you, Anna" he said, "Get some sleep. I'll see you in the morning."

And he went back into his own room, and he locked the door behind him.

Chapter 68 ❀ Anna

Anna had an idea. It was a *really good one*, she thought, but she had to act fast. She jogged quickly through the maze of offices, until she saw the sign for the stage production manager. She pushed the door open, and nearly ran into a tall man with a closely trimmed beard. He was pushing a cart with wheels that was stacked with record albums and some electronic equipment. He stepped back in surprise. "Hello! May I help you?" he asked. He had a slight French accent, and he seemed irritated with her, and in a hurry.

"Hi, so sorry, sir…I'm Anna Smithson—one of the pair skaters in tonight's show." Anna was still trying to catch her breath. "Are you the sound mixer?"

"I am the production *manager*. I don't do the actual mixing. I supervise it."

"Oh good! Could you have someone switch our program song? *Please* don't tell me it's too late."

He gave her a doubtful look. "You want to change your musical selection—*now*—for *tonight's performance?*"

"Yes…please?"

He frowned. "But, we go live in…" he looked at his watch. "Less than two hours. Won't you have a problem with…?"

"No. There won't be any problems. We need to use this song—instead of the one that's scheduled for us—Brown and Smithson."

She handed him a record album. The group of four black men was pictured on the front, standing in front of an open prison door, climbing on the bars. He pulled the record out of its cover. The song "Break Out" was circled on the label.

She watched as he rolled his eyes at her, his jaws working back and forth. "Hmm. This is a fairly new release. Very controversial," he said, as if he was thinking out loud. "A few minutes more, and you'd have missed me completely. I am on my way up there, to cue the program, so—I guess we can cut this one in on time…" He gave her another inquisitive look. "You're absolutely sure *this* is the song you want?"

"Yes, I would like to replace: "Heaven Sent Love" with "Break Out"…please."

He nodded. He seemed to suddenly recognize her. "Oh…you're the girl who ice dances with the *Negro*…"

She nodded. The way he looked at her made her feel uneasy.

"What's he like? I mean *really like*…*hmm?* He must enjoy having *you* as his partner…no?" He said, moving closer toward her.

She backed away. She didn't like him, or the way he was acting. Was he flirting with her? Or…

She realized that he was implying something…sexual. She felt a need to defend herself, and Abe, too, and she had a sudden urge to punch him. Her father would have smacked him, she thought.

Instead, she started whisper and to count back from 10, and taking deep breaths, to keep from getting too mad. He looked at her strangely. She didn't care. She had to stay calm, to get his help—but he had no business judging her—or implying…

She knew that she and Abe would face a lot of people like him. She would have to deal with them—not with hate, or violence—but with patience, understanding…and by telling the truth.

"Sir, I resent your implication. Mister Brown is a good, honest person—and so am I. My personal life is none of your business." She felt close to losing control, her eyes squinting, her hands clenched into tight fists.

The manager backed away. "Sorry, lady. I didn't mean to…" He looked at her, almost as if he respected her, and he said, "There's no problem. None at all. I'll make the change."

But as he closed the door and locked it, he turned to her, and said with a slight sneer, "Lots of luck, lady."

Chapter 69 ❋ Anna

"You did *what*?" cried Abe. A couple of skaters nearby in the warm-up rink looked over at him. The grand entry had finished, and the first pair had completed their turn on the ice.

"I had to, Abe," Anna said, swallowing hard.

"What were you thinking? I don't...Daisy will—"

She gave him a pleading look, trying to make him stop and listen. She raised her chin, she said, with conviction: "You and I are going to have sex—tonight."

That stopped him all right, she thought with a grin. He stared at her. "We're going to have sex—*tonight?* What does that have to do with the music—?"

"Nothing. No. It's not what you think. We're going to have sex—*here*—on the ice—in front of God, and everybody!"

"Have you gone crazy?"

Anna saw that a nearby couple was staring at them.

"Listen, Abe," she said, glancing at the skaters, and lowering her voice. "You know the Breakout dance—we both know it, by heart. It's—it's *our song!*"

His eyes were searching hers. The lines around his mouth were softening. She could tell he was starting to get her idea.

She continued on. "To hell with Daisy's pop song, Abe. This may be our only chance to really do our thing—and to share the message—*on live TV!*"

"Our message?" he said. "What message?"

"The message in the *song, silly!* You know, that love is the answer—for all races—for all people who are different—for people like Daisy—for J—and for *us—me and you!*"

"And our dance—it's our story." She whispered, excited, trying to keep her voice down. "Don't you *see?* We've done it all! We're different. We were arrested, and now we're in love. All we have to do is to act out how it was—and how we *really feel now!*"

"No more hiding our love..." he said thoughtfully.

"We tell the whole world about what's happened to us!" she repeated, giggling.

He looked down at her, and suddenly he grabbed her arm. "Come with me. Hurry!"

They skated past the curious faces of the other pairs, his strong strides pulling her behind him, into the dressing area. He stopped in front of a table with full length mirrors behind it. The temporary alcove had been set up for last-minute make-up and costume checks. There were cans of hairspray, brushes, combs, blow dryers, tissue boxes, and scissors scattered there, for anyone to use.

Abe reached for a pair of scissors.

"What are those for?" she asked, with suspicion.

"Give me your arm," he said gravely.

She looked at him with alarm. "Abe, what are you going to do?"

"Trust me...we don't have much time. *Give me your arm!*"

She took a breath, and held out her left arm. He slid the scissors carefully under the cloth of her costume near her shoulder, and made a long slit in her sleeve, ending just above her wrist.

"Now, the other side." He made the same long cut into her right sleeve.

She bent her elbow, and saw what he'd done. Her arm was showing through, and it changed the look of her top from a traditional, very conservative one, to one that was very sexy.

He knelt down in front of her on his good knee, steadying himself against the table's edge.

"Now what are you doing?" she asked him.

He didn't answer, and he began to cut her skirt into strips of varying widths, starting at the hemline.

"Oh, my God, Abe, you're a genius!"

When he finished, she twirled around, and strips of her skirt flew out in all directions.

"You do me next," he said with a suggestive raise of his eyebrow and a smirk. She glanced at his face, and wondered why he was chuckling. She must have missed something, she thought.

"Never mind...I'll explain...later!" he laughed.

He handed her the scissors.

She stepped back a step, and considered what she could do to change the harsh, formal look of his black jacket, and matching full length, formal pants. She crouched down, and started to cut strips up into the bottoms of his trousers half way up to his knees. Then she motioned for him to turn him around, and she cut strips into the tails of his tux. Standing, they exchanged looks of appraisal. Then then stood in front of one of the mirrors, and laughed at their reflections.

"OK—ready!" she announced.

"Not yet." He replied, smiling broadly, as he turned, and took her in his arms. "Just one more thing." He brought his lips within an inch of hers, and he stopped.

She was all ready to taste him, feel his kiss. She felt her body moving toward him, her mouth straining to feel his mouth, as if their lips were made of magnets.

"If I start kissing you now, I won't stop..." he whispered. "But right now, we have to focus..."

She couldn't speak. She felt like her heart was in her throat. She could hear it beating, and felt the blood rushing through her head. He didn't move any closer, nor did he back away. He just stood still. She felt his warm breath on her lips. Her arms were aching, wanting to pull him against her, and hold him there.

"Do you feel that?" he said in a strange deep voice that was unlike anything she'd ever heard before. Desire ripped through her body. Suddenly she didn't care about their performance out there. She just wanted him to touch her right here, to kiss her, all over, like had started to do last night on the floor...

She barely nodded.

"Good," he said. "Now...hold onto that feeling, Ice Woman. And let's go do it on the ice."

Chapter 70 ❋ Abe

The house lights came up, and the announcer was interviewing the skating experts about the performance of the pair who were just finishing.

Abe held Anna's hand. They were at the gate, ready to enter the arena. This was it. They were going to deliver their message—or make fools of themselves—and poor Daisy, too…He felt sorry for Daze, but he was glad that Anna had made the change in their program.

It was a great idea, and it was the right thing to do. He was sure if it now.

He watched the kids collecting the flowers from the ice. He saw the little Negro boy, and waved at him. The kids' futures were at stake. Jaheen had reminded him that he was now a role model for racial equality, and his daughter had been right.

Love was the answer. Love was the only thing that would heal the violence, and save the world from hate. Love would bring peace to all races—and to all of mankind. History had tried to teach him that, but it took falling in love with an Irish orphan for him to learn it.

He looked down at Anna. She was radiant. And she was ready. Unlike the cold fingers he'd tried so hard to warm before their last two performances, her hand was hot, and firmly pressing into his palm.

He wasn't listening to the commentary, but he'd heard: "timing was off" and "lack of energy," and he closed his mind to the idea that they were going to be analyzed by experts. He didn't care about the show; he cared about the message. He remembered that day in the warehouse—that dark day—when he'd been arrested and charged with "public indecency" for dancing to the words in a song that said love heals all conflict, pain and suffering.

Now he wondered how this audience would accept those very same dance moves here tonight. His own palms were growing warm and wet, as those memories, and the pain in his face from the attack by the police, came flooding back.

"Our next pair is from the United States." The announcer said. "They hail from Atlanta, Georgia: Abraham Lincoln Brown and Margaret Ann Smithson!"

The spotlight flashed in Abe's eyes and it lit up a strip of shiny ice. There was a small rippling of applause. He was sure he'd heard Jaheen say, "Go, Dad!" And his legs went weak for a quick moment. Jaheen was going to witness— how had Anna put it?—Sex on ice?

He took some slow deep breaths. He now believed that sex was a beautiful thing. He hadn't for much of his life, but, since knowing Anna, he'd learned that sex could be a part of loving someone...and what could be more amazing than that?

He caught Anna's attention. She gave him a quick nod, and a look that reminded him to focus.

She was right, he thought. *Focus!*

It was time to show the world who and what they really were all about. After tonight, they could look each other—or anyone else—with honesty, and not lie anymore, about how they believed in the power of love to heal— themselves—and the world.

There would be no acting tonight. Their performance was going to be real, because their love was real...and they had nothing to hide. Where they crazy? Maybe. But all he wanted to do right now was do the Breakout dance, with his Ice Woman.

He pulled her to a stop on the center mark. He suddenly realized that he didn't know how they would start their dance. They hadn't worked the song from the very beginning. He shot Anna a questioning look, but she just grinned at him and nodded.

Then, she turned her back on him, and put her hands on her hips. He copied her, and turned his back on her, too. The crowd was quiet, and they stood there, in the great silent hall, back-to-back, not touching, waiting for the music to start.

He knew the song would begin with a loud, hard driving rock beat, and that the introduction was repeated twice. He decided to wait for her to make the first move. He figured that he had a fifty-fifty chance of guessing right, but he planned to peek at her, just to be sure. If he was wrong, he was ready to jump in, and take the first lead.

The song had two themes; one was about falling into forbidden love that trapped people, like animals in a cage. The second theme described how love can free them—just like love saves the world...because love heals prejudice, violence...There was a line in the middle of the song about how being in love with the "wrong" person can hurt people. "The Breakout" was, just as Anna had said, their own story.

The drum beats began. He turned his head to look at Anna, and watched her take the first opening steps. He'd guessed right: she turned on him with a flirty expression, coming on to him, teasing him with her big eyes, wide smile, and her open arms. He mirrored what she'd done, adding his own style of flirting with her.

As if they were connected by some unknown kind of magic, they danced together, holding each other, just as they'd done on roller skates in the abandoned warehouse.

Then, he heard a low, rumbling noise. Surprised by the sound, he tripped slightly, but she caught him quickly, making it look like it had been a part of their routine. He looked around, and realized that it wasn't the cops coming after him…The sound was applause. It was applause, coming from the crowd!

They dove and dipped, teasing, and spinning each other. He felt the lyrics coming alive, erupting from somewhere deep within him. They stared each other down, smiling, grinning, and mouthing words with the music. She didn't miss a beat, and neither did he.

He'd never seen her stretch so far back in her spins. Then she grabbed him, and pulled him close to her—and then pushed him away, hard…so hard he had to struggle to regain his balance. She was perfect—and so hot!

Anna raced across the arena so fast, the spotlights had to work to keep up with her. He followed her, as fast as he could go, catching her. He grabbed her roughly, trying to kiss her, stopping just short of doing it, as they'd agreed to do. She refused him, pushing him away. Then, he did his own arena run, and she followed him fast, pulling him in for a kiss that he refused to give her. He couldn't pay attention to it, or he knew that would lose his timing, but he heard the audience clapping, keeping time with the beat.

When the part came about love hurting, they both reached up and locked forearms, blocking one another, tossing their heads back, and then they separated, each skating backward, away from each other. There was no mistaking the roar from the crowd. The screeches and whoops filled the air.

The audience's noises faded, and the song transitioned into the sultry, suggestive second theme. Anna changed her style from acting aggressively to one that appeared soft and loving—and very sexy.

They were back in the center now, and the descriptions of passionate love seemed to take her over. He saw Anna open her arms to him. She stared straight into his eyes, and she ran her hands down his chest—almost touching him. And then, my God, he thought, she was running her hands down the front of her own body!

Miming the lwords, as she had the day of their arrest, he followed her lead as they pulled into one another, and melted into a slow spin that brought their thighs pressed together. Their timing was perfect, as if they'd done this dance hundreds of times. Their eyes were locked on each other. He couldn't look away if he'd wanted to…

At the last word "love," they brought their faces together, and, as Abe had done in the dressing room. He stopped and held his mouth close to hers. He heard the crowd go wild with screaming, yelling, and wolf-whistling.

The song was closing now, and he had no idea how they were going to end it. He didn't want it to end. He saw a determined look flash in Anna's eyes, and he knew she had one of her crazy ideas.

She pulled him in next to her, and with strength that he didn't know she had, and she slowly tripped him, pushing him down, until he was lying flat on his back. She slid herself down on the ice next to him, just as the last notes of the music were sounding. She grabbed his hand, and, making a fist with hers, she held their clasped hands up toward the white light above them…and the audience went wild.

"Well, that was…I don't know, Stacey…How would you describe that ah—very *unusual*—performance? The crowd here in Montreal seems to be lovin' it!" said the announcer over the loudspeaker, laughing.

They helped each other to stand up. They waved and bowed, making two 360-degree turns. The audience was not quieting down, so they made another full circle, and then they skated together toward the gate, trying to avoid all the piles of flowers that had been thrown out on the ice for them.

The applause and yelling continued, echoing so loudly that it nearly drowned out the announcers' voices: "Matt, that was a…an amazing display, I must say."

"Yes, indeed, this pair seems to have won this audience over tonight. I hope, well, I just hope the kiddies were all in bed asleep, though. It was pretty *racy*—oops, excuse me—I meant…ah…it was a very *sexy* dance!"

Chapter 71 ❋ Emily

Emily sat on the edge of her chair next to Jaheen, watching her mother skate out of the arena. Daisy had left in hurry, reminding them to stay in the box until the end of the show, when she'd come back to take them to the after-party and a taped viewing of the TV show.

Emily felt like covering her ears, because the applause and the yelling around her was so loud. She wasn't sure why the crowd seemed to like her mother's new routine so much. She'd liked the other dance better. The one that her mother and Mr. Brown—Abe—he'd kept reminding her to call him *Abe*—had just done was too weird.

J seemed to like it though. She was jumping up and down and still clapping.

Tonight's dance had too much adult romance stuff in it. But, Emily had to admit, there were some cool times, during their new routine, when the two of them had skated so close like they looked like they were only one person.

When the song talked about love, she'd thought about Sammy, the boy she liked at school. He confused her—sometimes he seemed to like her, other times he just ignored her, but she still wondered what it would be like to hug him—the way her mom had hugged Mr.—Abe.

"Man!" called Jaheen, raising her voice over the noise, clapping loudly. "The audience *really* loved them! They didn't mess up one time, either! And, Em...didn't you just *love* their new outfits?"

"Yeah, they really liked them tonight," Emily agreed, turning around, scanning the crowd. Lots of people in the crowd were smiling, and nodding, and some were standing up, and others were still clapping.

"Wow! And look at all of those *flowers*—they've got a *ton* of them! There's—isn't he the *cutest?*" Jaheen's eyes were huge as she watched the Negro boy skater, collecting flowers from the ice.

When the noise finally died down, J said, "Em, someday, that'll be me down there. People will clap for me like that, and I'll have so many flowers, I won't be able to fit them all in the apartment I'm going to have—right here, in Montreal!"

Chapter 72 ❋ Anna

Skating into the warm-up rink, Anna tried to catch her breath. She sat down in one of the chairs, and leaned her head and back against the half-wall. Abe stood, half-bent over, next to her, holding onto the wall, breathing hard. She looked up at him, and saw that his eyes were glazed over, as if he was in shock, and maybe still trying to figure out what had just happened, like she was.

"You two shouldn't hold your breath so much. How many times have I told you to breathe with every step?" Daisy's stern voice came from somewhere over Anna's head. She tilted her head up, she saw Daisy's face looking down at her.

Anna jumped up, and spun around to face her coach. "I'm so sorry, Daisy. I should have talked it over with you first...but..."

Abe moved closer to Anna, as if to protect her from Daisy.

Daisy reached out, putting one hand on Anna's shoulder and the other on Abe's, and said sternly, "Anna, Abe, my job was to prepare you for anything that could happen out there." Then, her voice softened. "Of course, I didn't expect you two to *create* a crisis—and knowing you two, I probably should have expected it...But, that's not important—"

"The important thing is that we did it—and we couldn't have done it without you, Daisy," Abe cut her off.

Daisy looked at him, shook her head slowly, and smiled. "You continue to surprise me. You know, you and your partner here, have been the most...most...*challenging* people I've ever coached in my *entire* career...Even more than those temperamental Olympic types—if you can believe it...And, you know, I've loved every minute..."

"Oh Daze, I love you, too" said Anna, relief washing over her as she leaned over the wall, and grabbed Daisy for a long hug.

"Come on, you get in here, too, Abe...a threesome!" laughed Daisy. "You guys were right on the money tonight. You're an amazing pair, you know that, don't you? It's almost like..." She stepped back and stared at them, raising her perfect eyebrows, and wiping her misty eyes.

"Like we're in love?" said Anna, feeling a huge smile flood her face.

Daisy nodded. "And now the whole world knows it, too—at least everyone here..." she indicated the arena with her arm, "and everyone else who saw you on live TV tonight."

Chapter 73 ❀ Jaheen

The hospitality room was filled with rows of chairs facing four of the biggest TV sets that Jaheen had ever seen. The tables had huge silver serving dishes heaping with casseroles, salads, seafood and desserts. Bowls of chips, crackers, colorful dips, and cheeses filled the rolling trays that were placed next to the open bar.

Skaters, coaches, families, and their guests were eating and talking—sharing experiences and stories about the show. Some seemed happy. Others looked sad and disappointed.

Jaheen happily eavesdropped on conversations as she filled her plate to overflowing. There was so many delicious treats to choose from! She tried to take in everything that was happening. To her, everyone seemed sophisticated and elegant. She recognized many of the skaters from the show, and had learned about them from reading the program, from cover to cover several times.

The skaters were easy to spot; they moved like ballet dancers. As she slowly returned to her table, she made a special effort to stand extra tall, and walk as straight as she could, keeping her chin high, as Daisy—*her very own coach*—had taught her. She didn't care if Daisy was gay or not. What did her sex-ways have to do with anything? Daisy French was *her* coach—the best coach in the whole world!

Her father gave her a questioning look as she sat down next to him. "Is your back hurting, honey?" he asked.

"No, Dad!" She laughed at him. "I'm practicing—I'm walking like a professional skater, just like Daisy taught me."

"Ah. That's good," he said, biting into a forkful of shrimp salad. He seemed really happy, and *really* tired.

"I'm glad to hear that *somebody* listens to me," Daisy commented, smiling. Jaheen glanced up and saw a pretend-mad look pass from Daisy to her father, and from her father to Emily's mom.

The lights blinked on and off, and a man in a suit with a beard stood up in front of the room. Mrs. Smithson looked at him, she dropped her juice glass. She looked upset. It was almost like she knew that guy, Jaheen thought.

"Ladies and gentlemen. Your kind attention, please!"

The room got quiet. The sounds of her dad helping to wipe up Mrs. Smithson's broken glass seemed really loud.

The man with the beard ignored them, and kept talking. "We're ready to run the tape of tonight's performances. What you will see here, is what TV audiences saw, live, in their own homes—minus the commercials, of course!" He smiled, and waited while some people laughed. Then, he continued speaking. "As you know, professional commentary was added as a way to inform viewers—to educate them—about the magnificent sport of ice skating."

Jaheen nodded in agreement. The more people who knew about her sport, the better, she thought.

The room got dark, and the TV screens lit up with the first scenes of tonight's grand entry. There was a lot of whispering in the room. Jaheen excitedly began to relive each moment of the evening as she watched the tape playing. "Look, there you are, Dad!" she said in his ear, in a low voice. She saw him nod out of the corner of her eye, while he kept his eyes on the screen, and ate handfuls of potato chips.

Emily was sitting next to her mother. "There you are mom!" Mrs. Smithson smiled and said, "That's me, all right...Wow! I need to lose some weight!"

"No you don't, honey. Everybody looks fat on TV. You're fine." Daisy whispered.

As each pair came and went, Jaheen's excitement grew. Seeing her father on *TV*, out there, in front of all those people, was going to be *so cool!*

"There you are, Dad! Look!" Jaheen jiggled in her chair. She saw Emily laughing at her.

"Um...yeah...that's me...Shh, hush now." her father answered, his finger on his lips.

There they were, her dad and Mrs. Smithson—her dad wouldn't allow her to call her Anna, even though Emily's mom had said it was okay. He had said it wouldn't be polite.

Jaheen watched them as they found their place in the center of the rink, and the music started, but the commentator's and announcers voices were very loud, and it wasn't easy to hear the words of the song.

Why were they talking so much—and so loud? It hadn't been like that during their *real* performance! Jaheen was confused.

The skating expert said: "This pair is highly unconventional—not at all representative of the fine tradition of pair skating...Other skaters chose to skate to classical music here tonight...And those—ah, are very, unusual—costumes. The name of the designer wasn't supplied..." There was a pause, and Jaheen could hear some applause from the arena in the background, but the announcer's voice came on again, and it seemed to be even louder this time.

And Jaheen noticed that all of the clapping and calling from the audience that she'd heard from her box seat had been drowned out by the commentator's final speech: "Their synchronous moves are certainly well timed, as you can see. I'm sure that weeks of training, and hours and hours of practice, were needed to execute these steps so precisely. They certainly have synergy…"

Jaheen looked over at her father, who was staring at Mrs. Smithson. Daisy was shaking her head, as if the things that the commentator said weren't true.

Before her father's performance had even ended, the beginning of a commercial flashed onto the screen. Then, the picture went dark for a second, and then the next pair was shown entering the arena for their turn on the ice.

Why had they cut out the end of her dad's dance?

* * *

"I can't believe what he did to us!" Anna said. She was still upset about the way that sound manager had cut the finale out of their act.

She and Abe were sitting on the stuffed armchairs, in front of the window of her suite. His legs were propped up on the edge of her chair, and she was rubbing his ankles through his socks. He stared out the window, and he took a drink from the water glass in his hand.

Anna looked at her half-filled cup of water on the table between them, but she didn't want to Abe to move enough to reach for it. They were supposed to be resting, hydrating, and relaxing—Daisy's orders. Anna watched the lights of the city flicker in the falling snow, and she loved the way Abe's leg muscles and bones felt strong and hard, under her fingers.

"I know, baby. It wasn't right. The *real* audience loved us. Never forget that…"

"Yeah, they did! I heard them—clapping and cheering, and…" She sighed and shook her head. "Is there no real freedom—freedom to be different—to be who you really are—*anywhere* in this world?"

She felt sad. Not for herself this time, but for people—people who were different. He put down his glass and reached for her hand. He pulled her into his lap, and he wrapped his arms around her.

"I know how you feel." He kissed her forehead, and held her to him, like he done for Jaheen, when she was little, when her feelings had been hurt.

"It's not okay. But it's the way our world is, and we have to face it—and do what we can to change things—when we can." He was sounding like a teacher, but she found it comforting.

She nodded. "We tried—to send our message…It was about being free to love…"

"People who stood up for freedom: Lincoln, Doctor King, Kennedy…It got them killed, hon, but their message—like ours—the message will live on…and maybe someday, things will change…Love is a strong thing. It's stronger than hate…"

Anna looked up at him, feeling a strange sense of worry starting to gnaw at her. "You don't think that what we did tonight will, you know…put us—or the girls—in some kind of danger, do you? Because—oh my God, I didn't think…"

"Hey…don't worry." He paused, and kissed the top of her head again. "We'll be fine. We're leaving in the morning. I'm glad that you—that we—did our dance. Sometimes you just gotta do what's right…no matter what."

"Umm" Anna replied softly. She knew that he was trying to reassure her, but she wasn't totally convinced—and her worries continued to play in the back of her mind. "I hope you're right." She snuggled deeper against him.

"Just think about all of the good things we did tonight, Anna. You know, we literally shredded some of old ways of thinking, when we cut up those outfits!"

They both laughed.

"Yeah," she said. "And we went out there and told everybody who we are—about our music, and about what we believe in."

He playfully rubbed the top of her head. "And remember, when we heard all of that applause? Our audience loved us. They got the message. The TV people may have cut it out, but people heard it. Don't forget that."

"Abraham Lincoln Brown, I love you," she said, looking up at him.

"I love you, too—so much..." His lips brushed against her forehead, and her cheeks, and then he found her mouth.

Between long kisses, he whispered so quietly that she almost didn't hear his words: "When we get clear from our divorce paperwork, will you marry me, Anna?"

She gasped, and sat up, bumping him in the chest with her elbow.

"Sorry...Really? You're asking me to marry you?"

He jumped, holding his chest where she had hit him, and looked at her. He grinned, and he chuckled. "Surprised?"

"Well, now, yes...I am."

"Good. Because, it was my turn—you know, to surprise you."

She didn't understand, and she gave him a squint-eyed, questioning look.

"Hey, fair and square. You surprised me by changing our entire program in—ah, what…about an hour? And so, I've asked you to marry me for—um, a lifetime." he was laughing out loud now. "So, by then, I figure, we'll be even."

She was giggling like a teenager in love. She jumped on top of him, her legs straddling his lap, her arms locked around his back, and she knew that he'd probably guessed her answer.

Chapter 74 ❀ Anna

Rain splashed against the side of the plane like it was being sprayed with a garden hose. Anna let the turbulence rock her from side to side. She tried to relax.

Just go with it, Abe had suggested, before he'd fallen asleep. Abe said that he believed in Martin Luther King's philosophy—finding peace in yourself, wherever you went, no matter what was happening. Well, she thought that was certainly easier said than done—especially at thirty thousand feet off the ground!

Abe's regular breathing told her that he was asleep. But, even while he slept, his fingers were firmly wrapped around hers; their hands were hidden under the thin gray airline blanket. The first class cabin staff were *extremely* attentive, and so, in order to avoid any disapproving looks and comments, she and Abe had agreed that it was probably better to keep their public acts of affection to a minimum.

But when they were married...married! She was going to be married to Abe! She still couldn't believe it. She couldn't wait to get back to Atlanta—only because it meant her new life with him could start—soon.

But not soon enough. She'd be going back to the guest room in Bill's house, for Emily's sake, as if nothing had changed, until her divorce was final. And Abe had his own legal concerns to finish with Georgie.

The plane was circling the gray city below now, bouncing like a ship on the ocean in a hurricane, flying through low clouds that blocked the sun.

"We are beginning our descent into the Atlanta area. Please fasten your seat belts, and remain seated until the plane has come to a complete stop." The stewardess said.

Abe stirred. When he saw her watching him, his face softened into a happy grin. "Hi," he said. "It's great...to have you next to me when I wake up." He looked around, and then he kissed her mouth quickly.

She smiled at him, losing herself in the liquid gold flecks in his eyes. Immediately, she remembered last night. He'd slept with her, in her bed—the whole night.

She'd enticed him there. She giggled about it now, as she pictured Abe's look of surprise when he'd first seen her completely naked. She would never forget that moment.

After she'd gotten up from his lap to use the bathroom, she'd come up behind his chair—and he'd been looking out the window. She'd bend down, and put the little red box, in one of his hands, and a small bottle of champagne in the other.

Because she was hugging him from behind his chair, and her face was pressed against his good side, he couldn't see that she no longer was wearing pajamas.

He'd taken out one of the condom packets and had studied the wrapper.

"What's this for?" he'd asked, reading the back of the red foil packet.

"You know what it's for, Abe. It protects people from, you know, diseases."

He'd kept staring at it. "Honey, I haven't used one of these since I was in high school—and it really didn't work out too well then."

"Why not?"

"It broke. Maybe I didn't put it on right. I don't know."

"Well, now, you see, this one is—it says right here—it's extra-large. I think they make them stronger now."

"And you know this…because?" he'd laughed at her.

She remembered feeling her cheeks get hot.

"I don't. Bill and I never used them. We should have…but, then that's where my beautiful daughter Emily came from."

He'd laughed. "Ditto: my Jaheen!"

But then his voice had changed, and he'd suddenly sounded very serious. "Anna, if you got pregnant, would you…have my child?" He'd turned to look at her then.

She'd never forget the look of shock on his face. He'd look her up and down, and, at first, she'd wanted to run back into the bathroom. But he'd reached for her with such tenderness, the next thing she knew they were kissing, hugging, and she was undressing him…

Finally, she'd been able to speak. Between kisses, she'd whispered: "I would be so happy if that happened, Abe. To have your child would be—a gift…a gift—of love."

The rest of the night's memories had blurred together. Their warm, wet kisses, the way he touched her everywhere…they couldn't stop exploring each other's bodies. The room got so hot, Abe had to get up, and turn on the air conditioning.

She couldn't stop staring at his body—the way he walked and moved. The light from the city below was muted by the snow, but it was bright enough to illuminate him, as if he glowed in the dark.

He was so different from Bill! Bill looked like a little boy, compared to Abe! Even when Abe was not excited, he'd seemed so strong, so powerful. The color of his penis was rich and dark, like chocolate; he was unlike anything she'd ever imagined. He was…he was *absolutely beautiful.*

They'd never opened up the package of condoms—or the champagne. The bottle and the little red box were somewhere below them now, riding in the cargo hold, packed away in her suitcase.

When she moved in her seat, she could still feel Abe inside of her. She'd felt him there, every time she looked at him. The soreness between her legs was like her physical connection to him, and it helped make the magic that had happened between them seem more real.

She thought about how much Abe had become a part of her life in such a short time. That night in Montreal, when they'd first kissed, a door had opened between their minds and bodies, but last night, they'd both walked through the door, and they had discovered something wonderful—something that no one could ever take away. She wondered when they could be together again, and make love again.…With all her heart, she wanted it to be soon…and forever.

* * *

The stairs had been rolled out and set against the plane's cold silver sides. Anna watched Daisy and the girls ducking through the exit door, waving as they went, covering their heads with their coats, and laughing at the fierce wind.

Anna searched under her seat for one of her shoes. She guessed that it must have slipped behind their seats during that terribly bumpy landing. Abe was standing in the aisle, waiting for her with a patient smile, while she crawled around on the floor.

"You go ahead, Abe. I'll meet you at the baggage claim, okay? We're holding everyone up here…" Anna said from under the seat. "So sorry!" she said to a passenger

350

who had been blocked by her leg that was sticking out in the aisle.

She felt clumsy, as usual, and she was embarrassed, but she was so happy that there was someone who said he loved her for who she was, just the way she was.

"OK, baby," he said, grinning at her. And, to the surprise, and to the obvious disapproval of the man behind him, Abe added, with a wink: "I'll miss you!"

For months to come, Anna would replay that last scene on the plane, over and over, in her mind. Abe's face, his smile, the wink...telling her that he'd miss her...

During the police investigations of the shooting, the arrest, the reporters, the news interviews, and—worst of all—the long hours of waiting at the hospital, praying for him to pull through, Anna comforted herself with the memories of those last days and nights that she shared with Abe.

She'd picture the way he grinned when he was happy, and the way his eyes looked wet and soft with desire for her body.

She'd hear his jokes, remember kissing him on the couch, and think about being with him on the floor, in his lap, on the bed...

But in the darkest and most painful moments, whenever she missed him the most, she'd replay the messages of love and hope that they'd shared with the world, when they'd danced together that night, on the ice, in Montreal.

Chapter 75 ❋ Daisy

Daisy sat in the coaches' box, directly above the judges' table. She'd just watched her most talented student perform flawlessly in regional competition. Daisy was certain that this young skater was Olympic material; the girl's determination was as fierce as Daisy had seen in any child—or adult, for the matter.

But this young woman was all about performing "her way," and she tested Daisy's skills as a coach more than any other student she'd ever worked with—except for one special pair, who had kept her on edge nearly every day of their work together.

Daisy stood up abruptly, her hips aching from sitting, frozen with tension, to her seat during the grueling performance. Maybe she was getting too old for this—and she should *really* retire—for good next time. Stretching, her thigh bumped the side of the wheelchair that had been crowded in the aisle next to her.

"Hey, watch it there, little lady!" Abe's loud voice made her jump.

"Sorry, Abe! It's your daughter—she's...she's just too much!" Daisy laughed. "Another win. I hope it doesn't go to her head..."

"Really? It's not like you, to get so—involved with your students," he said, grinning up at her.

"Na, I like to keep my professional distance," she chuckled softly.

Daisy looked down at Abe, and she searched his tired brown eyes for clues to what he was thinking. He'd seen so much pain, she thought. He'd suffered too much—and it just wasn't fair. He was such good, kind man. And a great skater, too—like father, like daughter...

Were athletic skills inherited? She wondered. They seemed to be, in this family anyway.

She turned to keep a watchful eye on Jaheen, as she collected her medal. Daisy sighed, thinking things should have been—could have been—different.... She was happy for Jaheen, of course, but that should have been Abe—and Anna—out there...

But Abe was going to be okay. He was on the mend. The long, hard surgeries had worked well. His knees had been rebuilt, and the steel rods in his thigh, where the horrible bullets had shattered his legs, were healing. He'd never skate again, but, thank God, he had a real chance at walking now.

She looked down at him, and she saw the pride in his eyes as he followed Jaheen, who was practically floating on top of the ice, taking her victory round.

"She has your gift," Daisy said to Abe, a few tears starting to burn her eyes.

"She's very good," Abe said calmly. There was plenty of fatherly love in his voice...But had she heard a hint of sadness there, too? Abe was great at hiding his feelings, so it wasn't always easy to read him, even after all that they'd been through together.

Daisy saw Abe's ex-wife Georgie, and her new guy-soon-to-be-husband, Joe, walking toward to the exit gate, waiting for Jaheen. They were clapping and waving at J. Daisy smiled at them. There *were* happy endings—for some people.

Would there ever be one for her?

Daisy hoped so.

She turned Carol's ring around on her finger. One day, Daisy wished, she and Carol would marry—for real—and the whole world would know that they loved each other. But there was still too much senseless hate, and fear of people who were different, to get married yet. Maybe they would go to another country someday...

"I'm happy for Georgie," Abe said quietly.

Daisy nodded. She still thought about Bill too often, and that nightmare at the airport. Bill's hatred, and his sick need to control Anna had driven him to try to destroy Abe's life. No one had guessed that seeing that live TV performance in New York, would have pushed Bill Smithson so far over the edge.

Bill's parents had been devastated, and now they were trying to make up for what their only son had done. But all their money and lawyers hadn't kept Bill out of prison—and Daisy was pleased that her publicity skills ensured that the case had lots of exposure in the press. She wondered if Bill would ever change. Maybe he'd do some serious thinking during the hellish years he would spend in jail—and figure out that only love—not hate—brought peace to the mind and heart.

Bill's parents were going to counseling with Emily. Em was following in her mother's brave footsteps—having to grow up too fast, and face her fears. Daisy was happy to hear that Em was still planning to study art in France in a couple of years—and she certainly could, because of the generous trust fund that her grandparents had set aside for her education.

Eventually, Daisy hoped, time, and love, would heal them all.

But it would take lots of time, and lots of love...

The skating children had finished collecting Jaheen's flowers off of the ice. Jaheen was glowing. She grinned, and waved frantically, as she accepted the armful of floral bouquets from one of the Club kids—a little Asian girl.

Daisy watched Jaheen skate out of the rink and fall into her mother's waiting arms, flowers flying everywhere.

And what was Joe doing?

Joe picking up the flowers.

Was he really hugging J now?

Yes, he was!

That was so good for J, Daisy thought. More happy endings.

Daisy sat down again, in order to get back to her business. She keyed some numbers into her calculator. This win meant that Jaheen would be attending Olympic training in Colorado Springs with her—and Carol would be going along with them, too. Daisy smiled at the thought of openly sharing a life together with Carol—and living in their new condo in the mountains.

Thanks to the huge civil lawsuit settlement that had been negotiated by Georgie's lawyer and Bill's parents' attorneys—all of Jaheen's training expenses would be covered, with plenty of money to spare, for her education as well. Abe had insisted on a college fund, and Jaheen had decided to become a social worker, like her mother.

"Ah, hey, ma'am, could you please sit down, so that I can watch my daughter?" Abe asked. "If you hadn't noticed, somebody left me sitting here, all alone, in this damn wheelchair."

The woman who was blocking his view turned toward him. She was hugely pregnant. She was so big, Daisy was afraid that she was going to pop out little Abe Junior any second now, right here, in the stadium. Anna was wiping tears from her face with her hand, and, as usual, she was not doing a very good job of it.

"Sure thing, Ice-Pop," Anna giggled. Her smile lit up her wet freckles, and her flaming red hair was as bright, and as fly-away wild as Daisy had ever seen it, but Anna was glowing from the inside, as if she was human candle.

Abe reached into his pocket and held out a tissue. Anna grabbed it, and she blew her nose. She reached over and took Abe's face in her hands, tissue and all, and she kissed him with a tenderness that ended Daisy's effort to stop her own tears.

"I'm so sorry…" Anna said sweetly, looking at him as if she was caring for the most precious, most important person in the entire universe.

"Hey, Mom…remember what Abe always says?" said Emily, winking at Daisy, "Stop apologizing…and start doing what makes you happy."

Anna sniffled. She took her daughter's hand, and she squeezed it. "Thanks, Em! Out of the mouth of babes…"

"Yep…I wonder what this little guy's gonna say about that," laughed Abe, lightly running his hand across Anna's stomach, his gold Las Vegas wedding chapel band flashing in the house lights.

Reaching up for his wife's arms, Abe said, "Now bring those sweet lips of yours right here, Ice Woman, so I can show you what an Ice Dad can *really* do…"

They kissed for so long, Daisy wondered how they were able to breathe.

"What did I tell you two about holding your breath?" she asked them, with a pretend sigh.

They both turned to look at her. Daisy saw two honest Irish green ones, and two wise, bright brown ones.

Which eyes were the color of happiness?

She looked from one to the other, but she couldn't tell; that kind of happiness just didn't have a color, Daisy decided with a nod.

"Thank you, Daze—for—" said Anna, crying and smiling at the same time. She pulled Daisy into her big belly for a hug and a bump that nearly knocked her over.

"—*for everything!*" Abe finished for his wife. As always, he seemed to know exactly what Anna wanted—and he would give her whatever she needed—now—and after they'd moved to Montreal, as soon as their baby was born.

Daisy saw Abe turn to his daughter—skating around Georgie and Joe. She saw him look down at the empty rink. Maybe he was remembering what it was like to move his body, flying like the wind, over the ice. Maybe he was grieving the past—adjusting to the changes in his life—or, perhaps, he was just wondering about his future…

Daisy didn't know, for sure.

But suddenly, Abe turned to the people around him, and his grin grew big, like a jack-o-lantern, and Daisy thought she saw some teeth she'd never seen before.

Where had he been hiding that kind of a smile?

Daisy could clearly see the love in his eyes, and the happiness in the people around him who loved him, too.

Had it been worth it—all that they'd gone through—to find that kind of love?

Daisy smiled.

She knew the answer, even before she'd finished asking the question.